Hope at Christmas

Also by Nancy Naigle

Christmas Joy
Christmas Angels
The Christmas Shop
A Heartfelt Christmas Promise

Visit www.NancyNaigle.com for a
list of all Nancy's novels.

Hope at Christmas

Nancy Naigle

St. Martin's Paperbacks

This is a work of fiction. All of the characters, organizations, and events portrayed in this novel are either products of the author's imagination or are used fictitiously.

Published in the United States by St. Martin's Paperbacks, an imprint of St. Martin's Publishing Group.

HOPE AT CHRISTMAS

Copyright © 2017 by Nancy Lee Naigle.

All rights reserved.

For information, address St. Martin's Publishing Group, 120 Broadway, New York, NY 10271.

www.stmartins.com

Library of Congress Catalog Card Number: 2017028158

ISBN: 978-1-250-76454-6

Our books may be purchased in bulk for promotional, educational, or business use. Please contact your local bookseller or the Macmillan Corporate and Premium Sales Department at 1-800-221-7945, ext. 5442, or by email at MacmillanSpecialMarkets@macmillan.com.

Printed in the United States of America

St. Martin's Griffin edition / October 2017
St. Martin's Paperbacks edition 2020

10 9 8 7 6 5 4 3 2 1

To Pam Murray

*for her encouragement and support
through the years*

Acknowledgments

Grateful thanks to my editor, Eileen Rothschild, for the chance to share heartwarming stories with readers, and to the entire team at St. Martin's Press, who have made my manuscript shine as bright as a Christmas star.

To my wonderful agent, Kevan Lyon, thank you for creating this opportunity, and always keeping my focus on the writing. A true blessing. I've never felt better.

To my mom, thank you for the endless hours of support and motivation, read after read, rewrite after rewrite. You taught me to always dream big. We've done this together.

To Gwen Lucas. Your unflagging support through all of this is a gift I treasure, and the laughs we have keep me sane. I know I drive you crazy, but that makes it more like family, right?

And to Andrew, who rearranged his schedule and gave up time in the saddle as I worked on this book. I know it's not always easy to adjust your life to someone else's deadline, but you did it. Thanks. Now go saddle up the horses, Box and Tooter—it's time for another big trail ride.

Chapter One

Sydney Ragsdale pulled her car along the curb in front of the elementary school and faced her daughter with a go-get-'em kiddo smile. "Have a wonderful day, RayAnne."

"It's school, Mom."

The eye rolling was new, starting once they'd moved here last week, and she hoped it would leave as quickly as it had arrived. As aggravating as that was, her daughter's heavy sigh tugged at Sydney's heart. The divorce had been hard on them both.

Sydney's grandparents had left her the old Hopewell farmhouse when they passed away. It was a place full of happy memories, and with the move, it felt like a life raft in a rocky sea. A fresh start for her and RayAnne.

Unfortunately, to her daughter the idea of moving from Atlanta to tiny Hopewell, North Carolina, in November, after the school year had already started, had been worse than the divorce itself.

The move had been a necessary step in Sydney's self-preservation. It wasn't easy rebuilding your life when you'd been married for most of it. She'd prayed that moving to Hopewell might turn into a great mother-daughter adventure for them, but so far that hadn't been the case.

Managing a ten-year-old with an attitude was turning out to be harder than finding a decent job. She'd almost given up hope of finding a job at all when the call came from Peabody's a whole three months after her interview. It had been a long shot to begin with, but it was near the old farmhouse so she'd given it her best effort. The job offer was a blessing indeed, though the timing couldn't have been worse. School had already started, and the holidays were upon them.

Sydney watched her daughter schlep up the walkway to Hopewell Elementary School. Back in Atlanta, RayAnne had been so happy that she'd practically skipped from the car to class.

Her gut twisting, Sydney wished her marriage to Jon hadn't fallen apart and that the three of them were still one big, happy family. But then that had been a big lie. Tears puddled against the frame of Sydney's sunglasses, and she was too darned tired to even sweep them away. She sucked in a long slow breath to keep her composure.

Was moving to Hopewell a mistake?

Had it been a necessary step to regain her independence, or was it just a disguise for running away?

A car honked behind her. She waved an apology as she moved forward in the drop-off lane.

As she pulled out of the parking lot, her mind clicked through happy mother-and-daughter moments she'd pictured in this quiet little town. Laughs. Love. Lasting memories.

She eased out onto the street and glanced in her rearview mirror, barely recognizing herself in the reflection. Fluffing her bangs, she tugged the rubber band from her hair to release the messy bun. "Why am I letting Jon get to me like this?" she said aloud. She stared at herself. The answer was simple. Divorce hurts. She was broken. Wounded. His infidelity had torn her in a way she wasn't sure would ever heal. And some days this was the best she could do.

She drove up to the next block and swerved into the parking lot of the Piggly Wiggly, declaring, "I'm better than this." She shut down the car and shuffled through the console for a piece of paper and a pen.

"This has to stop." So did talking to herself, but right now that was about all she had. Tomorrow. She'd stop talking to herself tomorrow.

Rather than go back to the house and feel sorry for herself, she'd make a plan. It's what she'd always done to make sure she and Jon met *his* goals. Why was she treating her life any differently?

She tapped the pen against the steering wheel, then leaned forward and started writing.

> Step One: Get a job. *Check*.
> Step Two: Get out of Dodge. *Fine. So she made it out of Atlanta. Check!!*

It never hurt to start a plan with a few easy, achievable, or *already done* tasks to get things rolling. It's why she usually had "make the bed" at the top of her chore list.

> Step Three: Get involved locally to meet some people.
> Step Four: Regain my confidence.
> Step Five: Get into the holiday spirit.
> And the Finale: Get this divorce from Jon finalized and behind me, and never put all my eggs in one man's basket again.

After months of Jon still controlling her through his purse strings even though they had separated, the generous job offer from Peabody's had enabled her to move to Hopewell and stand on her own two feet. Free of Jon's hold.

Uprooting RayAnne had been such a hard decision, but she needed to set an example for her daughter, to show her that even when dealt a cruddy hand in life, one can respond with grace, strength, and independence.

Determined to make this a day that would change her path, she made the short drive to Main Street and parked.

She got out of the car and breathed in the fresh air. It was quiet as she walked down Main Street. The retail area was only two short blocks, unless you counted the mansion that sat across the way. Well, it hadn't been a residence for as far back as she could remember. Back then it had been a bookstore called The Book Bea. Her very favorite place in town when she was a little girl.

She smiled at a memory of The Book Bea. For the longest time she'd thought the word *bee* had been misspelled on the sign in front of the bookstore. It wasn't until she'd told her grandmother she wanted to help fix the sign that she'd learned that it was a play on words. The bookstore had been named after its owner, Bea Marion.

Sydney looked both ways, which was barely necessary with the light traffic, then crossed the street.

The thick wooden sign had been sandblasted, similar to those signs on fancy beach houses on the Outer Banks. The background of the perfect oval was bright cobalt blue, just the way she remembered it. The shop name, THE BOOK BEA, stood out in 3D next to a stack of colorful books with little yellow-and-black bumblebees circling above them, looking as cheerful today as it had twenty years ago.

She took a picture of the sign with her phone. An OPEN sign hung in the window of the front door.

It's still here! she thought excitedly.

She tucked her phone back into her purse as she walked between the perfectly shaped box hedges that flanked the sidewalk leading to The Book Bea's front door, giving it a dignified air. Winter was beginning to fade the landscape, but the grass on the other side was still thick and green, making her want to kick off her clogs and walk barefoot through it on the unseasonably warm day.

She was tempted to buy a paperback and lie in the grass and read the day away, only she needed to be frugal until her job started after the first of the year. Couldn't hurt to browse, though.

Fond memories of trips with her grandparents to the bookstore rushed back. Hours spent scouring the shelves, getting lost in those stories, and trying to make a decision on which book to buy had been both agonizing and exciting.

She climbed the stairs to the huge old turn-of-the-century house. The wide front porch was painted a playful basil green against the glossy white wooden railing, giving it a soft southern air. Rockers in various colors popped like wildflowers swaying in a gentle breeze, making it hard to believe Christmas was just around the corner.

She'd so hoped that she'd be able to share a white Christmas with RayAnne this year. It would have been her daughter's first, but it didn't look too likely. Sydney left her snow dreams behind as she pushed open the screen door and was met with a blast of cool air conditioning as she walked inside.

Her footsteps echoed against the age-old wooden floors as she headed for the bookshelves. She'd found comfort here as a young girl. Books had always rescued her, and she'd never stopped trusting a good book to bring her joy, erase her fears, and give her strength. That same excitement swirled inside her. The place even still smelled of warm cookies. Like nothing had changed.

"Good morning," a shaky voice carried across the room.

Sydney swiveled to her right. The tall wooden counter still stood in front of the bay window. A bony hand waved in the air, looking almost detached from its body, like some leftover Halloween prop.

Could Miss Bea still be working here? Sydney marveled. *She'd always sat behind that counter, where you could barely see her unless you were really looking.*

"Hi." Sydney walked toward the counter to satisfy her curiosity. "How are you today?"

"Fabulous, Darling. Always fabulous. The only way to be."

Sydney's cheeks tugged as she smiled. *Miss Bea had always said that.*

The woman stood and stepped around the counter.

There was no mistaking the tall red-haired woman. Yes, she was older, and much thinner than Sydney recalled, but the signature hair and artistic attire were one hundred percent Miss Bea. Bright lime-green reading glasses hung from a colorful strand of beads around her neck. Her long black jacket, like a duster a cowboy might have worn back in the day, swung gracefully from her shoulders to her knees.

"Welcome, dear. Are you looking for something special today?"

Memories? A safe place to get my footing back? she thought.

But Sydney could hardly answer Bea's question with either of those responses. "I need a good book to take me away for a little while."

"Ah, then you've come to the right place. The Book Bea has been doing that for years. I have all the best sellers, and some of the best-kept secrets, too." Bea raised her glasses and put them on, giving Sydney the once-over. "I was going to ask if you were passing through, but you look so familiar."

Sydney laughed. "People have always said that I favor my grandmother. I'm Carmen and Bret Rockford's granddaughter."

"Yes. That's it." Bea snapped her fingers and then pulled her hands to her hips. "I remember you. Braids and bruised knees."

"I was so clumsy back then. I grew out of that."

"Thank goodness. Used to think we should maybe bubble-wrap you."

Sydney remembered Miss Bea saying that the summer Sydney had fallen off her bike and skinned both knees.

"Bless her soul," Bea said, studying Sydney's face. "You do favor Carmen. Such a lovely woman. Your grandparents really are missed around here."

"Sydney Ragsdale now." She reached to shake Bea's hand. "I moved into their old place over on Green Needles Lane."

"I'd heard that someone was moving in there. So happy to hear that it's you. That house has been empty too long."

"I know. I had great intentions of using it as a vacation

getaway after they passed, but my husband never seemed to know how to take a break."

"Well, that's not good for anyone. What changed his mind?"

"There was no changing his mind."

"He's out of the picture now, I take it." Bea *tsked*, peering over her glasses, then letting them fall to her hefty bosom.

"Yes, ma'am. Totally out of the picture."

"Well, then we'll file that history on one of the bookshelves in the back," Bea teased.

"We'd have to find a spot in the children's section for him based on the age of his new love interest."

"Ouch. Don't know what gets into men sometimes. I swear they just go crazy." Bea swept a hand in the air. "Good riddance."

Sydney wished it were that easy.

"Take a look around. Let me know if I can help you find anything." Bea walked back around the counter and sat in a plush green armchair. "And stay out of the children's section, nothing good there for you anymore. If you know what I mean."

She meant Jon, Sydney realized. *Funny.*

The rest of this town seemed smaller than she remembered, but The Book Bea still felt as big and magical as ever. The big antique cash register that had looked old when she was ten still lorded over the ornate counter and was every bit as awe-inspiring today. The intricate brass casing had to be from the early 1900s but was still polished to a glimmering shine. The glossy circular buttons on the metal-keyed arms, like an old typewriter, probably took full force to press down. But the heft of the old machine looked so sturdy and strong. Secure. And there was beauty in that.

The smell of books, knowledge, and old ink may have been in her imagination, but it all worked like some kind of happiness pheromone. Suddenly, being replaced by a young model didn't feel like an insult as much as plain idiocy on Jon's part. The next time she had a pity party over that, she'd try to remember how amazing all these aged things still were. She could be special and unique, and age with a purpose too. Thirty-something wasn't that old, but he'd made her regret it.

She wandered back toward the bookcases. Thick carpets lay in the high-traffic areas, plush beneath her feet in some places and worn to the hardwood flooring below in others from years of customers.

"I'm just going to look around a bit, if that's okay," Sydney said.

"Help yourself. No hurries in The Book Bea."

After meandering through the stacks Sydney couldn't resist picking up a few books. Finally, she headed toward the cash register, setting her selections in a neat stack there. "I remember coming to town with Gram. It took hours to run errands, but she always made time to let me pick out a book. It was the best part of the day."

"Such a nice memory."

"It is." Feeling a little dizzy from the trip down memory lane, she leaned against the counter to steady herself. "She'd hold my hand as we walked down the street. Back then Hopewell seemed like a big bustling place to me. Gram parked in the same spot right in front of Lucky's Diner. I noticed it's not there any longer."

"That old diner has been gone for years. Lucky died and seems he took his luck with him, because nothing else that's gone into that space has made a nickel."

"Too bad. I remember his fried green tomato sandwiches."

"They were delicious, but there are still good eats around here. That hasn't changed."

Sydney could use one of those yummy sandwiches about now, too. "I remembered Hopewell seeming so much bigger. Now, I think I could walk the whole town twice and still be done before lunch time."

"Hopewell is pretty much the same unless you count the new gas station and fast-food restaurant at the interstate exit. Then again, what were you? Ten or twelve years old?"

"I guess everything seems bigger when you're ten years old."

"Probably, but if it makes you feel any better, Hopewell does seem bigger in the summertime, when people are back outside and the sidewalks are busy." She smiled and with a tilt of her head, she said, "But you hold on to those childhood memories."

"I will. They're great ones." The Nancy Drew hardbacks with the yellow-gold spines were still lined up on the long shelf in her old room. She could almost feel the excitement that used to swirl inside her when Gram and Pop would bring her here to buy a new book—sometimes two—and the way she'd clung to her precious purchase on the ride home, hardly able to resist the urge to read in the car even if that always made her car sick.

"So, what besides that rat of a husband helped you land back here in Hopewell?"

"I need to make my own life, and since I had the house here it just made sense. Jon was still controlling me while he built a whole new life for himself. It was time for that to stop." Saying it out loud was a bit empowering. "I just hope my ten-year-old daughter adjusts."

"She will. You loved this town at that age. She'll see what's special about it, too. And she'll make friends."

"Sure hope so. She's not very happy with me right now."

"You'll have to bring her in. We have a children's book club on Saturday mornings. If she's half the reader you were, she'll enjoy that."

"RayAnne loves to read. Thanks, Miss Bea. I'll do that," she said, sliding her books across the counter.

"You can just call me Bea, dear." She rang up the purchase. "If there's anything I can do to help you settle in, just ask. I know everyone in this town."

Sydney rested her elbows on the tall counter. "I need to keep myself busy until I start my job after the first of the year."

"Really? What is it exactly that you do?"

Jon had never wanted her to work, so her résumé was lean.

"Well," Sydney faltered for words. "All I've ever been is a mom and a wife, but I have a business degree. I did graphic arts for my ex, but that was all freelance stuff. My work won him a couple of his biggest contracts, so I think I have something to offer there."

"Being a mother and a wife is underrated. Budgets, schedules, creativity, project planning, and patience. I'd say any good CEO should have all of that." Bea's expression was sincere.

Sydney worried that even with more than ten years in that role, raising RayAnne through all of this change and working full-time was going to be more than she was ready for, but she couldn't slip into that worrisome dark place again.

"It takes all kinds of skills to accomplish the demands on a mother. So, you must be the new hire over at Peabody's."

"I am. How did you know?"

Bea's soft grin turned up on the corners in a bit of a smirk. "Nice thing about owning The Book Bea is I get all of the scoops. The folks who own Peabody's shop here. Nice family. I heard they are doing the marketing for a new movie studio, and a boot company. Things are going really well for them. That's big news in a town like this. They're good people. You're going to love working with them."

"Thank you. Now if I can stay busy through the holidays without going crazy until I start working, then I'll be fine. My daughter is leaving as soon as school gets out to spend Christmas with her dad. It's going to be really quiet without her around."

"You know . . ." Bea pressed a finger to her lips. "I could use a little help around here."

Sydney knew that her face probably lit up like a jack-o-lantern. Hopefully not a totally goofy one, but a pleasant, smiling one.

"Don't get too excited. The pay is lousy, and the job is a little of this and that, and only through the holidays. I can add the bonus of free books, though. If you're interested."

"Really?" Sydney could really use some extra cash. She wasn't on a super-tight budget, but she needed to be careful. No matter what, there was no way she'd ask Jon for money, even if they had to resort to eating cereal for breakfast, lunch, and dinner.

"Yes. It would be a huge help."

"I'll do it," Sydney said. "Of course I will."

She felt like dancing a jig. Heck, swinging Bea in a do-si-do seemed appropriate, but she held her feet firmly to the ground. "Thank you so much. I won't let you down."

The rows and rows of bookcases held a feeling of

order that was welcoming in the chaos of her life these days. And how those bookshelves seemed orderly amid the varying sizes, thicknesses, and colors of the spines was interesting. Yes, this place might just be the ticket to getting a little order in her own house.

"When can you start?" Bea asked.

"How about now? I don't have to pick up RayAnne until school lets out at three."

"Excellent." Bea pointed to the left side of the checkout counter. There was a stack of boxes labeled CHRISTMAS piled next to an artificial tree that had dust clinging to its limbs. "I've got to start decorating the store, but the arthritis has really been giving me a holy terror lately. Maybe we could start there."

"I can definitely do that," Sydney said, and then a sinking feeling settled over her as she recalled that she'd never hung a single Christmas light in her life. Not because she couldn't, but because as a kid her daddy had had that honor, and once she'd married Jon he'd always handled it. Oh well, time to step up.

Bea leaned forward and whispered. "At least I was smart enough to leave all the outside lights up at the end of the season last year. One flip of the switch and folks passing by will think we've been busy as bees in here." Bea gave Sydney a playful wink. "Bees. Bea. Get it?"

"Yes. I get it." Sydney laughed. A little too hearty as it conjured up a very unladylike snort, but it was freeing to laugh over something silly.

Yes, working here, even for just a few weeks, would be a good thing. Plus, she hadn't planned to decorate, since RayAnne would be leaving soon to stay the whole Christmas vacation with her dad.

"I'm so excited to help you out over the holidays," Sydney said.

Bea's smile spread wide, little lipstick lines dancing in the wrinkles around her lips. She clapped her hands, and then held them to her heart. "Thank you, dear. You already know the layout of the store, it's never changed since I opened it. There is a washroom and storage area just under the staircase. And a small office back there." She reached into the register and pulled out a key on a keychain with a metal enamel bee on it. "Here's a key in case you need it. This is going to be a really good way to end the year."

Sydney set her purse on the counter. Step five on Sydney's list was to get into the holiday spirit, and this seemed to be the perfect way to begin. "I should be able to make some good progress before I have to pick up RayAnne. Shall we get started?"

Bea came around the counter and pulled her into a hug. "I had a feeling today was going to be extra special. So good to see you again, Sydney."

Her mood lifted, and the tight worry was replaced with peaceful relief from her accomplishments today. And Bea's hug helped more than she'd ever know. The old woman smelled of peppermint Life Savers and sugar cookies, and her hug held the kindness that Sydney hadn't felt since the last time she'd seen Gram. "I'm glad we crossed paths today. I needed this," she said to Bea.

Bea stepped back and took Sydney's hand into hers. "I think we may have needed each other today." She led Sydney toward the front of the store. "I usually decorate this window for the holiday, but I can't crawl around like I used to. Could you come up with a display for it? The town folks kind of count on our decorations as part of the caroling tour."

"The caroling tour?"

"Oh yes. Each of the merchants sponsors a song. It's

quite popular. Even folks from neighboring counties join in. The carolers start in front of any shop. Each storefront gives away a different song page, and we provide the music on a loop. By the end of the night each participant has a whole Christmas songbook as a keepsake."

"That sounds like fun."

"It is."

"How do you pick a song?"

"We don't pick them out ourselves. The mayor assigns them randomly the day after Thanksgiving. The town makes the song sheets up for us. They'll deliver them to us closer to the event. Mine is 'O Christmas Tree' this year."

Sydney tried to maintain a pleasant smile, but that dusty old Christmas tree she'd seen next to the counter wasn't going to cut it. Certainly not as the main feature of the window to represent the song. She was going to have to think fast. She hoped the smile she pasted over her grimace looked confident. "I'll come up with something innovative and eye-catching for the window to go with that carol."

Bea's smile softened. "We'll have to use what we've got here. I'm afraid I don't have a budget for decorations this year."

"Don't you worry about that. I have just the thing." She glanced around the room with absolutely no idea what she could do, but she wasn't about to admit defeat on hour one of her new job. "And I believe we have everything we need right here. With one exception."

"What's that?"

"I'll bring RayAnne over after school to give me a hand."

"Have her pick out a couple of books for helping."

"She'll love that. Thank you."

A set of wind chimes sent a rich, muted sound through the room. Sydney followed the sound to a set of brass tubes hanging from a wooden dragonfly sculpture above the cash register. Thin fishing line ran from the chimes just below the coffered ceiling all the way to the doorway. Clever. And way more pleasant than those door alarms so many people used in their shops.

The UPS man wheeled in a cart with two boxes on it. "Good morning, Miss Bea. Got two for you. It's been a while. Thought maybe you were cheating on me with another delivery man."

Bea giggled like a flirty teenager. "You know that would never happen. Just haven't been ordering much, but can't get through the holidays without one last shipment of Christmas books."

"You know I'll be back to pick up the missus a couple of those Christmas novels. She counts on those in her stocking."

"And I've got the wrapping paper and ribbon just waiting on you." She gave him a playful wink.

He dropped the boxes next to the counter. "You have a good day now."

Sydney reached for the pair of scissors on the counter. "How about I go ahead and unpack these and put them on display so the customers can have at them? I'll work on the decorations after hours. Less clutter for your customers."

"You don't mind?"

"Not at all. And the decorations will be a fun mother-daughter project." Sydney unpacked the boxes, stacking the books along the edge of the counter. A small table holding ink pens and other impulse-buy items caught her eye. Those things could fit on the counter right near the register.

It didn't take long to create a nice little arrangement at the checkout, and then she got right down to work on the Christmas book display. The shiny foil covers looked pretty enough without additional decoration, but maybe she could come up with something festive once she and RayAnne figured out what they'd do for the window display.

She checked her watch. How had that much time already swept by? "Bea, I need to run and pick up RayAnne. We'll be back in a while to work on the decorations."

"Thanks, Sydney. Take your key. No need to rush. If I'm not here just make yourself at home."

Sydney suddenly fought back tears. So much had shifted since this morning. "Thank you so much, Bea, for trusting me and giving me a chance to get my feet under me before I start my new job. This is exactly what I needed. How can I ever thank you enough?"

"Don't be silly. You were meant to come in here today. Trust your journey, dear. It will take you where you're supposed to go."

"I sure hope so, because I'll tell you that the journey I've been on for the past year has not been a pleasant one."

Bea nodded. "I can tell. There's trouble in your eyes. We'll sit and talk about it one day when you're ready. But I'll say this much: Your troubles will pass and you will see that something better is ahead of you. Some*one* better, if I were to say what was really on my mind."

And hadn't she done just that? Said what she wanted to say? At least she hadn't spouted that "one door closes another opens" hogwash. Sydney didn't plan to walk through anyone's door any time soon, if ever, anyway. "I'll be glad to have the troubles pass, but I'm not looking for anyone. I've decided solo is the way to go. No heart-break. No lies. No problem."

Bea just grinned. "Sure, dear."

So Bea was a hopeless romantic. She could believe what she wanted, but what Sydney believed was that it wouldn't hurt RayAnne one bit to see that a woman didn't need a man and that you had to work for the things you wanted.

"Tomorrow you will walk into a Christmas wonder-land." Sydney picked up her purse and headed out the door feeling about three inches taller. She smiled at every tree along the path and every puffy white cloud in the sky. Wrapping her fingers around the strap of her shoulder bag, she waited at the stoplight to cross over.

As she walked to her car, she took a closer look at the other shop windows along Main Street. Her competitive nature was already shifting into high gear.

She took in a deep breath and then blew out all the negative energy, letting it seal up like a bubble and float away, just like she'd read to do in one of the books that she'd downloaded about surviving the stress of di-vorce.

That deep breath was the first one that felt like it might actually work. Thank goodness, because she'd tried just about everything.

Sydney walked past the bike shop, cleverly named Wheelies. The shiny bike in the window caught her eye. It would be a splurge. Probably not a smart one in their situation, but one shiny gift was all she could do, so she wanted it to be a good one. Ten minutes later she walked out of Wheelie's as the owner hung a SOLD card from the handlebars of RayAnne's Christmas present. She'd told

RayAnne they'd celebrate Christmas when she got back from being with her dad. That seemed a long ways off.

Sydney wondered if the splurge would look more like a pet rock following Jon's fancy getaway. Expensive gifts were Jon's love language. Always had been, and she had no doubt he'd go overboard more than usual this year with all that was going on.

Next door, Cookie Doe, a bakery with its glass case filled with all kinds of desserts, had her mouth watering. She walked inside, and the scent of sugar and frosting and something slightly peanutty wrapped around her. She knew exactly what she was going to buy the instant she laid eyes on it.

"Three peanut butter cookies, please."

"Just took them out of the oven a little while ago. Probably still warm," said the man behind the counter.

"Doesn't get much better than that." As she waited for them to be packaged up, she turned and looked at his window display. A three-story gingerbread house filled most of it, and cookies in the shape of snowflakes hung from wide white satin ribbon, each with shiny frosty white icing and those little BB-looking silver dragées. The window was simple and elegant.

Less is more, Sydney thought.

The man behind the counter thrust a white wax paper bag her way. She paid for the cookies then stepped outside, stopping only to snap a quick picture for inspiration before heading to her car.

On the way to the school, Sydney hoped the cookies might allow for a momentary return of her daughter's sweet attitude. Her little daddy's girl blamed her for Jon leaving them. RayAnne was mad. And hurt. And some days Sydney couldn't help but wonder how much of it *was* her own fault. If she'd only done . . .

She stopped herself. There'd be no more of that. She had been a good wife, doggone it. The divorce was not her fault, which was all the more reason for her to move on.

Trying to ease the heavy burden of worry, she shoved her hand into the bag of cookies.

At the stoplight she took a bite.

There really wasn't much a homemade peanut butter cookie couldn't make better. At least for a minute.

Chapter Two

Mac turned his back to the chalkboard and faced his students. It was almost impossible to keep their attention during the last school week before Christmas vacation. Not that he could blame them. He was looking forward to the holiday, too, so he'd taken a departure from the planned curriculum. "Our topic this week is the history of the National Christmas Tree Lighting."

The classroom of teens hooted and hollered. He knew it wasn't because they loved the topic but because they thought it was an easy one. He didn't mind; he'd help them find their Christmas spirit.

"If someone will get the lights, I've got a documentary for you today."

"You rock, Mr. MacAlee," Bubba Monroe hollered from the back of the room as he leapt from his desk and raced to man the light switch.

"There'll still be a quiz. So listen up, and take notes. Anyone know when the White House had its first Christmas tree?"

His size made it easy to command a room, and being the baseball coach didn't hurt. He was tough, but these kids worked hard and had earned a break.

"1492," a kid in the back yelled.

"Uh, no. That would be when Columbus sailed the ocean blue. It started with President Calvin Coolidge in 1923 with a forty-eight-foot fir. This movie will take you through all of the traditions and how they've changed over the years."

Mac pressed play on the video panel. "Bubba, lights please."

The room dimmed and then filled with the sound of jingling sleigh bells and a deep, rich voice-over. Mac settled in behind his desk, reviewing his calendar and list of to-dos.

The video ran until just a few minutes before the bell. He turned up the lights and stepped back in front of his class. Rubbing his hands together, he asked, "Anyone learn anything new?"

Every student nodded.

"Good. Here's your homework."

A collective groan rolled across the room.

He withheld a grin. "Each of you needs to go out and find a piece of holiday trivia from pre-1920."

The bell rang, and notebooks slapped closed like a clap of thunder.

"You'll each report on what you learned tomorrow. Don't disappoint me."

As the kids made a scramble for the door, Mac straightened the desks and raised the blinds, going through his normal end-of-day routine.

His son, Seth, was in middle school, and they released an hour after his high schoolers. That gave Mac an hour to get things done.

At twelve years old, Seth wasn't keen on the idea of carpooling with his dad to and from school, but ever since Genna left them, Mac had felt the need to be as present as possible, and that short ride guaranteed them time together before Seth got absorbed into after-school activities.

He closed his classroom door behind him and walked the empty hall.

"Have a great afternoon, Mac."

He recognized his co-worker's voice immediately. He didn't even have to look, but he did to be polite, then lifted his hand in the air. "Good night, Miranda." She had a knack for popping up whenever he was alone. He'd hoped the wave and the fact he hadn't broken stride would deter her, but she jogged over to catch up with him.

"A bunch of us are meeting up for drinks tonight at the Billy Goat Grill. You coming?"

"No." He shoved his hands into his jacket pockets. "Can't. I have plans."

Her shoulders dropped. "Come on. You never do anything fun. Get a sitter."

She was cute, but not his type even if he was looking. Which he was not. "Thanks. Maybe next time."

"You always say that." She pouted, and even pouting she was pretty, but the last thing he needed was a woman to distract him. He had a son to raise, and he'd already proved that he couldn't make a marriage work. He had no intention of putting himself back in that position again no matter how difficult it was being a single parent. "Thanks for the invite. I've got to go pick up Seth." He turned and made a beeline for the door.

"If you change your mind you know where we are," she called after him. "And if you need a sitter I can get you the name of my neighbor."

He gave her a quick nod as the door closed behind him.

He hoped she wouldn't follow him out to the parking

lot. Last time she'd cornered him in the teacher's lounge, and he'd thought he might have to hurdle her to escape.

He reached his parking spot and climbed into the front seat of his Dodge pickup. A quick glance in his rearview confirmed there was no sign of her.

He started the truck, drove across the block to the middle school, and parked in the last spot in the lot as he did each afternoon. A deal he'd made with Seth so as to not cramp his style. Style? At twelve? Mac didn't remember worrying about that kind of stuff at that age. He had a feeling the older Seth got the less cool Mac was going to seem.

As the row of yellow school buses rolled out of the lot, Seth came around the corner of the building with his camo backpack hooked under his thumbs. He was growing so fast this year that the poor guy couldn't seem to keep any weight on him. He was tall and lanky, like Mac had been at the same age. Mac now understood why his mother always seemed to be shoving food at him as a kid. Sometimes Mac worried people might think Seth wasn't getting enough food at home. Seth's slender build was pretty much where Seth's physical similarities with Mac ended. Seth had his mother's sandy hair and green eyes, and a complexion that burned at the first kiss of sunshine.

He and Seth exchanged manly nods and grunts as Seth jumped into the truck and slunk down in the seat, putting one of his blue Puma sneakers up on the dash.

Mac gave him the look, and Seth dropped his foot to the floor.

Sometimes it was nice to be able to communicate with a simple head gesture or grunt.

"Hungry?" Mac asked.

"Starved to death."

Mac lifted a brow.

Seth rolled his eyes. "Fine. I'm not starving to death. Yes. I'm hungry. Burgers from the hut?"

Mac nodded and pulled away from the curb. During baseball season he worked a lot of nights. During the holidays, he had a special job. A secret one that Seth didn't know about. The same one he'd had since the year Genna was pregnant with Seth. On the nights he worked, they grabbed dinner on the way home unless Seth wasn't hungry. Then he'd just let Seth ransack the cupboards with the sitter while he was gone.

"The usual?" Mac asked as he pulled through the drive-thru.

Seth nodded.

Twenty minutes later they were in front of their house. Seth had already devoured most of his fries, but Mac couldn't be mad. The truck smelled of salty fries and freshly grilled burgers. They went inside and ate at the kitchen island.

"Homework?" Mac asked.

"Nope." Seth pushed his long skater-style bangs across his face. "Christmas break's almost here. The teachers are being cool."

Mac hoped his students were saying the same thing about him to their parents tonight.

RayAnne waved goodbye to a group of girls standing in front of the school.

RayAnne was making friends already. Maybe she'd been worried over nothing, Sydney thought.

RayAnne opened the car door and slung her book bag onto the floor, then flopped into the passenger seat. Not exactly the greeting Sydney had expected from the little girl who'd been skipping and waving to others just a moment ago.

"How was your day?"

"Fine." RayAnne stared out the window.

"Just fine?"

"It was school. With no friends. What did you think it would be like?"

"Well, aren't you just a little slice of heaven this afternoon." Wishing she'd kept that to herself, Sydney steadied her smile, which wasn't all that easy with her teeth clamped. *I'm the parent here.* "I see you met some new friends. That's exciting."

"I don't even know them yet."

"It's a start though. People are nice here, right?"

"I don't know."

When all else fails, peanut butter cookies solve everything. "Brought you something."

RayAnne didn't even turn to look, and did she just roll her eyes? Sydney had thought this wouldn't happen until she was at least a teenager.

Sydney leaned back, grabbed the bakery bag from behind the seat, and set it in RayAnne's lap.

RayAnne looked down at the white paper bag, and then glanced over at Sydney.

"They're your favorite," Sydney said with a big smile.

RayAnne lifted the bag. As soon as she opened it, the peanut butter smell filled the car. She couldn't hold back a smile no matter how hard she wanted to, and Sydney silently scored one for the mom team.

RayAnne pulled a cookie out of the bag and took a bite. "Oh. My. Gosh. These are so good."

"You're welcome."

"Thanks, Mom."

And there was the sweet girl she'd raised. "I've got another surprise for you, too."

RayAnne quit chewing for a three count, looking like she was searching the windshield for a guess.

Sydney patted her leg.

"Dad?" RayAnne asked hopefully. "He loves peanut butter cookies as much as I do, and there's another one in the bag."

"No, honey." Sydney squeezed her hand. Buying cookies for Jon was the last thing she'd do. "This doesn't have anything to do with your dad. It's a surprise for *us*. A fun one."

"Hope it's better than moving to stupid Hopewell." RayAnne's huff hit Sydney like slap.

1 . . . 2 . . . 3 . . . Sydney counted. *She's just upset. It's not personal.* "This isn't easy on me either, you know."

"Yes, ma'am."

But RayAnne's response had been low, and that was almost worse than the huffing and puffing. Why was it that Jon was the one who'd broken the marriage and yet she ended up having to be the bad guy? "We're going to a place that I absolutely loved when I was your age."

"That long ago and it's still here?"

"Hey, it wasn't that long ago."

"Like a kazillion years." But RayAnne was smiling.

"Only *half* a kazillion."

RayAnne took the other cookie out of the bag and happily munched on it as they drove down Main Street.

Sydney parallel parked in the last block, and got out of the car. "Come on. It's just up the road here, and trust me, you're going to love this."

"Somehow I doubt it." Begrudgingly, RayAnne got

out, but she couldn't have moved slower if she'd been walking on stilts . . . backward.

Around each of the signposts at the street corners, wooden planter boxes were boasting winter flowers blooming in an array of colors. Pansies poured over the edge, and orange flowers with deep-purple upper petals and softer purple outlines snuggled next to equally bright orange, pink, and yellow ones. And although that wasn't Christmas-y in the least, it somehow looked just right below the giant, green, lamppost-mounted zig-zag Z-Christmas tree art.

Sydney was determined not to let RayAnne pass judgment until they went inside The Book Bea and got started.

They crossed over Elm Street, and Sydney stopped in front of the sidewalk that led to The Book Bea. "Here we are."

RayAnne stopped. "A bookstore? Seriously, Mom?"

"Come on. We're going to decorate the front window for Miss Bea. It'll put us in the Christmas spirit."

"Can't we just decorate our own house?"

"We already talked about that," Sydney said. "With you spending the holidays with your dad, it doesn't make sense to buy a tree and do all that just for me."

"But won't you be sad with no tree? You love Christmas."

"I'll be fine. Don't worry about me. What I love, baby girl, is you." She tapped her on the nose. "Please let's do this. It's a nice thing to do for Miss Bea, and I'm going to help her through the holidays. Besides, we always have fun decorating together. It's tradition."

"This is not *our* tradition. Dad should come here, or we can both go there. Then we can have tradition."

"That would be awkward with your dad's girlfriend hanging around, don't you think?"

"You could stay in a hotel. She'd go away when she saw what a great family we are together."

"That's not going to happen. You need to put that thought right out of your mind."

"You'd have fun skiing with us. Remember how we—"

"RayAnne . . ." Sydney's hands balled tight. She was tired of remembering all those things that would never be again. She shook her hands out and took a breath, trying to steady her voice. "I know you wish things would change, but your dad made his decision. He's moved on. It changes my life with him, but not yours."

"It's not fair. You shouldn't give up. You're prettier than she is. You have to try."

"Oh sweetie, it's not about who's pretty." Did anything good ever really come out of a divorce? Because it felt like there was nothing but constant readjusting and shifting to keep things from collapsing. "It's complicated. I don't expect you to understand. Heck, even I don't really understand."

"It's stupid."

"Well, you know what? You're right, but it's what we've got to deal with, kiddo." She wrapped her arm around her daughter. The sweet little girl that she and Jon had worked so hard to have. She never thought she'd be raising her alone. "Now come on. Humor me. We'll both feel better."

"I doubt it."

"Well, then let your half-a-kazillion-year-old mom feel better, okay?"

"Fine."

"Great." She took RayAnne's hand. "Miss Bea has owned this bookstore since I was a little girl. I used to love coming here. It's a cool old house, and she's a sweet old lady. She needs our help. We're going to decorate this place like it's never been decorated before!"

"Okay," RayAnne conceded.

"I knew you'd like the idea." Sydney and RayAnne walked up to the door of The Book Bea hand in hand. "We're back," Sydney called out as she pushed open the front door.

"Right here, girls." Bea placed a gold-rimmed teacup on the counter. "You must be RayAnne."

"Yes, ma'am."

"It is so nice to meet you." She reached for RayAnne's hands and took them into her own. "You are such a beautiful young lady." The old woman glanced over at Sydney then back at RayAnne. "I can see the resemblance. You two could almost be sisters."

RayAnne laughed nervously. "Thank you."

"I appreciate your help so much. This decorating is a bit overdue actually. I'm a little worn out these days, as much as I hate to admit it."

"Mom and I are a good team. We'll turn this place into a winter wonderland."

"You two are angels coming to help me like this."

"I think I like being an angel," RayAnne said.

"I wonder, Sydney, if you wouldn't mind if I headed on home while you two work on the window. I think I'll just close a little early tonight."

"We wouldn't mind at all. But I can take care of any customers that come in while we're here."

"Would you?"

"Of course. It would be our pleasure."

"You're already doing so much."

"Don't be silly. We're just getting settled in this town. It will be nice for us to have a mother-daughter project and meet some new neighbors while we're at it."

"Well, in that case I'm going to let you girls get to it. Do you have your key?"

"I sure do. We'll lock up when we leave."

Bea started making her way slowly toward the door, then stopped. "Did your mother tell you about the Christmas caroling, RayAnne?"

"No, ma'am."

"Ask her about it. I think you should plan on coming. It's really a lot of fun. Oh, and there's a little treat of some kind at each stop. Like hot chocolate or cookies or candy. And singing. Lots of singing of Christmas carols." Bea wagged a finger at Sydney. "Tell her all about it."

"I like to sing. Mom, can we?"

"Of course, if you haven't already left to go spend the holiday with your dad. We'll check the calendar."

RayAnne bounced. "And Miss Bea, if I'm here we can help you that night, too."

"That would be delightful. We'll all have a glorious time. Caroling in Hopewell is quite magical really." Bea's eyes danced. "My sweet husband started the tradition. He had such a wonderful voice. Deep and pure as a church organ. When he sang 'O Holy Night' . . . everyone fell silent and listened. Still hits me right in the heart when I think of it." She closed her eyes and raised her hand to her heart as if she could hear him singing right at that moment.

Sydney glanced over at RayAnne, who nodded and reached for her mother's hand.

"I miss him still. Especially at the holidays."

"How long has he been gone?" Sydney asked.

"Twenty-one years."

"That's a long time ago," RayAnne said.

"Yes, it is dear, but the heart doesn't forget so quickly."

Bea's eyes teared. "You know, Sydney, don't confuse someone misusing trust or honesty with your ability to love or be loved. That's very different. You gals don't work too late."

Sydney heard Bea's advice. But Bea didn't know what it was like to have her heart trampled, and once was enough. Sydney watched Bea walk down the sidewalk to her car, then Sydney turned toward RayAnne in the empty store and did a cheerleader leap into the air. "Okay, you ready for this?"

"Mom. You are *not* a cheerleader anymore."

And darn if her daughter hadn't looked around like she'd have been embarrassed for anyone to have seen that. "Don't be a party pooper. It's Christmas! We can have as much fun as we want." She wrapped her hands around each of RayAnne's wrists, leaned back and started side-stepping until they were both turning in a circle so fast that the bookshelves seemed to make a colorful kaleidoscope around them. "Remember doing this?"

Laughing like twin schoolgirls, they stopped twirling in a flurry of huffs and giggles and fell onto the floor. "You're crazy, Mom!"

"We need more fun like this, kiddo. Don't you think?"

Sydney got up from the floor, half out of breath, and walked over to the stack of dusty boxes.

"Are those boxes full of decorations?" RayAnne said. "Doesn't look like very many."

Sydney pulled her mouth to the side and made a funny face. "Yes, and some of them are pretty old. We might have to get creative."

"Well, Miss Bea is pretty old, too. I'm glad we're here to help her." RayAnne walked over to the boxes and then ran her fingers over the Christmas tree. "Mom, this is kind of icky."

"I know. Maybe we can clean it." Sydney plucked a couple tissues from a box on the counter. "See what you can do."

RayAnne worked on the tree for a good thirty minutes while Sydney unpacked the decorations, setting the prettiest stuff aside for the front window.

Sydney walked over and turned the sign on the door to CLOSED and turned the lock. "How's it going, kiddo?"

RayAnne pressed the tissue against the dusty needles and wiped at the residue. "Not so good. Look."

Sydney peered closer, then moaned. "Think people would believe that's snow?"

"Nope," she said. "Not even with a sign that said it was snow." A second attempt with some glass cleaner didn't yield any better results. "This is a disaster, Mom."

"I have an idea," Sydney said. "I passed a sign earlier today that said they are selling Christmas trees at some place called Santa's Village. Let's go see how much a live tree will cost."

Chapter Three

Mac crumpled the wrappers from their dinner and stuffed them into the paper bag, which he then tossed from the dining room into the trash can in the kitchen.

Never missed.

Never failed to perk him up, either.

He checked his watch. "Hey, Seth, I've got about an hour to kill before I have to head to work tonight. Want to go four-wheeling?"

Seth bolted back into the room, his eyes wide. "Heck, yeah!"

"Go change clothes. I'll meet you out front."

Seth was bounding up the stairs, leaving the scent of ketchup and french fries in his wake, before Mac could even get out of his chair. Mac wished Seth would react like that when they talked about Christmas, but instead he always shut down. Seth's mom, Genna, had left them on Christmas Eve. It had been a long time ago, but the scar remained.

Mac went to the garage and pulled the two four-wheelers to the driveway. His property was only two acres, but it backed up to a twenty-five-acre tract that had once been part of a golf course. The owners' kid had been one of Mac's star first basemen at Hopewell

High and went on to get a scholarship to Duke. The kid's parents had been so happy about that scholarship that they'd given Mac permission to use that property whenever he wanted. The first year he and Seth had hiked every inch of it, and even camped out. It was like having your own Boy Scout campground in the backyard.

Back then Seth had been easy to impress. Impressing a twelve-year-old was a bit tougher. But the four-wheelers had been just as exciting for Mac as they had been for Seth.

Seth hopped from the top stair to the garage floor.

"You're gonna break your fool neck one of these days." But Mac was joking because he'd been exactly the same way, adventurous to a fault, when he was that age.

"Naw." Seth pulled on his protective gear and helmet and then did a flying leap onto the seat of his blue four-wheeler and revved it up.

Mac started his ATV and then strapped on his helmet. Locking eyes with Seth, he then patted the top of his helmet with a flat palm twice.

Seth responded with the same gesture followed by a thumbs up.

That signal was their checkpoint, signifying they were buckled up and ready to go.

Mac twisted the throttle and led the way to the back entrance of the old golf course. They'd worn a path through the property, and this time of year everything was dying off, giving them a pretty smooth ride.

The gate wasn't locked, but the chain draped between the two poles kept most people out. Mac got off of his four-wheeler, unwrapped the chain, and pushed the left poll gate until it caught on a clump of dried broom straw.

Mac waved Seth through, then hopped back on his ride and caught up to him.

As usual, Seth headed left at the fork. His favorite spot was in the old sand trap off what used to be hole seven when Mac played golf here with his dad. Mac puttered around in circles while Seth hot-dogged his ATV, doing doughnuts in the sand and sending rooster tails into the air.

The cool thing about driving four-wheelers was that no matter if it was hot, cold, wet, dry, or snowy, they always had a good time. No two rides were the same.

The alarm on Mac's phone vibrated in his pocket.

He waved his arms above his head, their signal for time to go in. Seth wheeled his ATV into one last circle, then headed back toward the gate.

Seth pulled through and waited for Mac to catch up and close the gate.

Mac gave Seth the nod to lead the way back home.

They were pulling back up to the house when Haley came walking over, carrying a covered dish.

The newlywed lived in Norfolk, Virginia, now, but was staying with her parents over the holidays since her husband had shipped out. She'd confided in Mac that she wasn't sure which was harder, being a military wife away from her husband or staying with her parents.

And so it began that Haley had offered to watch Seth on the three days Mac worked his holiday part-time job. She wasn't so miserable when she spent time with Seth, and to Seth it wasn't like being with a babysitter. A win-win for everyone, two nights a week and on Saturdays.

"Looks like you two have been having some big fun again," she said.

Seth pulled off his helmet and hung it over the handlebar. "It was awesome."

Mac pushed his ATV into the garage and then helped Seth park his.

"I made some cookies." Turning to Seth, Haley said, "I thought maybe the two of us could decorate them together tonight."

Seth slapped his hands against his jeans, sending up a puff of dust. "Do we get to eat some, too?"

"Well, of course we do," she said. "What's the fun of decorating Christmas cookies if we don't eat any?"

"What's the fun of Christmas at all?" Seth said.

"You can't be serious." Haley put the cookies on the workbench, and she pulled her hands to her hips. "Who doesn't love Christmas? Except the Grinch. Or Scrooge?"

Seth shrugged. "How about we just decorate them so they taste good?"

Haley gave him a suspicious glance. "Tell you what. You can decorate yours however you want. I'm making mine with a Christmas theme, Mr. Scrooge."

Seth raised his hand and gave her a high five. "Cool by me."

"Save me a Christmas cookie. I'm particularly fond of red and green." Mac wished he could make a good excuse for Seth's behavior, but Haley knew the story. Mac loved Christmas, and all he could do was hope that one of these days he'd find a way to renew that spirit in Seth.

"He'll come around," Haley said with a wink.

"I better go get changed or I'm going to be late. Thanks for coming over to hang out with Seth again tonight."

"Go on. I've got this." Haley gathered her things and headed inside with Seth right behind her.

When Mac came back downstairs, Haley and Seth were having an easy conversation in the kitchen. "I'm headed out. Shoot me a text if you need anything on my way back."

"We'll be fine," Haley assured him.

Anyone who could handle his angsty twelve-year-old got big points. And he liked that she didn't knuckle under to Seth's moods. Was he crazy to hope that by the time he got home, Seth would be decorating holiday-shaped cookies in red and green?

Mac drove over to Santa's Village. Eleven months out of the year it was the 4-H campground, but every December for the last thirteen years this place transformed into a snowy miniature town spreading holiday cheer. It was easy for Mac to remember when it all started because that was the year Genna had been pregnant with Seth.

He'd taken the job as a part-time Santa Claus to earn a little extra money to splurge on something special for his new family. He'd been so excited to become a father.

Santa's Village had been a roaring success, raising lots of money for the town to help its residents in need. The town was even able to set up a scholarship fund. Each year they reinvested a little more money into the event, and now Santa's Village sparkled so bright in both lights and opportunity that the real North Pole would have trouble competing.

Mac was honored to be a part of the team, doing his part as Santa every Tuesday, Thursday, and Saturday since they'd started the tradition.

It took the local Ruritan Club, and every extra hand they could harness, over two weeks to prepare the site and turn the old barn and equestrian center into a magical place. Over the years they'd perfected putting up the lights and setting up the Hollywood-set fronts that transformed the place. This year they'd added a snow machine.

Okay, so it wasn't real snow, but bubbles that blew from the hay doors at the top of the barn. They looked just like snow as they drifted down, landing in the mounds of faux snow piled up on the sides of the toy shop next to the barn.

Working here made him feel like a kid again.

A few years ago a major department store had gone out of business and the town had purchased a cast of electronic elves at the auction. Those pointy-eared robotic elves hammered and sawed for hours on end. Kids lined up in front of the long window of the toy shop, watching in awe.

Mac parked his truck behind the tree lot so he could keep a low profile as he headed to his dressing room. He was the best-kept secret at Santa's Village. Sure, a few adults knew it was him beneath the red suit and high-quality beard, but none of his students, or even Seth, knew that he was Santa.

The smell of pine hit him as soon as he got out of his truck. There wasn't a candle or spray that could replace the scent of a real Christmas tree. He weaved through the cut trees, checking out the stock and eyeing the largest ones. Brightly colored tassels indicated the price of each tree. It didn't matter though. He wanted the biggest one that would fit in his house, no matter what the price.

"Hey, Mac. Need help picking out your tree tonight?" A man wearing a red flannel shirt waved in his direction.

Mac walked over and shook the man's hand. "No. Too early for us. We'll do that next weekend. Always two Sundays before Christmas. Tradition. You know I want the biggest one you've got."

"I've got just the one. See y'all next weekend." Just

then a couple with four children in tow grabbed the guy's attention to buy a small four-foot tree.

Mac slipped through the back gate and turned to the left, where a row of buildings, really big wooden sheds on skids, had been lined up like Main Street at the North Pole.

Candy-striped poles held directional signs to all the main hot spots. Some were paid vendors, but the most popular place on the street aside from Santa was Mocha Zone, manned by the local Scout troops. They sold fresh cookies and served complimentary hot chocolate with marshmallows. It was their biggest fundraiser of the year. Even though the hot chocolate was free, the tip box yielded more money each year than they'd ever earned when they'd charged for it.

Another building specialized in wrapping the gifts people bought from the other shops. The last couple of nights they were open that place would be lined up half-way down the street with men doing their last-minute shopping.

He glanced over at his station—Santa's Snow Castle.

A line was already forming.

Mac dipped into an alley between Santa's Toy Shop and the reindeer barn. They only had three deer, but no one seemed to care, or even bother to ask about the rest of them. An empty stall held a sign on an artist's easel that said Rudolph had returned to the island of misfit toys to visit friends before the big trip. It still tickled him.

Mac took a quick look around to be sure no one was watching, then turned left into the locker room to change into his Santa suit.

When he stepped back outside, he was in character. Santa to the core.

Tonight the air was warm, and all the padding it took to make him look like the big, jolly guy would make for a long couple of hours. He hoped the weather would cool soon like the forecast promised, because cooler temperatures put everyone in the holiday spirit.

He walked outside and headed for his post. Rebecca, a tall blonde dressed as an elf, stood next to the red velvet ropes lining the walkway to Santa's chair. In candy cane–striped stockings, and a green-and-white dress with bells that jingled when she walked, her costume wasn't a typical Santa's helper costume, but her exuberant smile and easy way with the kids had made her a favorite, which is why this was her third year in a row working at Santa's Snow Castle.

Rebecca had taken the job as head elf to a whole new level.

By the time Mac was coming in the back door of Santa's Snow Castle, Rebecca had already texted him the list of the first five kids' names along with tidbits mentioned by their parents.

One of the kids must have spotted him, because a cheer began to rise from the crowd. It wasn't easy to sneak around in a red suit and white beard. Mac placed his hands on his padded belly and leaned back, treating them to his best *ho-ho-ho*.

The kids cheered, and parents grinned like they were reliving their own childhood dreams all over again.

Mac had a feeling this was how a rock star felt on a full venue night. Sort of.

He waved as he took his spot on the oversized throne-like chair. The back towered a good two feet above his head, while dramatic arches on each side of him created a whimsical backdrop for pictures. He tucked his phone into a secret pocket, so he could get messages from his head elf throughout the night without anyone noticing.

The first child in line, a towheaded boy who looked to be about five, was bouncing around like an over-anxious offensive lineman. At least there'd be no penalty for it here. Mac watched the little boy's mother whisper something to him before she let go of his hand. He chuckled, knowing from the look on the young woman's face that she'd told him to calm down and walk, because when he jettisoned toward Mac his mom shrugged and huffed out a long breath.

But Mac didn't mind one bit. He spread his arms and braced himself for the impact.

Ooopmh. That little guy was a solid hit, definitely some football in that kid's future. Mac swept him up and onto his lap in one motion. "How are you, Dylan?"

The little boy swallowed a big gulp of air. "Santa! You remember me. I knew you would. I was so good this year. So much better than last year. Good all the time. Good. Good. Good."

"I thought you were on the nice list. What is it you want from Santa this year?"

Little Dylan eyed him, then tugged on the beard.

Mac intercepted the assault, thankful that sticky glue worked so well, then belted out a hearty, "Ouch!"

Dylan looked nervous. "I'm sorry. I shouldn't have pulled your beard."

"I accept your apology."

Dylan blew out a loud sigh, and then the floodgates opened. Dylan started rattling off a list that would have made a toy company CEO shiver in excitement over the profit potential. The capacity a child had for Christmas wishes and wants boggled Mac's mind. At an age kids still struggled to remember all the ABCs, they could run down every toy that had been advertised over the last thirty days.

He listened intently.

"And the remote control car you got me last year broke when Dad tried to use it so I think some of the elves might have made a mistake on it. Could I have a better one this year?"

"Thank you for letting me know. I'll have to see if we have any more of the super duty dad-proof remote control vehicles. Sounds like that's what you need this year. What's your favorite color?"

"Red. Really fast red."

"Okay. I think we just made some of those." Mac's dad had been one of those kind of dads, too. The kind that always broke one of his toys on Christmas Day, usually before he'd even had a chance to play with it himself. Always such a bummer. His dad had been a big kid until the day he died ten years ago. Even breaking a few of Seth's toys over the years. Mac came by his love of Christmas from him.

Little Dylan was still rolling. "Mom and Dad make good cookies. We'll leave some for you so you won't be hungry going to everybody's house."

"Thank you. And my reindeer get hungry, too. Do you think you could leave a carrot for them?"

"I'm not sure." Dylan held his finger to his pursed lips. "How about an apple?"

"I think that would be fine. Merry Christmas, Dylan."

And no sooner had Dylan cleared the steps than a set of twins marched toward him in matching red dresses with lacy collars and black patent leather shoes. He was pretty sure the one on the left already had a blister from those new shoes by the way she was walking.

"Merry Christmas. Have you been good this year?"

Both heads nodded. He glanced at the phone positioned above their heads. Rebecca rocked the Intel. "Lisa," he said nodding to his left. "And Lori. Do you both want the same things for Christmas?"

"Yes!"

"Well, that will make it double fun. What would you like this year?"

The line of children went on for two hours straight, but even though Mac was tired, sweaty, and missing his son, he really didn't mind. This time of year was magic to him, and these moments refilled his well. Enough to last all year long.

Chapter Four

Sydney and RayAnne stopped and ate dinner, then drove over to Santa's Village. Peppermint-striped candy canes and crystal-blue snowflakes glowed from every row marker in the parking lot. Families walked hand in hand, weaving their way toward the busy entrance.

Sydney was reminded again how different Hopewell was from Atlanta. People seemed quite willing to patiently wait for parents to load up their children and strap them into car seats to get a good parking spot. A young mother chased after her son who had already broken free from her twice. She finally swung him up on her hip even though he was over half her height. He wriggled in her arms as they passed a tree decorated in chasing lights and moved toward a minivan.

Sydney remembered those days when RayAnne seemed capable of out-Houdini-ing her in less time than it took Sydney to blink.

RayAnne rose up in her seat. "I didn't think there were this many cars in the whole town of Hopewell!"

"Must be a pretty popular place." Sydney cruised down three aisles before finally finding an open parking spot.

"It looks pretty cool." RayAnne pressed her hands

against the window. "Like the North Pole. Look, Mom. It's like a town."

"Bea said it was worth the trip. Looks like everybody is here."

"Hope I don't see anyone from school," RayAnne said as she got out of the car. "They'd think I'm such a dork. I'd never hear the end of it."

RayAnne swung between child and diva at the speed of a cheetah these days. "Well, if you do, that means they were here too. Right? So how could they really say anything?"

RayAnne perked up. "Yeah. Guess you're right."

"See. Nothing to worry about." But Sydney knew how cruel kids could be, and RayAnne was the new kid at school. Even so, the last thing she wanted was to cheat her daughter out of her last years of Santa fun.

They walked past a long line of children with their parents waiting to have their chance to visit with Santa Claus. RayAnne dipped her head and forged ahead, following the signs to the tree lot on the other side of the property.

Sydney slowed down, watching as the man in the red suit lifted a young girl onto his lap. Memories of RayAnne at that age warmed her. Back then she'd been able to put RayAnne in a dress without a fuss. Funny how a few years could change all that. She and Jon had fought about telling RayAnne the truth about Santa, but Sydney refused to be the one to ruin the magic . . . even if RayAnne already knew. At the age of ten that was probably the case, but Jon had always preached, "If you don't believe, you don't receive," so the ruse went on.

Santa leaned in nodding, speaking to the little girl, then smiling, as she enthusiastically ran down her wish

list. Actually counting things off on her fingers until a
gentle *ho-ho-ho* rolled through the air.

The little girl leapt from his lap and ran into her
mother's arms with a grin as bright as the North Star itself. "I love Santa," she said.

Sydney's hand went to her heart. Absorbing the sweet
moment she turned to find RayAnne standing there with
her arms crossed and hip cocked. There was that attitude. If it wasn't bad enough her marriage had fallen
apart, her daughter acting out like a hormonal teenager
at just ten was about to send Sydney right over the edge
of sanity to crazyland. Everyone kept telling her not to
worry. Kids are resilient; she'll be fine, they'd say. That
was easy to say when you weren't the one dealing with it
on a daily basis. Most days she wasn't sure if either
one of them would ever be fine again.

"Thought we were looking for a tree." RayAnne's
snipped words broke the moment.

"We are," Sydney said. "I was just checking things
out. Did you want to visit Santa while we're here? We
have time."

"No-oo. You said you'd take me home to our regular
Santa on Saturday."

That she had, although boy did she regret it now. It
would be a long drive all the way back to Atlanta, but at
the time she'd felt so guilty about the move that she'd
have promised RayAnne anything. "Right." Guess her
wish that RayAnne would forget wasn't going to come
true.

Santa held a pose as the elf took another picture. Anxious parents loomed nearby, waving at their child to look
in the direction of the camera.

Sydney remembered the first time RayAnne had

climbed into Santa's lap. No crying. No fussing. No fear. She was still pretty fearless.

A light flashed, and another moment had been captured. Someday that child's grandchildren would probably look at that picture and talk about how Christmases used to be.

Somewhere in her old photo albums there was a picture of her and Jon together on Santa's lap, before they were married. They were so carefree then. Things changed over the course of a marriage. She wondered if he and his girlfriend were sitting on Santa's lap somewhere, grinning for a candid shot this year. It knotted her gut to think about it.

She turned and headed toward the tree lot. RayAnne walked a few steps ahead of her. Sometimes she seemed so grown up for her age. But like the weather here in the south, that was unpredictable and could change at any moment.

They walked into the tree lot and meandered through the trees.

"Dad would have liked this one," RayAnne said, tugging on a tall, thin, long-needled tree.

"Yeah, looks just like what he'd pick out." Sydney kept walking. She didn't give a hoot what Jon liked anymore, and keeping those comments to herself was sometimes not the easiest to do.

A sign held a grid of flag colors and prices. Even the cheapest trees were more than she cared to spend for a window display for a part-time job, and Bea had been clear she had no budget. Every dollar had its place in the budget until Sydney started her new job at the beginning of the year.

She let out a heavy sigh. She wanted the store window to be wonderful. For Bea. For RayAnne. But as wonderful as a live tree would be, it didn't make sense to tap her savings to buy one. There had to be another option.

She swept a glance around Santa's Village. They had more decorations in this one small space than many businesses would garner in a lifetime.

With the theme at The Book Bea being "O Christmas Tree," it only seemed natural that there had to be a tree in the window display. But that dingy artificial one seemed like such a downer. All the decorating in the world wasn't going to transform it. The one in her attic was too tall. That wouldn't work, either.

The decorations on the street lampposts caught her eye again.

The fringy garland gave her an idea. She'd seen someone post something last year on Pinterest that was cool, and very different. And really perfect for a bookstore, too. Could she pull it off? Only one way to find out.

"RayAnne. Where are you?" Sydney backtracked until she found her still standing next to the tree that she'd said her dad would like. "We're going to try something different for the tree."

"But I like this one."

"I know you do, but it's not money well spent. Come on." Sydney had taken at least ten steps before she realized RayAnne wasn't following her. "What are you doing?"

"I don't know why we can't buy this tree. It's perfect."

Sydney felt her calm losing its hold. "It's not perfect, RayAnne. It's way too big for the window at The Book Bea. And we're not spending that much money on something for two weeks."

"So that's how it's going to be from now on. Dad gets

to do whatever he wants with all the money and you're going to be, like, broke all the time. This sucks."

Sydney spun around. "Don't take that tone with me, RayAnne. Just stop it. I'm sad. You're sad. But this is the hand we've been dealt. And yes, your dad will always have more money than me but he will never love you more than I do." Sydney wished she'd held it in. Her jaw was tight but her lip trembled.

RayAnne was right. This did suck.

She didn't bother to wait for RayAnne. She headed straight to the car, got in, slammed the door, and cradled the steering wheel, hoping like heck she wasn't going to cry.

And maybe that's what happens when you hold it all in for too long with no one to talk to. Everything comes out in one big blubbering mess. And not an easy one to clean up.

RayAnne opened the door and slipped into the passenger seat. Sydney had no idea how long it had been.

"I'm sorry, Mom."

"You're right. It does suck. I don't know who I'm fooling."

"We're going to be fine," RayAnne said.

Her daughter laid a hand on her shoulder, and that just made the tears fall again. Maybe she should've let RayAnne stay with Jon. It's what she'd wanted. It had been completely selfish of her to think RayAnne would be better off with her just because she was her mother. All she'd wanted was to show RayAnne they could be happy together. They didn't need all the monetary things that Jon so easily provided.

"Mom, tell me the idea for the window."

"It probably won't even work," Sydney said. Besides, she was exhausted now. All that pep and vigor she'd felt earlier today had drained like someone had pulled the plug. She knew better than to overpromise and under-deliver, but that was exactly what she was about to do. She hated that. She wanted so badly to do a good job, but she had nothing to decorate with, and RayAnne's heart wasn't really in it.

"Let's try it. I'll help. Besides we don't want to let Miss Bea down."

"How'd you get to be so smart?"

"Lucky, I guess." RayAnne hugged her and then put her seatbelt on. "I love you, Mom. I didn't mean to make you sad."

Sydney dug for a napkin in the console and blew her nose. "Okay, let's start over." She twisted the key in the ignition and pulled out onto the street, heading for The Book Bea.

This time of night it was easy to get a parking spot right out in front of The Book Bea.

Sydney and RayAnne walked up the steps, and Syd-ney used her key to unlock the door. Inside she waved her hand along the wall through the darkness, searching for the light switches.

Being in this place renewed her strength and confi-dence.

Finally, she flipped the switch and the lights flick-ered on. "Okay. Here's what I need you to do," she said to RayAnne. "Take the book cart over there and go down each aisle and pull books that have red or white or green spines on them. I say we start with sixty and see where we get. Twenty big ones. Twenty medium and twenty small books if possible."

RayAnne's face lit up. "Cool. Okay. I can totally do

that." She took off like she was on that show with the shopping cart races. Down one aisle and heading toward the next, the clunk of books hitting the cart breaking the quiet.

Sydney grabbed a round end table from beside an overstuffed chair near the children's section and carried it to the display window.

The deep bay window was four feet deep at the widest spot and probably close to eight feet wide—her best guess without a tape measure. Plenty of room. She cleared out the books that had been displayed on three different risers in the window, saving the books with red, white, or green spines to add to the collection RayAnne was rounding up.

She lifted the table into the display area, then wiggled it into the center. Things were starting to take shape in her mind. She began to hum "O Christmas Tree," then stepped down from the window and went to sort decorations into three piles.

1. What they could definitely use
2. And what they maybe could use in an emergency
3. What really should be tossed

Sydney went to the boxes stacked like one giant wedding cake next to the counter.

One of the boxes was full of brand new miniature LED Christmas lights. Jackpot!

Maybe someone had sprinkled a little Christmas magic on them while they'd been at Santa's Village. Feeling renewed hope, she sat on the floor opening four boxes of lights. One by one she strung them together, plugging one end into the next. It wasn't so hard to do.

"Got the books," RayAnne said, sliding to a stop just in front of her. "What are you doing?"

"I found twinkle lights. I think this should be just enough lights to frame the front window. I hope they work."

RayAnne said, "Crossing my fingers!"

Sydney squeezed her eyes shut and plugged them in. Luckily, the glow of the blue lights was so bright she didn't have to open her eyes to know they worked.

RayAnne squealed in excitement. "They're pretty. So much prettier than the lights we always had on our tree back home."

"Indeed," Sydney said. Only what was really going through her head was *I don't need you, Jon Ragsdale.* Okay, so maybe it was a tiny win when kept in perspective, but it felt huge today. Jon had always handled the Christmas lights. A task that he'd always made seem so daunting, and it had turned out to be quite doable.

He'd always insisted on those big multicolored bulbs, too. So that's exactly what they'd had. Every single year. She'd always thought these teeny LED lights were so pretty, and she was right. She loved the way they glowed.

She was starting to realize that she'd made an awful lot of concessions in their relationship. She could get used to being completely independent.

Sydney draped a long strand of lights across her outstretched arms then handed the rest to RayAnne to hold.

"Hold this hammer and nails while I climb up."

"You're going to hammer?" RayAnne looked at Sydney like she was planning to walk into an MMA match.

"Sure."

"Do you know how?"

"Sure." Certainly she had hung a picture or something

over the years. Stepping up onto the red metal step stool, she draped the strand of lights over her neck and reached toward RayAnne for the hammer.

"I don't think this is a good idea. What if we break the window?"

Sydney froze for a millisecond. "Oh, it'll be fine."

RayAnne reluctantly handed over the hammer and two nails. "Here you go." Then she stepped back.

"Where are you going? You don't trust me?"

RayAnne pulled her lips together and giggled.

"I see how you are. We're a good team. Trust me, we'll be fine."

Sydney pinched a nail between her finger and thumb and held it in place against the frame of the window, then lifted the hammer and swung it. The nail sailed across the room.

RayAnne laughed out loud and raced over to retrieve the shiny nail.

"Whoops."

"Three strikes and you're out, Mom."

"Funny." Sydney put the other nail in the same spot and pressed it into the wood just a little to hold it steadier this time. The first three whacks landed nicely, then confidence overcame her and she swung one last time a little harder, landing right against the glass window.

Her heart sank. She was almost afraid to look.

RayAnne sucked in a breath and raced to the window. "Did it break?"

Sydney winced and took a close look at the glass. But no, the window hadn't broken. "We got lucky."

"We? You got lucky. This wasn't my idea," RayAnne said.

"Got a better one?"

RayAnne walked over to the window and pressed her

finger against the inside frame of the window. "How about these?"

Sydney lowered herself to see what RayAnne was talking about. Tiny adhesive-backed hooks lined the window at about eighteen-inch intervals. They'd probably been there for years.

"Why didn't we notice those before?"

"Because they're like see-through."

"True," Sydney said. "I think we'll go that route." A much better plan, because as much as she hated to admit it, RayAnne was right. This could've ended in an embarrassing and expensive mistake that she couldn't afford. "Let's try those hooks." It only took a few minutes to hang the lights.

The day's hot weather was now being pushed out by evening rain. She felt sorry for all those people who had been standing in line to see Santa, because it sure looked like things were getting ready to be a complete washout.

The drops splattered against the porch roof, creating a melodic background to their project. The forecast called for colder temperatures soon. That could mean snow. She'd never been here for a Christmas though, so she really wasn't all that sure what to expect.

If these raindrops had been snowflakes, they'd be socked in tomorrow for sure.

Stringing the lights, she remembered how when Gram passed and left the property to her, she'd dreamed of her little family spending white Christmases here in Hopewell. Jon chopping wood for the fireplace, then holding RayAnne on his shoulders to decorate the high parts of the tree, because of course they'd buy a tree that rose all the way to the tippy-top of those old twelve-foot-high ceilings. All three of them wearing new Christmas pajamas and sipping hot cocoa by the fire after they'd decorated the tree. Of course, none of that had ever happened. Jon had never agreed to spend even a weekend here, much less a whole holiday.

She stepped down from the stool and guided the last inches of lights into place around the side of the window. She could still hear Jon saying, so matter-of-factly, that Christmas should be spent at home. But then he was the one sweeping their daughter off to some lodge in West Virginia.

In hindsight, what he'd really meant was that it would have been harder for him to squeeze in visits with that girlfriend of his had they ventured away for the holidays. And when Sydney's former best friend told her that Jon had taken that girl to the Arts Council Holiday gala the last two years, when she still thought they were a happy family, it had about broken her. Jon knew her interest in the Arts Council events, and so had her friends. She'd even helped create the co-branding logo on the corporate sponsorship with the Arts Council. If it hadn't been for her, Jon may never have landed their account. He'd always been so adamant that he didn't want to go, but really he just hadn't wanted to go with her. Everyone knew, but she'd never suspected a thing. That still stung.

She swallowed back the bitter taste that left in her mouth.

The dark thought threatened to dampen her mood. It still made her mad that she'd had no idea that Jon had been carrying on for over two years before he'd up and left her.

Good thoughts. New life. Positive focus. Better things are ahead, she chanted to herself.

That mantra had kept her sane . . . so far.

She pulled the wire tight so the bulbs lined up in a straight row.

"That looks perfect!" RayAnne danced below her as she reached her hands in the air, feeding more lights to her.

The tiny lights cast a heavenly glow against the wet glass—raindrops reflecting the light in a way that reminded her of the warm blue waters of the Caribbean. This time of night back in Atlanta would be bustling, but it was quiet here. Or maybe all hours were slow in a town this size.

Easier to decorate without a crowd anyway, she thought.

Working here part-time with Bea was a huge stroke of luck. She hadn't felt this capable in a long time.

The Book Bea was where she'd found her love for reading, and if she could do that for someone else, wasn't that reason enough to dedicate her time to it? She felt like she belonged here in The Book Bea. And she needed that more than anything right now.

For the first time this year as she grappled for a hold on to something, anything, she felt like she was in the right place at the right time and that what she'd reached for was in her hand.

"Go out front and tell me if they look good," Sydney said.

RayAnne unlocked the door and ran outside, holding one hand above her head like that was going to protect her from the light rain. Squinting, she gave Sydney the thumbs up and ran back inside. "Man, that rain is cold."

"They said it was going to cool off."

"Didn't think it would cool down that fast. It was warm when we were at the tree lot."

"Guess the weather is a little less predictable here," Sydney said.

"Won't that be weird if Dad takes me to go skiing somewhere with snow and you have it right here anyway?"

"Could happen." She wasn't going to let the mention of Jon ruin her mood again. Better to shift the topic. "Okay, so here's what we're going to do. Let's start stacking all of the books you've collected by size. Big ones first."

With the two of them, it didn't take long to split the inventory into three piles of similarly sized books.

Sydney climbed back into the window and then reached toward RayAnne. "Start handing me books. The big ones first."

"I still don't know what we're doing."

"If it works, you will in just a few moments." Sydney laid a row of books flat, spine out, in a circle. Then another overlapping the previous row.

RayAnne kept a steady stream of books coming Sydney's way.

After a few rows of stacking RayAnne hollered, "Cool! It's going to be a tree out of books."

"Yep." Sydney stood, inching back against the window for a better look. The red, green, and white books did give it a nice holiday feeling, and it was actually starting to take the conical shape she'd been hoping for. "Before we get too far, go grab that strand of big colored bulbs over by the counter and bring it to me."

RayAnne came back carrying them like they were boa constrictors.

"Plug them in and see if they come on."

She plugged them into the wall, but nothing happened. "Ruh. Roh," RayAnne said.

"Hmm," Sydney said. That was the problem with those old lights. One bad light and nothing lit. "Hand me the other end."

She started wiggling each of the bulbs, and RayAnne took her lead and started at the opposite end. All of a sudden the strand came to life.

Sydney cheered.

"Awesome!" RayAnne leaped into the air. "Now what?"

Sydney wove the wire through a small space in the back of the book tree and then started tucking the bulbs between the gaps in the books.

The colorful bulbs played nicely against the glossy book covers.

"Mom, it's going to be beautiful! Like magic. I bet this will be the best display this place has ever had."

"I hope so."

They went back to work stacking and then weaving more lights throughout the pockets in the structure until they had a three-foot tree sitting atop that table.

She hoped everything was going to go this well in Hopewell.

Chapter Five

The crowd at Santa's Village was thinning out. Mac lifted the last child from his knee and set him to the ground.

He rose and gave a hearty *ho-ho-ho* for anyone still within earshot, committed to the role until he made it all the way back to his dressing room.

Proud of his role as Santa, he couldn't wait until Seth was old enough that he could tell him all about the experience. Now that Seth was twelve the whole Santa magic had pretty much imploded, but Mac hadn't been able to bring himself to completely confirm Seth's misgivings about Santa. Even just a seed of doubt that it could be true was enough to hang on to.

Mac pulled off his heavy plush coat and hung it on the hanger behind the door. His t-shirt was damp from the bulky costume. The air cooled his skin. He stepped closer to the mirror and carefully squeezed oil onto his finger, rubbed it into his skin just above the beard, and then eased the sticky backing of the beard from his face. In thirteen years he'd pretty much perfected the act. Just sticky enough to keep the kids from pulling his beard from his face, but not so much that he gave himself an unplanned epidermal peel in the process of re-moving it.

He stacked all his gear in the order he'd put it back on, then closed his locker.

Just as Mac came out of the dressing room, Rebecca entered the building with the pushcart that held the print-ing equipment for the photos. "That was the busiest first night I remember. Seems like parents are ahead of schedule this year."

"It did seem busier than usual. If this keeps up we might be out of business early this year."

"Wishful thinking. I'm beginning to think that more people are hearing about our extra-special Santa and making the drive to see you. We had several folks from outside the county tonight. I'm going to start asking, just so we can track it."

"You did a great job out there. Thanks."

"Thank you for bringing me back again. I really ap-preciate your support, you know."

"You earned it."

"I was a brat that first year. I didn't want this job." She looked down at the crazy leggings and outfit. "I was the last person you should've hired. I'm lucky you did."

"I saw a young lady determined to focus on her goals. There was something special about you. If I had a daughter like you in college, I'd hope someone would do the same for her. Don't shortchange yourself. You're great with the kids, and even better at managing those parents."

"They're harder to handle than the kids!"

"Exactly. I've had other people in that role that were older and should have been more mature who couldn't keep things in order. You've got the gift."

"Well, working for a Santa like you doesn't hurt. And it's fair to say this will help me with handling patients when I finally graduate from nursing school."

The first year they'd worked together Rebecca had come to him at the end of the first week and apologized for being less than enthusiastic. She'd said after being there for a week she felt like he was the real deal once he put on that outfit.

"Did you need a lift?"

"Nope. I've got a car this year."

Mac was surprised. Money was always lean for her family. "That's great news."

"Well, not really. Dad got a DUI. Lost his license. So, I've got his car."

"Sorry, Rebecca. I thought he was doing so much better."

"We all did. What he got better at was hiding his drinking." She shrugged. "It's okay. I'm learning to roll with whatever comes my way. As upset as I was, it kind of ended up in my favor."

"That's a good attitude. Still sorry that happened to you though. You should come spend the holidays with Seth and me. Of course, my Santa gig is still under wraps. You might be the only person in this town under twenty-five that knows Santa's true identity." Only the mayor, Bea, and a few other long-timers knew, and that was the way he liked it. Rebecca had that going for her, too. Rehiring her meant keeping that circle small.

She zipped her lip. "No one will ever hear it from me."

"I know. But seriously. You're welcome at our place. My neighbors are planning to come over, and their daughter is home. Her husband is in the Navy. He shipped out so she's staying with her parents for the holidays. She's been helping me with Seth. The more the merrier."

"Thanks, Mr. Mac. I might take you up on that." She put the cart in the storage room and turned the combination lock. "I'll see you Saturday."

It was tough when kids got dealt that kind of stuff. At least she'd been able to stay on track with her studies despite the bumps along the way.

Mac drove straight home. It was still early enough to catch some decent TV before he had to turn in so he'd be fresh for work in the morning. When the two jobs overlapped it was a grueling schedule. But winter break started next week, and he'd be fine until then.

Mac walked into his house to the mixed sounds of music from Seth's room upstairs and the television downstairs.

"Hey, Mac," Haley called out from the sofa.

"Everything go okay tonight?"

"Yep. We decorated all of the cookies. Put some aside for you, too."

"Did Seth give in to calling them Christmas cookies?"

"Sure did. I saved you one of those just to prove it."

Mac rubbed his belly. If he wasn't careful he wouldn't need the padding at the end of the season with all of her cooking. Maybe he'd just take them to work for lunch tomorrow. "Did he finish his homework?"

"Yes. And he has some things for you to sign for him. Don't let him forget to tell you."

"Seth. I'm home, buddy," Mac called up the stairs.

Could have been a herd of thundering mustangs coming down the stairs from the sound of it, rather than a twelve-year-old shaggy-haired boy. "Hey, Dad."

Mac ruffled his hand through Seth's hair. Genna would probably be horrified that he'd let Seth grow his hair like that. She'd always been so finicky, but all the kids on the soccer team seemed to be doing it, and Seth liked it. No harm. No foul. And Genna wasn't around.

"Thanks for the cookies, Haley. It was fun."

"You got it, buddy. See you Saturday?"

Seth clapped his hand in the air for a high-five with her as she walked past him to go back home.

Mac walked into the kitchen and poured himself a tall glass of iced tea.

Seth backed up to the kitchen island and hoisted himself up on the counter. "Did you have a good night tonight?"

"Yeah. It was. How about yours?"

"Didn't have much homework. Cookies were cool. Haley is nice. When are we putting up our Christmas tree?"

"You anxious?"

"Maybe. Was just kind of thinking about it."

Sometimes he looked at Seth and all he could see was Genna. He knew Seth still missed her, but they rarely spoke of it. Which was just as well, because he could never forgive her for what she'd done.

"We usually don't put up the tree until next weekend, but I guess we can bring the stuff down from the attic so we can get an early start."

"Cool. Think we could pop popcorn and string it like we did that one year?"

That was the first year Genna had left. His mom and dad had come and spent the holiday with them to help him out. It had been one hard Christmas to get through, but they'd all tried like crazy to be sure Seth would be the least impacted. Somehow.

They *had* managed to leave Seth with at least one special memory that year. You never know what will last a lifetime. Hard to believe it had been six years ago that they'd strung popcorn.

"Yeah. We could do that," Mac said. "If we don't eat it all. I know how you are about hogging popcorn."

"I just have to eat it fast before you do. But that's cool. I think we can do it." Seth turned and headed toward the stairs. With one hand on the bannister, he stopped and turned back. "Must be really hard for Haley to be away from her husband at Christmas."

"Yes, son. I'm sure it is. Military wives give quite a bit for our freedom, too." He wasn't sure whether to feel proud of Seth for his obvious compassion to Haley's situation, or like hell that his son knew what it felt like to be separated from someone who was still around. *Damn Genna for leaving like that,* he thought. He would call Genna and ask her to come visit Seth for his son's sake, except he didn't know where she was, and quite honestly he wasn't sure it would end well anyway. That woman didn't have brakes. She just kept moving. She'd always told him that. Only he'd never thought that would be the case with their son.

"I'm glad Haley's staying with her mom and dad," Seth said. "And us. Ya know, not alone back in Virginia by herself. Did you know her husband won't be back until, like, February?"

"I knew he was going to be gone for the holidays. Did you ask her about it?"

"Yeah. She said he's on a ship that's bigger than my school. She seemed happy to talk about him even though she's really sad that he's gone."

Was there a message in that innocent statement? Did Seth still miss Genna? Did he silently still hold out hope she might come back? There was no filling the noticeable gap that her exit had left, and no matter how hard Mac tried to do double-duty, deep down he knew that it wasn't the same.

Sydney opened the front door to the farmhouse. The rain overnight had caused the temperature to drop drastically. A brisk breeze had her backpedaling into the room.

"We're going to need our coats this morning."

"I'll get them." RayAnne snagged them off the hooks in the hall and ran back over to the door.

They pulled on their jackets and headed out to the car.

RayAnne rattled on about The Book Bea the whole way to school, and that made Sydney's morning. She loved seeing her daughter acting like her old self. A good day indeed.

She dropped off RayAnne at school, and then went straight over to The Book Bea.

To her delight the book tree looked just as beautiful in the daylight from the street. She let herself into the store and began turning on the lights.

Being in this place gave her a surge of renewed energy. More than a fancy, highly caffeinated cup of coffee could, which was nice since she would have to drive over an hour just to find a Starbucks.

She walked through the store, taking in every feature. She'd been so busy yesterday that she hadn't really had the time. In the reading nook there was a coffee station. Paper cups were there for customers, but there was also a whole rack of coffee mugs for sale. Some funny. Some geared more toward the love of books and friendship. One in particular caught her eye. A deep-blue ceramic mug with a quote from *Pride and Preju-dice,* by Jane Austen:

MY COURAGE ALWAYS RISES
WITH EVERY ATTEMPT TO INTIMIDATE ME.

Bea had recommended *Pride and Prejudice* to her the summer she'd turned thirteen. It was still one of her favorites. She remembered carrying that book out of the store that day, like she'd just earned the rites of passage to adulthood.

The read didn't make nearly as much sense to her at the time as it had in the rereads over the years, but every time she read it she fell in love with love all over again. That book had made it through her teen years, college, and moves as a married woman. It was on the shelf in the living room right now.

And boy did this quote seem appropriate for what she was going through in her life now.

She walked over to the register and wrote up a sales ticket. "A treat to myself." Then she rang up the sale and put the money in the register.

She started a pot of coffee and refilled the decanter of water for tea drinkers who might stop in later. There was a journal next to the coffee station, and a small card invited readers to share what they were reading and favorite things around town.

Sydney sat in an overstuffed chair and read some of the entries as the coffee brewed.

I love The Book Bea. Sitting here reading brings balance that a mother of twins never gets at home. I'm reading Jane Austen for the first time. Thanks for the recommendation, Bea.

Passing through Hopewell on our way to
Asheville to visit the Biltmore. I have a feeling
this might end up my favorite stop on the trip.
You were such a joy to visit with while our
children picked out books to keep them busy
on the ride. This place has healing properties.
Nice to meet you, Miss Bea. Best wishes from
the Pyatt family.

Reading In for a Penny. Love these over-fifty
ladies. Thanks for telling me about this hys-
terical southern series. Love the shenanigans
they get into on those capers.—Gloria on
Penny Hill Lane.

Hearing the last gurgles and sputter from the coffee
pot, Sydney got up and fixed herself some coffee in her
new mug.

"Here's to the first real turning point in my new life."
She toasted herself, feeling more courageous already.

She tucked the journal back into its spot and then
went back to the storage room to see what else might be
there to finish the window display. It was still missing a
little something-something, although she couldn't put
her finger on what that was.

The storage room was orderly. Cleaning supplies together. Office supplies on a separate shelf. Sydney
sucked in a breath when she spotted the stack of fabric.
Tablecloths, fabric, and quilts. She lifted them off of
the shelf and placed them on a worktable to get a better
look. Some of them were obviously vintage. Handiwork
you didn't see much these days and fine fabric that had
yellowed slightly with age. Her hand swept across a slip-
pery fabric tucked between two quilts.

Jackpot.

Probably forgotten, the remnant still had the store tag on it. Eighty-nine cents a yard. On sale. The thin fabric had a silvery sheen too it. It would be the perfect back-drop for the window. She'd spread packing peanuts on the floor last night and that gave a whimsical snowy look, but it wasn't perfect. This could be the sparkly accent she needed.

She unfolded the fabric and pulled it through her hands lengthwise, spreading her arms out with each measure to guesstimate how much was there. Six arms wide had to be at least eight yards of material or so. It should be plenty.

Her heart galloped as she gathered the fabric into her arms and grabbed her cup of coffee. Moving swiftly through the store, she hoped she could make the change before Bea arrived.

She stood at the edge of the window and tossed the fabric into the window display. It caught air like a para-chute and drifted down into a delicate blanket of rises and falls on top of the layer of packing peanuts.

Just like freshly fallen snow.

Gently nudging the fabric around the base of the table she was able to cover the entire floor.

So good!

She jogged back to the storage room where she and RayAnne had put the leftover holiday supplies the night before and dug through the box with glass ornaments. With twelve brightly colored ornaments carefully cra-dled in her arms, she went back out front.

It only took a minute to scatter the bright ornaments around the base of the display. She found six boxes and wrapped them in the shiny foil. Purple, blue, red, green, silver, and gold. She topped each box with a perfect wire ribbon bow of bright blue, to match The Book Bea logo, then placed them beneath the book tree.

"Now all I need is a tree topper," she said with satisfaction. But Bea should help, too, so Sydney decided to wait and give Bea the chance to come up with that when she got there.

Thrilled with the window, she turned on the old CD player, grabbed a dust cloth from the counter, and began working her way through the shelves, tidying and dusting as she went. An easy process that seemed to be removing not only the dust that had settled, but also the cobwebs in her own mind.

People were starting to move down Main Street, so even though it was early, she flipped the sign from CLOSED to OPEN.

She put the dusting cloth away in the cabinet under the cash register and checked for any to-do lists that Bea may have left lying around.

The chimes sent a soothing sound through The Book Bea as the door swept open.

"Good morning," Bea called out. "That window is breathtaking." Bea looked like the Michelin Man, in a big oversized down coat, with a scarf wrapped at least three times around her neck and over her head.

"Thank you! I'm so glad you like it." Sydney crossed the room and helped Bea with her coat.

"You're quite the early bird," Bea said.

"Hope you don't mind."

"Not at all." Bea wrestled with the scarf.

"Let me help you with that." Sydney found one end and began looping it away. "How long is this thing?"

Bea laughed. "You know. I'm an early bird too, so lots of mornings I'll just get up and come in and knit until it's time to open the doors. I have to admit this is one of those projects that I got to knitting and just forgot to stop."

"I'm half-tempted to call the Guinness World Book of Records to come out and do an official measure of this thing. The colors are great though. I've always wondered if I could learn how to knit."

"It's so easy. I can teach you."

"Really? That would be a great project for me while RayAnne is away with her dad. I'll pick up some yarn."

"Don't bother. I have tons. I'll get you started." Bea walked over to the display window. "It's just beautiful. Thank you so much."

"We enjoyed doing it."

"Of course, you did. That's what makes holidays special. Doing things with the ones we love."

Sydney pressed her lips together. As much as it still hurt, Jon had been the only man in her heart the last fourteen years, and finding the magic in anything lately was hard. She loved spending time with her daughter, but it wasn't the same as spending time with a partner. She just didn't think there'd be room for that again in her life.

It wasn't Jon that she missed as much as it was the companionship, the partnership, of someone else enjoying the moment with her. Sharing a laugh. A soft kiss. The brush of a hand. A passing glance.

"I see that look, Sydney."

"What?"

"You're afraid. You're locking yourself down because of your husband's stupidity. Don't do it. No ma'am. You're going to see something better is ahead of you. Some*one* better."

"I'm not looking for anyone."

"Well, that's good. Because you won't find him if

you're looking for him. Just live life and keep your heart open."

"Bea, that's all very sweet, but I can't take another broken heart. I haven't even survived this one yet."

"That's just silly talk. You're a very young woman. You will find real love. It will be different next time."

Next time? "I've got a daughter to raise. She's my priority."

"And she should be. But don't let a broken heart keep you from being open to something even more special down the road. Some of us end up with a few more heartbreaks than others. Hopefully this one was your last."

"It will be. I'm going to see to that."

"Believe me. Happiness lies ahead of you. With or without someone. But I have a feeling you are the perfect piece to someone else's puzzled life."

"I'll take the happiness, but I'll pass on the puzzle."

"Do me a favor," Bea said. "Just remember . . . you are the gift."

The twinkle in Bea's eye made Sydney giggle. The Book Bea had a huge romance novel selection, and Sydney bet that Bea had read each one of them multiple times. "It's been so long I wouldn't recognize happiness if it bopped me over the head. And someone else? I'm not ready for that. I probably wouldn't even recognize that."

"Oh, sweetie, I guarantee you'll know it. When you do, you won't second-guess what they're thinking. There will be an unspoken understanding. And you'll see. Finally, things will become easy again. Just keep yourself open. And honey, your perfect happiness isn't always about a person. I believe that."

Sydney breathed in deeply. Reuniting with Bea was more than she could have ever hoped for, and darn if that just didn't make her want to break down into a mush pile of tears.

"I'm thankful for you, Bea. I don't know about all that romantic hooey, but your friendship has already changed things for the better." For the past ten months she'd been trying to get past the death of her marriage. Waking up on Valentine's Day to a chocolate heart next to her pillow wasn't unusual, but the note with it had caught her completely off guard. A goodbye note. He'd found someone new, and he was sorry. Which she couldn't have agreed with more. Jon had left a candy heart in RayAnne's room, too, but with no note. He left Sydney to explain his absence.

That day had come with no warning. A total surprise. To her at least, but not to her friends. From their comments, it seemed that they all knew that Jon hadn't been happy for a long while.

Bea's voice brought her back. Which was good, because she was tired of reliving those moments.

"I have a feeling the rest of your life is beginning to unfold in a very special way. You, my dear, can handle anything." Bea wiggled her brows, then spun on her heel and headed over to pour herself a cup of tea.

Sydney stood there wondering how one old woman could make her feel so much stronger. Then, a tall red-haired man rapped on the front window, giving her a start. It was Wes, the man who owned the bike shop.

"The window display looks great," he said with a wide grin and a thumbs up. "Are you working here with Bea?" he asked as he walked inside.

"Yes. Just for the holidays. I started yesterday."

"Good. I still can't believe she's going to close down after the holidays. Won't be the same without this place."

"Closing?"

Wes clamped his jaw tight. "She didn't tell you?" He shook his head. "It's been on the downlow. Only a few people know. Dang. Don't tell her I said anything." He looked past her, then whispered. "Here she comes. Our secret?"

"Of course." Only she couldn't even process the possibility. This place was Bea's whole life. She loved it more than anything. Why would she do that? And selfishly, Sydney needed this place to be here.

"Good morning, Wes." Bea's voice was vibrant and optimistic. "How's business down at the bike shop?"

"It's Christmas. Best time of the year." He rubbed his hands together and blew into them. "Not sure how we went from summer to winter in two days though. I wasn't prepared for this today."

"So you two have met?" Bea glanced between Sydney and Wes.

"I bought RayAnne a bike for Christmas. Wes helped me make a decision. I had no idea how many factors went into picking out the right bike."

"Candy apple–red mountain bike. She'll love it," he said.

"I'd have picked pink," Sydney said. "But my ex turned my precious little princess into a sports fanatic, starting with the St. Louis Cardinals baseball onesie he'd bought to take her home from the hospital in." It was weird to refer to Jon as her ex. Technically he wasn't yet, but he was way closer to an ex than a husband, so she may as well get used to it.

Bea said, "There's not a thing wrong with that. I used to be Tarzan and make the boys be Jane or Cheetah when I was a kid. I was quite scrappy."

Wes laughed. "Still are."

"I'll take that as a compliment," Bea said.

"Meant to be one. I just stopped by to see if you needed any help. But it looks like you've got things under control."

Bea and Sydney exchanged a smile. "We sure do," they both said.

"Then I'll let you girls get back to it. Give a holler if you need anything. Happy to help out, or send one of the boys down." He headed for the door, then tucked his chin beneath his collar as he took the stairs two at a time back toward the sidewalk.

"Wes and his wife are always so helpful. Such a nice couple." Bea watched him turn down Main Street. "It's still out there, Sydney. Don't lose sight of it."

Enough of that already. Sydney was dying to ask about the store, but she'd have to wait until Bea was ready to tell her.

"So, about the window. We need one last thing."

Bea looked confused. "I think it's perfect the way it is."

"Not yet. We need a tree topper. It will give us a little more height. So keep your eye out for something we can use. It needs a flat bottom so I can sit it astride that top book. Meanwhile, care to give me a crash course on the items you think we should focus on selling over the next two weeks until Christmas?"

"Absolutely." Bea motioned Sydney to follow her through the store, pointing out perfect gift items. "Now these are my all-time favorites. The two new novels will sell themselves. But this pop-up Christmas book is extra special. Look at this."

Sydney stepped closer as Bea gently opened the book, laying it flat so that the pop-ups fully engaged. Not only was it three dimensional, but delicate die-cuts gave vivid detail and texture to each page.

"It's gorgeous. So intricate."

"North Carolina author. Amazing story to go with it, too."

Sydney snapped her fingers. "This is it, Bea!"

"What?"

"The tree topper. We can open one of these books on the top of the tree. I can tuck a little light right into the scene. It will be gorgeous." She flipped through the pages. "This one. The village with the church in the middle. What do you think?"

"I love that idea."

"Me too. Only the hard part will be picking which scene to use. I like this one with the nativity, too." Sydney took another copy off the stack. "Come on, let's try it out."

In the window Sydney opened the book flat and set it on top of the tree. As she turned the pages, the pop-ups came to life. She flipped through each one until she hit the one she knew was perfect. The nativity scene. Wise men, animals, and all.

Bea took an audible gasp. "That's perfect!"

"I was just thinking the same thing." Sydney straightened the book so the scene could be viewed from the front window or within the store. "I think I can use that little battery pack light set to light up the manger and the star. We'll no doubt sell the last copy of this book right out of the window, but that's fine. It's a gorgeous book."

"A keepsake," Bea agreed.

Sydney stepped down from the window and swept her hands against her jeans.

"It's the best window display this store has ever had. Breathtaking."

"Thank you." A wave of satisfaction soared through her. "Yeah, it did turn out good." She raised a finger in the air. "Oh, and I made this bin for the song sheets out of some stuff in the back room. I hope you don't mind."

She dragged the box she'd attached to a plant stand that had seen better days out from behind the counter. "I was feeling creative. Plus, you can use it for other things throughout the year."

"I believe you have fallen in love with my store all over again."

Sydney looked across the room. She had. Or maybe she'd never stopped. This place held great memories. The stories she'd been introduced to here had molded the curves of her heart. "I'm excited to share the experience with RayAnne, too. Which reminds me. I was supposed to take her back to Atlanta this weekend if that's not a problem. But then I promise that I'm all yours through the holidays if you don't mind RayAnne hanging around. Her dad will be picking her up Wednesday afternoon as soon as school lets out for the Christmas break."

Bea waved a hand in the air. "Not a problem. I'm flexible."

"I made the promise to take her back to Atlanta to see her favorite Santa a long time ago, and I wish I hadn't now. She's so tied to the traditions we had as a family. I think it's just going to make it harder for her, but a promise is a promise."

"We have a wonderful Santa here at our Santa's Village if y'all change your mind."

"I saw him there yesterday. He really does look the

part. We loved all the shops and stuff there. Kind of a magical place."

"We're quite proud of Santa's Village. I'm glad you got a chance to go by there."

"Me too," Sydney said, just as the first customer of their day walked in.

The hours swept by, and Sydney was surprised by how many customers the store had throughout the day. She was in the middle of helping a customer put together a Christmas gift for her sister when Bea came over. "How's it going over here?"

"It's going great, Miss Bea." The customer lifted the small basket that contained the items Sydney had helped her select. "I'm so excited. My sister is going to love this stuff."

Bea glanced into the basket. "I see there are a few things for you in there, too, Diane."

"You know me so well. I'm using that one-for-her and one-for-me approach to shopping this year. Those bracelets are adorable. I'm checking things off my list."

"I had you on my list today, too. My call list to tell you about Mary Kay's new release. I'm glad you stopped in."

"You know I can't pass up Mary Kay Andrews's new release."

"I'd be happy to gift wrap that for you," Bea said. "I still wrap the prettiest darn package in all of Hopewell."

Diane grinned. "Of course, you do. I was counting on that."

"And you've met Sydney. She's new in town."

"Not new to the town exactly," Sydney said. "I used to spend summers here with my grandparents, but new as in I've just moved here."

"Sydney?"

"Named after my dad—"

"—dy's daddy," Diane completed her sentence. "I know. I've heard you say that before."

Sydney paused.

"You're Sydney Rockford, aren't you?"

"I am."

"Oh my gosh. I'm Diane Hartman. No wonder you seemed like an old friend. You are!"

"I can't believe it's you." But now looking at her, she could almost see the little girl that she'd sat with in this very store, the two of them whispering about the books they'd fallen in love with. Those thick braids that Sydney had always coveted had been lopped off into a chic, short, fringy hairdo that looked more New York City runway than Hopewell.

Diane hitched a hand to her hip. "What brought you back?"

"Long story."

"I've thought of you so many times over the years. We've got to get together. I want to hear everything."

Bea touched Sydney's elbow. "Honey, it's about time for you to pick up your daughter."

"A daughter?" Diane held her hand to her heart. "I have a ten-year-old daughter and six-year-old son. We've got to catch up over a glass of wine."

"We do. It's great to see you again." Sydney glanced at her watch. "Oh, gosh. I'm going to be late. Thank you, Bea. Where has this day gone? I'm sorry. I do have to run, but let's talk."

"Miss Bea has my phone number."

Sydney grabbed her purse and coat and headed to the door. "Merry Christmas, Diane. It was so great to see you after all of these years." She pulled her coat on. "Goodbye, Bea. I'll see you on Sunday. Diane, I can't wait to catch up."

"Thanks, dear. Be careful tomorrow. I hear they're calling for some bad weather and it's coming from that way."

Sydney didn't even mind the nip in the air this afternoon. Hopewell seemed to be handing out warm hugs today, in the shape of friends.

Chapter Six

Saturday morning Sydney's alarm went off at six o'clock to allow them enough time to make it to the mall in Atlanta by lunchtime. A visit with Santa, a little shopping, and then dinner on their way home. It was going to be one long day, but Sydney wasn't about to complain about it. She only had a few more days with RayAnne before Jon came to pick her up for the holiday break.

Division of property hadn't been much of a problem. Those were just things that had been accumulated during happier times in their marriage. Easy to let go of now.

Having to split time with their daughter was an entirely different situation. Every time Jon picked RayAnne up and spoiled her to the nth degree, it was one more time Sydney had to listen to RayAnne say she wanted to live with him.

Heartbreaking. Not that RayAnne loved her dad more. In her heart, Sydney knew that wasn't the case. The problem was that all the money and fun seemed to be on his side of the fence, and the emotion and readjustments in her world. It wasn't a fair fight.

She already missed RayAnne like crazy and she hadn't even left yet.

Sydney hugged her robe close as she pushed her toes into her favorite slippers, then walked out into the hallway.

This old farmhouse was drafty. Replacing the windows was going to be something she'd have to do eventually, but camping in the living room in front of the fireplace was an economical option for the time being. If it was this cold now, how was it going to be when the real winter weather arrived?

The smell of coffee hit her before she got to the kitchen. Thank goodness for coffee on a timer. She poured a cup, suddenly wishing she'd brought her pretty new mug home with her. She hugged the warm mug to her as she turned on the television that hung near the kitchen table.

The local weatherman enthusiastically made his predictions for the next two days. Freezing temperatures and drizzly rain would create hazardous conditions.

Sydney walked over to the window and peered out. It didn't look good.

RayAnne came into the kitchen and pulled a chair from the table, the legs screeching against the hardwood floors.

"Good morning, sunshine." Sydney poured a glass of orange juice and sat down in the chair across from her. "Sleep good?"

"Ummhmm." She sipped the orange juice. "It's cold. Do we have any hot chocolate?"

"In the pantry."

RayAnne climbed out of her chair and put a mug of hot water in the microwave.

"The weather's not looking good."

RayAnne snapped her head around. "Mo-om."

"Icy conditions. I don't want to drive over the mountain to Atlanta in bad weather. It's just not worth the risk. I'm sorry."

"You promised."

"I'll take you to Santa's Village here in town. Bea says they have the best Santa ever. She would know."

"I like *our* Santa."

Sydney really didn't want to argue with RayAnne this morning. It wasn't like it was really the same Santa every year that they went to see. That was easy enough to tell by the pictures, but she couldn't say that to RayAnne. "I can't control the weather."

"Maybe it will clear up."

"Even if it clears up here, the weather is bad all the way to Atlanta. I know you're disappointed, but can we make the best of it?"

RayAnne stirred her hot chocolate.

The silent treatment? Sydney thought. "I'll check the hours for Santa today. I think it said ten to four on the sign when we were there the other day." She searched for their website on her phone. "It'll be fun. Come on. Say something."

"So I can go back to bed?"

"Yes. You can go back to bed. I'm going to make a fire in the fireplace to try to chase the chill away. You can sleep down here if you want. Go grab your pillow and quilt. We'll snuggle, have a late breakfast, and then go see Santa. Deal?"

"I guess." RayAnne slurped her hot chocolate, then lumbered down the hall and upstairs.

Sydney brought in a couple pieces of firewood from the porch and started a fire with one of those fire starter logs. It might be cheating, but it took her nearly a whole pad of matches just to light the edge of that paper. She wasn't up for learning to start a fire from scratch.

Colorful flames licked the air. She tented two small logs on either side of the starter, then poked at them to get them nestled with enough air between them to make them burn hot, just like the guy who'd delivered the logs had told her to do. She stepped back, warming her hands in front of the bright orange flames.

RayAnne came back downstairs with her pillow and quilt and spread out on the couch. "That's toasty. You did good, Mom."

"Thanks, kiddo. I'm getting better at it. That's for sure."

RayAnne laughed. "At least we didn't have to open the doors and windows to let the smoke out this time."

Sydney laughed. "That was a rookie mistake." But it had been funny after the fact. She sat down at the other end of the couch, gazing into the pretty flames and thinking about how quiet the house was going to be with RayAnne gone. She slid her legs out to her side and tucked them under RayAnne's quilt. RayAnne was already asleep.

By nine o'clock Sydney couldn't stay tucked in any longer, so she got up and started frying bacon. Enough for breakfast and some left to have bacon cheeseburgers that night. RayAnne's favorite.

When she heard RayAnne turn on the television in the other room, Sydney cracked the eggs and fixed breakfast. She arranged the food on the plate to look like a smiley face—eyes of eggs, bacon mouth, and a fresh orange slice nose.

She carried them out to the living room. "Hungry?"

"You woke me up with the bacon. Smells so good in here."

Sydney grinned. "Always works."

RayAnne took one of the plates and set it in her lap,

lifting a piece of bacon to her lips. "Think we could stop by The Book Bea today, too?

"Sure. You want to pick up some books for your trip?"

RayAnne shrugged. "I guess. And I thought we could say hello to Miss Bea. I like her."

"She's very nice."

"I can't believe it's less than a week before school's out."

And you leave, Sydney thought. "I know. It's going to be here before we know it. We probably should start figuring out what you're going to pack. I bought you some new socks. You'll need those for skiing. Your dad said something about needing some dressy clothes for dinner."

RayAnne rolled her eyes. "I liked it better when Dad and I just ate junk all the time. It's Ashley that likes to eat at those fancy places. Last time we had to eat raw fish. It was just gross. And she got mad when I didn't like it."

"Well, try to enjoy it. Not raw fish, but the places. You'll find that one day you'll enjoy going out to fancy places, too." Would've been nice if Jon had made the effort to take her to a few the last few years.

"I doubt that. I hate dresses."

"We can shop for a new one."

"No, thank you. I'd rather buy something good than a dress. I'll wear the stupid blue one."

"Suit yourself." That was going to be Jon's battle to fight. No sense in stressing herself out over it. She leaned over and gave RayAnne a hug. "I love you just the way you are, kiddo."

"Thanks, Mom."

Sydney finished her breakfast and took their plates into the kitchen before going upstairs to change. The leisurely morning had been an unexpected luxury. She took her time in the shower and even put on some makeup. Something she hadn't done in way too long. It felt nice to make an effort for no one but herself. She leaned closer to the mirror and applied lipstick, stepped back and pressed her lips together, then fluffed her hair.

"You about ready, RayAnne?"

"Already downstairs."

A good sign. Maybe today would be okay after all.

The drizzle had stopped, but it was still cold outside. Bundled in their winter jackets, Sydney and RayAnne headed into Santa's Village. Heat lamps had been set up, offering a warm place to thaw, but with so many people standing close together it really didn't feel that bad.

"Want to look around first?" Sydney asked.

"No. Let's talk to Santa first, then look around."

"Sounds like a plan." Sydney let RayAnne lead the way.

They stood in line, moving up a few steps at a time.

Sydney watched Santa. It looked like the same one who'd been there Thursday night, but then red suits and white beards had a way of looking the same.

The music coming from the speakers suddenly stopped mid-jingle, and the visitors who'd been singing along found themselves in an awkward a capella until a man's voice announced, "Hopewell Elementary School." A choir of children's voices rose from the ground to the heavy clouds hanging just above them in a chorus of "What Child Is This?"

"That's your school, RayAnne. Did you know they had a choir?"

She shook her head.

"They're really good."

RayAnne nodded and sang quietly along.

The line slowly moved closer to Santa Claus, who seemed to be in no hurry at all. One at a time he seemed to give his full attention to each child.

The song ended and everyone clapped.

The first five chords of "The First Noel" was all it took for RayAnne to recognize it. "My favorite one!"

A woman next to them leaned in. "Mine too."

They sang along as they continued to inch along in line.

A few minutes later a costumed character dressed up like a snowman walked along the line, handing out free pencils decorated with poinsettias from the local florist and a coupon for a discount on a cookie.

RayAnne thrummed her pencil in the air and then against her leg as she sang along to a chorus of "Rudolph the Red-Nosed Reindeer" coming over the speakers.

An ear-piercing squeal of "RayAnne!" came from across the way. Two girls ran across the lot, leaving their moms looking confused in the middle of Santa's Village.

The girls shared how *totally awesome* their visits with Santa had been, confirming how cool he was, and that every year they got what they asked for.

RayAnne's face lit up. "I know what I'm asking for then."

"What?"

RayAnne looked like she didn't want to tell them at first. Probably afraid the wish wouldn't come true if she shared it, but that was birthday wishes not Santa. Sydney hoped RayAnne was going to say a bike, since that's what she'd gotten her.

"A four-wheeler."

"No way," the auburn-haired girl said, looking impressed.

RayAnne stood taller. "They're cool. My dad got one for us, but then we had to move. So maybe Santa can bring me one."

Sydney's mood sank. That was not going to happen. There was no way she was buying her daughter a four-wheeler. They were dangerous. Jon had started all of that, not for RayAnne, but because he'd wanted one. And boy had there been a battle when he demanded it in the division of property, because RayAnne had felt like it was hers even if she'd ridden on the back most of the time. If RayAnne had any idea how easily Sydney had agreed to Jon's request for that four-wheeler she'd be mad at her for sure.

She hoped RayAnne hadn't been trying to guilt him into buying her one. Jon would never do that without talking to her—or would he? The next time they talked she might have to ask very specifically what his gift plans were for RayAnne.

RayAnne bounded back over to Sydney, cheerful and a bundle of energy. "The girls said the cookies here are the best." She waved the coupon in the air. "Can we get one?"

"We'll do that after we're done here."

Santa's head elf was a pretty blonde girl, complete with pointy ears and elf shoes that turned up a good three inches at the toes. Sydney wondered if the elf and Santa were somehow related. They seemed to have one of those unspoken communications that kept everything moving along smoothly.

RayAnne grabbed Sydney's hand. There were only a couple people in line in front of them finally. RayAnne's hand was sweaty, and Sydney gave it a little squeeze. At least if she was nervous it meant she still believed. At least a little.

The elf walked over to them. "First time visiting us?"

RayAnne nodded and glanced away.

"We just moved here," Sydney said.

"Welcome to Hopewell. It's a wonderful town. You're going to love it here. What's your name?" she asked.

"Ray."

"RayAnne," Sydney inserted. Jon had wanted a boy so badly that he'd practically ignored the fact that she was a girl. Sydney had never been a fan of that nickname. "Her dad is the only one who calls her Ray."

The elf typed the name into her tablet. "Don't be nervous, RayAnne. Looks like Santa has you on his nice list."

RayAnne's face lit up.

The elf turned to Sydney. "Would y'all like a picture? No obligation to buy unless you like it. They'll be on display in the gift shop when you exit."

"Yes, definitely."

"Mom!" RayAnne huffed in exaggeration. "I'm too old for a Santa picture!"

"Oh, just do it for me. You can give a copy to your dad for Christmas. He'll love it."

RayAnne pouted, letting out a little huff.

"Go ahead. Act a fool. Don't you think Santa can see you from just over there?" Sydney gave the elf another nod of confirmation.

The pout disappeared from RayAnne's face instantaneously.

The elf led them down the red velvet roped walkway leading to Santa. Sydney wondered if this was what it felt like to walk one of those red carpet events. As they got closer to Santa's Snow Castle she was surprised at just how intricate the details were. Something she'd expect of a big budget store in Atlanta, not tiny Hopewell. They'd certainly put a lot of effort into this display.

They waited patiently until there were only two women in front of them. *Those women have to be about my age,* Sydney thought. She'd overheard them say they were planning to ask Santa for new boyfriends this year.

"Have you looked into Santa's eyes?" one asked.

"Yes. I know Santa was supposed to have blue eyes, but I'm telling you those brown eyes of his send me absolutely over the North Pole. They look like dark chocolate. And you know how I love chocolate."

"I'd love to see him without that getup on. When I came last week I snuck a squeeze of his arm. I swear he has the biceps of a professional athlete."

"I'm dying to see his mouth. I'm going to tug on his beard and see if it pulls away," she giggled.

"I did last year and it is stuck tight. He's determined to keep that secret. Probably a felon on the run from the law."

"That would be my luck. Mom always said I was a bad-boy magnet."

"Everybody has baggage. He's probably a closet drunk. Might even have twenty nippers in his big old Santa boot right now."

"His nose is red. Isn't that a sign of drinking? Red wine makes people flush. That could be it . . . he's a wino."

"I'd drink with him. I'm telling you he's not a drunk. He's perfect. Kind. He listens. Even with us being totally inappropriate he won't be inappropriate. You watch."

The head elf came over and led the two women for their turn.

Sydney didn't find the humor in it at all. Yeah, she might be skeptical of love since Jon's betrayal, but even before all of that she wouldn't have found their behavior cute.

She couldn't help but stare as the two women traipsed up to Santa's Snow Castle. They were definitely working it, flirting so blatantly that Sydney was embarrassed for them. *Lord, please don't let me get that desperate,* she prayed. *Ever.*

It irritated her that they'd take up Santa's time when so many children were waiting in line.

The elf came back over. "You ready?"

"I guess. Do you have a name?" RayAnne asked.

"Of course, I do. My name is Rebecca."

"Hi, Rebecca. No offense but this Santa Claus isn't anything like our one at home. His beard doesn't even look real."

Rebecca straightened, and then leaned forward with her hands on her knees. "Give him a chance. He might not look like your old Santa, but I have worked for him a long, long time. I can promise you that there is something very special about this one."

Sydney flushed. *Sorry,* she mouthed to Rebecca.

"We were supposed to go back to our hometown in Atlanta today. The weather messed us up."

Rebecca nodded. "I understand. Sometimes things happen for a reason."

"Sorry, kiddo." How many times would she apologize for this today? *As many as it took.*

RayAnne sighed. "I know it's not your fault, Mom. I love you anyway."

"Love you, too." She wrapped her arms around her daughter and gave a humbled smile toward Rebecca.

"Moving is hard." Rebecca laid a gentle hand on

RayAnne's shoulder. "It's your turn next." She led them to the left side of Santa's Snow Castle where Sydney could wait, then led RayAnne up the stairs.

Sydney's throat tightened. Tears welled as every Santa visit over the years came crashing back. Always the three of them. Jon had always made time for the three of them to make this Santa visit each year. She'd never felt quite this lonely.

This Santa's padding looked just as faux as that cottony beard and eyebrows, but there was something genuine about him. The way he moved, cared, and didn't seem to be in a hurry at all. And his elf had a gentle and kind spirit, too.

Rebecca walked over and gave her a gentle smile. "Told you he was a good Santa. Everyone loves him."

Sydney watched him again. Still just as thoughtful and focused as he'd been earlier. Maybe this Santa did have a connection with the big guy.

"Ho-ho-ho. Who do I have here?" Mac held his arms wide, welcoming the little girl.

"RayAnne." She hesitated, then climbed onto his lap.

Mac liked to catch them off guard when they seemed a little suspicious. "You're not the RayAnne on the naughty list, are you?"

"No, sir."

"I didn't think so. She has blonde hair."

"You're probably confused because I just moved here with my mom."

"That's right. You were from . . ."

"Near Atlanta."

"Took the words right out of my mouth." Wasn't his first rodeo. He had a way of pulling details out of the kids so that they walked away thinking that he knew everything. Well, he did have a few tidbits from Rebecca to help, too. In this case, the young girl's nickname.

"Sometimes our lists need a little review. Do you think you've been a good girl this year?"

RayAnne hesitated. That didn't happen often, but he braced himself, because when they became thoughtful like that, there was usually more to the story.

"I think so. It's been a hard year. We had to move because my dad has a girlfriend. I'm afraid maybe it was something I did. Do you know?"

Mac let out a breath. "It's not something you did. You've been a good girl. It's not easy though."

"I miss him. But I miss all of us together most. It's sad."

"Have you talked to your parents about it?"

"I'm afraid to make them sad, too."

"I know they both love you very much. They want you to be happy. Never be afraid to talk to your parents about what's hurting your heart." Mac's throat tightened. He wondered what thoughts had gone through Seth's head about Genna leaving that he'd never voiced. "What's on your list this year?"

"I miss my dad. And now we moved. Dad is taking me skiing with his girlfriend so I won't even be home. Mom will be all alone. Can you bring something to Mom instead?"

"That's very kind, Ray. You are definitely on the nice list."

She leaned back, her mouth forming an O. "My daddy calls me that."

He winked. "I know. Our secret."

"If you could just find a present for Mom so she's happy again, that would be really good. I want a four-wheeler for Christmas. Daddy got one for us to ride, but he wouldn't let us bring it. So if he isn't going to give me one maybe you could bring that."

"You can be happy in your heart, and know that both of your parents love you no matter where they live. I want you to believe that. Can you do that for me?"

"Yes, sir." RayAnne lowered her head. "Do you have our new address?"

"I sure do." He tapped the side of his head. "Got your address right here. Don't you worry. I'll find you no matter where you go. Santa always knows where his favorite nice kids are. And remember that not all the gifts of Christmas are under the tree. Okay?"

"Thanks, Santa."

"You're welcome, RayAnne. Let's have a picture taken." He and RayAnne turned and faced the camera, and Rebecca snapped the picture. The little girl turned back and gave him a hug before skipping back to her mom.

Rebecca gestured them toward the exit.

"He's the real Santa, Mom," RayAnne gushed. "He knew everything. He's totally different, Mom. That *is* Santa." She looked back toward him with a wide grin.

This was exactly why he loved this job. He leaned over, picked up his mug of water and took a sip.

"Really, Mom. The bad weather was the best thing that could have happened today. I'm so glad I didn't miss this." She sucked in a big breath. "Love you, Mom."

Rebecca clapped her hands. "I know exactly how you feel. He's the only reason I work here. I was just telling your mom that."

Mac loved how Rebecca perpetuated the myth.

He noticed that RayAnne's pretty, dark-haired mother was staring at him. He smiled and waved.

She wiggled her fingers in an embarrassed wave back, then pressed her lips together in a smile that revealed a dimple in her left cheek.

And it just wasn't right for a woman so beautiful to be so sad that her daughter was worried. And what kind of man cheated on a woman like that? He silently hoped that Hopewell would change her life for the better.

Mac drove home, humming along to Tchaikovsky's "Waltz of the Flowers" from *The Nutcracker*.

He enjoyed the music at Santa's Village, too, but this music had a way of making him feel at peace. The rise and fall of the melody told a story without any words at all.

Tonight several of the houses on his route home had Christmas lights turned on. He and Seth would work on theirs that weekend.

Usually when Mac got home, Seth's bedroom light would be on. Not the case tonight. He hoped Seth hadn't gotten sick right before Christmas break.

He parked in front of the house and went in through the garage. The house was eerily quiet.

"Hey. Anyone around?"

"In here, Dad."

Mac followed his son's voice to the kitchen, where he and Haley sat on opposite ends of the table with a pile of markers between them.

"What are y'all up to?"

"Christmas cards," Seth said.

"School project?"

"No." Seth dipped his head, leaning closer to the glossy cardstock in front of him. "For our military people away from their families."

That caught Mac's attention. "That's really nice."

"Yeah, Haley and I were talking about it. She said that lots of people where she lives make cards and they send them overseas so everyone gets something from home. I told her I could draw pretty good."

"Yeah. Sandbagger. This kid is one heckuva an artist," Haley said.

"He is. Always had a knack for drawing. You should've seen the—"

"Dad. Don't tell that story."

"What?" Mac leaned on the kitchen counter next to the table. "You mean the one—"

"Where I painted a mural on the shed." He glared at his dad. "He always tells that story."

"Wasn't just any shed. Tell the rest of the story, Seth."

Seth laughed. "Yeah. So it was apparently the new neighbor's super expensive shed." Seth's nervous laugh bubbled. He had the best laugh. "Hey, I was expressing myself."

Haley joined in the laughter. "What did you draw?"

Seth cracked up. "A pterodactyl eating Barney."

"Barney the purple dinosaur?"

Mac said, "Yep. Seth never was a fan of that show."

"Clearly," she said. "Well, he's doing a good job here. Not one dinosaur in the bunch."

"Oh, he did a great job on the shed. Unfortunately, our new neighbors didn't turn out to be art lovers. I had to replace the T1-11 on that side of the building."

"Consider it an investment in my future as a Christmas card artist." Seth held up the card he'd just finished drawing.

"He's drawing. I'm coloring," Haley said. "Want to help?"

"Sure." Mac pulled out a chair and picked out a

marker. "I've been known to color inside the lines a time or two."

Seth handed him the card. "Here. You can color this one."

He held the folded piece of cardstock in his hand. Santa saluting a whimsical snowman wearing dog tags in front of a Christmas tree with a flag on the top held just the right balance of message and meaning. "This is really good, son."

"Thanks. Haley and I came up with the idea together."

"I think they'll really like it."

"Figured it was a good way to help," Seth said.

"It is." They sat at the table coloring in the cards until Haley finally got up. "I'm beat. I'll take some home with me to work on."

"Okay. And maybe I can make some more before it's time to mail them," Seth said.

"That would be great." Haley gathered her things. "I need to send them out by Wednesday or they won't make it on time."

"I'll make a bunch," Seth said. "I like doing this."

Mac got up and followed her to the door, paying her for her help. "Thanks so much. You've been a really good influence on Seth."

"He's a good kid. Seth overheard me talking to my husband on the phone tonight. Greg was talking about this project. Seth overheard us talking about it and had a million questions. He offered to help. It hadn't been my plan, just turned out to be a happy accident."

"It's great. I'm thrilled. Christmas has been tough on him since his mom left. I'm thankful he's found something to connect with for the holiday that is positive."

"He sure seems into it. I'm glad to have his help.

Makes me feel better, too. I'll see you Tuesday night," she said as she walked out the door.

Mac shut the door behind her and went back into the kitchen. "Think it's time to call it a night?"

"No school tomorrow. Can I work on this just a little longer?"

"Sure." Mac got a soda out of the refrigerator. "We'll decorate the outside of the house tomorrow. Looks like the wet weather is going to move out of here tonight."

"Sounds good."

Seth had drawn a Santa on the card. He had to have a little Christmas magic in that twelve-year-old heart.

"Dad, do you think we could go to the bookstore tomorrow? I have an idea, but I'm not sure how to draw it. Thought I could find a book with some pictures in it."

Mac felt a little like he'd been swept into someone else's house by mistake. "Sure. We can definitely do that."

"Cool."

"I'm going to jump in the shower." Mac started to walk out of the kitchen, then stopped. "Son, I'm proud of you. For this project. That's really mature of you to understand that, and to help like this."

"Yeah. I get it. It's hard when you want to be with someone and they aren't around."

Ouch. That hit the target. Didn't matter how hard he tried to be everything, the truth was Seth would always feel that gap that Genna had left.

"Besides. I really like drawing," Seth said. "I'm better at it than I remembered."

At least the kid knew what he was good at. More than Mac could say for most kids that age. Mac had never thought much about encouraging Seth in his artwork. They spent almost all their time outdoors or involved in sports. Seth was good at sports but never as into them as Mac had been at that age. This was where having two parents brought balance to a kid's world. He'd try to do better.

Chapter Seven

Sunday morning Sydney and RayAnne went to the early service at church so that Sydney could make it to the bookstore before it opened.

The old church was filled to capacity, and there was comfort in being able to pick up the worn hymnal and sing familiar songs.

With the last amen, everyone filed out slowly and orderly from the back to the front.

Sydney waited on RayAnne, who'd decided to try the youth group today instead, smiling as people walked by.

"Mom!" RayAnne ran up to her with a slender freckle-faced girl. "Can I go to Jenny's today?"

"Sydney?" Diane followed Jenny down the aisle. "We just keep bumping in to each other."

"Is Jenny your daughter?"

"Yes. What a small world. I guess we were going to connect one way or another with you being back in town. This is great. We'd love to have RayAnne over. Jenny's been talking about the new girl at school all week."

"Please, Mom!" RayAnne bounced with excitement.

"You sure it's no trouble?"

Diane hitched her handbag up on her shoulder. "She can stay for supper."

RayAnne folded her hands and pressed them beneath her chin. "Please. Please. Ple-ease?"

"Oh, Miss Dramatic here. How can I say no to that?"

The two girls squealed and bounced off to the side in a fit of giggles.

"Thank you, Diane."

"No problem. My house is girl central these days. I'll just drop her off at your place when we're done. Around six-thirty or seven?"

"We're staying at my grandparents' old place over on Green Needles Lane."

"I know exactly where that is. Let me know if there's anything I can do while y'all are getting settled in. My husband is pretty handy, too."

"I will. Thank you for inviting her over. Making some friends will surely help make the adjustment easier."

"Anytime. Trust me, she's going to love it here. Plus, if she can burn some energy out of Jenny it'll be a blessing for me, too." A small boy in a Carolina Panthers sweatshirt broke free from her hold. "Zach, come back here. Do you think we actually had that much energy at some point in our lives?" Zach ran over to the girls and then back to Diane and wrapped himself around her leg.

"I'm pretty sure we did."

Diane handed her a business card. "Our home number is on there too in case you haven't gotten it from Bea yet."

Sydney glanced at the card. Diane's husband owned the local gas station. "You sure you don't mind dropping her off? I can pick her up if that's easier."

"Not at all. Happy to do it. Tony's working late. It'll give me something to do, and get us out of the house." Diane glanced over at the girls. "They seem to really be hitting it off."

"Yeah, they do." Sydney dug into her purse and wrote her number on the back of an old appointment card. "Here's my number. Since your husband is working late, why don't you, Jenny, and Zach have dinner at our house? I'd love the company, and it would give us a chance to catch up. It'll make me feel better about you taking RayAnne for the day."

Diane took the card. "I would love that. The timing couldn't be more perfect."

"I'll see you then."

She watched as Diane herded the group of kids together and then through the parking lot to her minivan.

Cars were lined up at the traffic light on Main Street. The huge congregation made for a slow exit from the parking lot, so Sydney veered off of her path toward her car and headed toward The Book Bea. It was just a couple blocks away. She'd walk down, and come back and get her car later. The exercise wouldn't hurt her anyway.

Bea was already in the store when Sydney got there. The aroma of fresh coffee filled the air, and customers were already browsing.

"Am I late?" Sydney asked as she tucked her purse beneath the counter.

"No," Bea said. "Folks know I sometimes come in early. We're pretty relaxed about the hours these days."

"How are you today?" Sydney said to a woman who looked like she'd just come from church, too. "I can help you with that." Sydney punched the codes and prices into the register for each book. "Did you see there's a coloring book that goes with this one?"

"No. I didn't."

"Would you care to see it?"

"That would be a wonderful addition. Thank you."

"My pleasure." Sydney whisked around the counter

and picked up a coloring book and a pack of colored pencils. She waved them both in the air as she headed back to the register. "I tried these pencils out the other day. They're almost like crayons. Really neat. Don't know if you need them."

"Thank you. Yes, I'll take them both."

Bea looked pleased with the upsell.

A steady stream of customers filled the afternoon. Bea stayed busy at the checkout counter wrapping gifts, and Sydney waited on customers and rang them up.

"Can I help you?" Sydney asked a gentleman wearing a heavy wool coat and carrying a cardboard box.

"Why haven't we met?" He jostled the package to the crook of his left arm and extended his hand. "Mayor Blevins."

"The mayor?" Should she curtsy or something? "Hi there. I'm helping Bea out over the holidays. I just moved here." She motioned over her shoulder. "Well, not here here. Into my grandparents' old farmhouse on the other side of town."

"You're the Rockfords' granddaughter? I knew you'd come back and take care of that place eventually."

The words stung a little. It wasn't like she'd meant to shirk the responsibility that the inheritance had carried with it. She just never really thought much about it once Jon put the kibosh on using it as a vacation retreat.

The mayor looked her up and down. "You favor her. Carmen, that is. I can see it in those laughing blue eyes of yours."

"Thank you." Although she'd never seen the resemblance herself. It was hard to think of yourself as looking like an old woman. But her grandmother had been a kind and wonderful lady, so being compared to her was nice.

The mayor's head swiveled. "This place is really bustling today. I guess I can just give these to you. It's the song sheets for the town's caroling night coming up soon. You know about that, right?"

"Oh, great. Yes, we've been talking about that." She took the box. "I can take care of these."

"The window looks lovely by the way. I guess you had a little hand in that."

"My daughter and I worked on it together. It was fun, especially once we knew about the song so we could tie the display to the theme."

"Yes, perfectly!" The mayor edged his way back to the door. "I have several other deliveries to make. Tell Bea we'll see her at the chamber of commerce meeting next week." He headed for the door and then spun around. "Oh, and one more thing. Let her know that we have had a resounding number of early ticket purchases this year. Ask her to please double the number of those amazing treats she makes, will you? And ask her to put one aside for me. It's my favorite stop."

"Will do." Sydney said. A line of five people had accrued while she was talking with the mayor. Bea was ringing up customers, but the way she chit-chatted with every single person sure did slow down the progress at checkout.

Sydney walked over and started ringing up customers, letting Bea play hostess and talk folks into letting her wrap the presents for a cash tip in the big, foil-wrapped Folgers's can on the counter.

Finally, around five-thirty things quieted down. Sydney stepped away from the counter and made two cups of tea.

"Here." She handed one of them to Bea. "Drink up."

"Oh, thank you, Sydney." Bea blew across the rim of

her cup and took a sip, one finger still pressed in the center of the bow she'd been finishing up. She quickly swung the ribbon around and up and through and then tightened it. "There you go."

The wiry boy in front of her grinned. "Thank you, ma'am."

A dark-haired man with the deepest brown eyes Sydney had ever seen watched the boy from next in line.

"He yours?" Sydney asked.

The man nodded. "Yes. He is." He laid a stack of books on the counter.

"You must be proud."

"Oh yeah. Understatement."

Sydney quickly rang up the books. Two historical fiction novels, the latest bestselling crime fiction, and a coffee table book of military equipment. "You a veteran?"

He looked puzzled. "Oh, the book. No."

"Gift?"

"No. Seth, my son, he draws. He's making homemade cards for the troops. He was looking for inspiration."

"That's great. We used to do that where I lived. Well, with store-bought cards, but we got a big group of folks together to sign and address them. It's an awesome tradition."

"Yeah. Seth's really been into it."

"That's great. Balancing a little creative outlet and the Christmas spirit."

"Exactly."

"You know," Sydney said. "If you wanted to get a group of folks to help you with those, I'm sure we could set up some tables here for one night after work." Sydney regretted opening her mouth so quickly. The thought had just tumbled right out. It wasn't her place to offer, but surely Bea wouldn't mind. "I mean I could talk to Bea for you."

"Great. I didn't catch your name."

"Sydney Ragsdale."

"Nice to meet you, Sydney. I'm Kevin MacAlee, but everyone calls me Mac. Are you related to Bea? Visiting?"

"Oh, no. Just helping out over the holidays. I'm new to town."

"Welcome to Hopewell. Good to have some new folks coming into town. I'm sure I'll see you around."

And his brown eyes seemed to dance when he talked. How'd he do that? "Yeah. Probably." She hoped so, and that was completely unexpected. So were the flurries in her stomach right now. "Small town and all."

"Yeah. Small town." He signed the credit card slip and then stepped back, bumping into the woman behind him. "Sorry, ma'am. See you, Sydney. Nice meeting you."

Bea elbowed Sydney. "I see you met Mac. He's our most eligible bachelor, you know."

"Oh stop it. Get back to wrapping presents."

"Hopewell local boy. Went away to college then came right back here to teach."

"Not interested," Sydney said, hardly able to hold back the laugh at the ridiculous thought. Exhausted, she walked the last customer to the door herself. If she was this tired, she could only imagine how Bea felt. She flipped the sign on the door to CLOSED. "Wow," she said. "How do you handle this alone, Bea?"

Bea's laugh was as soothing as those chimes that hung above the counter. "It's not this busy all the time. The holiday rush. And quite honestly, I just work at my own pace. If anyone is in a big hurry, they know they can just leave me a list of what they've got and come back and settle up later."

"That seems risky. Do you always get your money?"

"Of course. No one would ever take advantage of me. It's like family around here, and like you, most of them have been coming here since they were just kids themselves."

Bea pulled the tray from the register and started separating tickets and money. "Help me tally these up. I think this may have been my best day all year."

"Sure." Sydney stacked the tickets and started a tally on the old calculator. The tape unfurled from the top with a chugga-chug-chug every time she hit the plus key.

"I like to close out the register every night if I can. Just helps me stay on top of things. I'm afraid if I get behind I'll never catch up."

"Nothing wrong with routine. Especially if it works for you."

Bea counted coins. "It's worked for over forty years."

"I'd say that's a pretty good track record."

Sydney finished tallying the tickets, then counted out the money in stacks by denomination, matching her totals to the ones Bea had written on a tablet.

Bea ran a tape against the final numbers, and then pressed the button that fed the paper out. She peered over the top of her glasses as she carefully penciled in the final figures in the old ledger. "Yes! I knew it. My biggest sales day all year. And I have you to thank for it."

"Me?"

"Yes. Don't think I didn't notice how you helped people find little extras to add to their purchase. The coloring books, and I think you may have sold me out of the literary coffee mugs. And if there's one copy of the latest bestseller by Nicholas Sparks, I'll be shocked."

"Well, that's an awesome book. I read it in one night."

"You've earned your keep. Thank you for happening in my store when you did."

But it was Sydney who felt like she should be thanking Bea. The last couple days had given her new hope that she could find a way to rebuild a good life with RayAnne, and maybe there was a chance to do that in Hopewell long term. She'd thought it might be a soft landing place just for a little while. She could gain practical work experience to build a résumé so they could move back to Atlanta, where all of RayAnne's old friends were. And with the passing of time, hopefully Sydney's friends would have forgotten all the drama between her and Jon. But maybe that wasn't the only long-term option.

"I think you've found your natural gift. You're great at helping people find what they didn't even know they wanted."

"Maybe you'll keep me on after the holiday and next year will be your best *year* yet." She was digging for information. Hoping that what Wes had said had been just a rumor.

"Oh, Sydney. I probably should have been more specific when I told you this job was just for the holidays."

Sydney's stomach took a backflip. It was true. *Here it comes,* she thought.

"I'm closing the doors of The Book Bea on New Year's Eve."

"But why? I don't understand. Business is good, and you seem to really love spending time with your customers."

"I do, but I'm too old to keep this kind of schedule anymore. It's time."

Sydney turned away, not wanting to show her disappointment. It was selfish after all. Bea had to be in her late seventies. She deserved the chance to slow down. But this was a good place. And Sydney needed it right now. "The town needs The Book Bea. It's more than just a store, it's part of the town's charm."

"That's so sweet of you."

"What if I help you? I could open and close every day. Or we could adjust the hours to help make it easier for you to work. Or you could have some days off. Maybe you do a short week like hair salons do with the 'closed on Mondays' thing."

"I've thought this through. It's time."

"Oh, Bea, working here the last couple days has been the best part of my whole year. I really hate to think the store's not going to be here anymore."

"It's more than just me growing old. I'm so behind the times. We need technology to keep up, and I just can't do it. I don't have any interest in learning all that new stuff, and I don't have the money to invest, either. But thank you. You're going to be the best part of this last season here."

"What are you doing with the building? I'm assuming you own it. Right?"

"Oh yes. My sweet husband bought it for me as a wedding gift. His family lived here in Hopewell their whole lives. When he brought me here to meet them, this old building was the town library. It was so enchanting."

Bea looked as if she'd drifted back fifty years in time. "When I saw it I told him that I dreamed of living here. It hadn't even been for sale at the time, but my sweet Henry was quite persuasive when he wanted to be."

"He sounds like a very special man."

"Oh, he was. Spoiled me like crazy."

"So, you actually lived here at one time."

"Yes. We'd hoped to fill every single bedroom with a big family. All eight of them. But we were never blessed with any children."

"I'm so sorry."

"Me too, dear, but in a way every child who passes through those doors is mine. At least they take a little piece of my heart from this store. That's been enough."

"Is there a reason you didn't put this place up for sale? I mean if you're closing and all." She realized she might be jinxing herself right out of an opportunity by asking, but she also didn't want to take advantage of Bea.

"I'd thought I'd sell the business, but there's no one locally that really loves this place like I do, and it wouldn't do to bring an outsider in. They wouldn't understand how things work around here. I'll probably let the building sit as is for a while until I figure it out. The tenants who rent the three upstairs apartments have all been so good. I hate to turn them out. There aren't too many places to rent in this town."

"Hadn't thought about that, but if you're willing to let it sit for a while, why not just stay open? I'll help. I love this place."

"Maybe I'll find someone to rent the downstairs out as another shop of some kind."

"Or maybe as a living space. The kitchen is still in working order, isn't it?"

"It would take so much work. I can't even really think about that. I really wish I'd found the right person to take it over from me. Someone like you."

"I would love to own this place. I don't know how I could do it, but if you really are thinking to sell The Book Bea, maybe I could buy it." And there she was again, letting the thoughts in her head roll right out to the universe without a second thought. She didn't have the means or the experience to run The Book Bea. What was she thinking?

Bea's face lit up. "I can't tell you how long I've waited in hopes that someone would want to take over my little store. I've prayed about it. And I've believed that someone was on their way."

"So many of the independent bookstores have closed back where we lived. It's hard to see that happen."

"We've remained profitable. That's not the problem."

"This place has a wonderful vibe to it. I feel alive when I'm in here. It's like . . . like an embrace."

"Yes." Bea snapped her fingers in the air. "That's exactly what I said the first time I saw it. I said Henry, when I walk inside that building I feel like I'm in an embrace so loving that nothing could happen to me. That's so funny that you used the same word. I felt such a peace come over me when I was here. I still do."

"I feel it too."

Sydney didn't know how she would do it. Or why she'd want to. Owning a business was a big undertaking, and she'd never been impulsive. But the old Sydney was someone she wanted to leave behind. The new Sydney should learn to follow her dreams even if it meant taking a risk. Maybe even build a legacy that she could share with her daughter. A legacy like The Book Bea.

Bea softened for a moment. "I got the feeling you weren't planning to put roots down here in Hopewell. That this was temporary for you."

"That's not my hope, but it is sort of the plan. I promised RayAnne we'd reassess staying in Hopewell after the school year, but it's not because I don't want to put roots down. My divorce has made things very complicated."

"Maybe it doesn't have to be. Sometimes it's a lot easier to uncomplicate things than it looks like when you're sitting in the middle of the mess. Take a step back. Maybe you were meant to stick around."

"Maybe." But was she fooling herself?

"Tell you what. I was planning to have someone pick up my entire inventory for a flat rate, just to expedite things. But if you really want to hang out here a little longer, I'll put that on hold. Then we'll take this a step at a time."

"But I can't make the promise that I'll stay right now."

"What if you change your mind-set? Really believe you'll stay, rather than just hope. And if things don't work out, then just promise you'll stick around long enough to help me with the liquidation. Is that a deal?"

Sydney wanted to be able to stay here so badly. Far away from Jon's stronghold. Raising her daughter in a small town with good people would be a good thing. She'd treasured the time she'd spent here with her grandparents. RayAnne could grow to love it here, too. She felt an excitement she hadn't felt in a long time.

"Yes. You most certainly have a deal on that." If she believed it, could it possibly come true? Crazier things had happened. *I believe,* she thought fervently.

"I'm so proud of you, Sydney. You can do this."

"I hope I won't let you down."

"Hope? You need to substitute every *hope* with *believe*."

She mentally slashed through the word *hope* and replaced it with *believe* in all capital letters. "I won't let you down."

"That's better. It's a big undertaking, but I believe

you could do even bigger things with this place than I ever have. The Book Bea has taken good care of me for decades. It would do the same for you."

Sydney scanned the room. Could this really be hers? As big as it was, it made her feel light and able. "It feels right somehow."

"There are good things for you in Hopewell."

"I hope—" She stopped herself. "I'm eager to see what that is."

"And I'll always be behind you. So later this week let's sit down and go through all the ledgers together. You need to know what you've got to start with. It will make every little change you make taking my old store into the next generation that much more exciting for you. You will breathe new life into The Book Bea."

"That's so sweet of you to say."

"I've made such wonderful friends because of this store. Not just locals, but people who stopped in and paid a visit and then kept in touch. You can't put a price on that. Friends are the true assets of your life. Not your house or cars or jewelry."

"You and I will be forever friends," Sydney said.

"Oh yes. You can count on that. There are other perks to being the owner of the bookstore, too."

Bea didn't need to sell Sydney on the idea. She was already fantasizing about it. "I know. It would be like having an unlimited personal book budget. I might have to learn how to read without cracking the spine though." Wouldn't that be awesome to have every single story and place right at your fingertips?

"Oh yes. That too, but I was referring to something a little less tangible. Through this store, I know things going on in people's lives before anyone else does. Sometimes before they even realize it themselves."

"Gossip?"

"Oh heavens, no. I'd never gossip."

Sydney tried not to smile, because she was quite certain that she'd call about ninety percent of Bea's conversations with her customers today just that. Gossip.

"More like being on the inside. When a customer buys a book, fiction or non-fiction, it usually ties to something going on in their lives. It's like getting a puzzle piece. Not a nice edge or corner piece, though. One of the murky middle ones that takes a while to figure out. It's like unweaving a mystery. I've always been a sucker for a good mystery."

The only puzzle Sydney wanted to solve right now was how she might be able to take over The Book Bea. Was it a good business decision for her in her new role as a single parent? The ledgers would show her the numbers, but did she really have what it took to run her own business?

Chapter Eight

Traffic was light as she left the bookstore to pick up her car at the church. As she walked down the sidewalk, strangers smiled. You couldn't spend much time in a town like this and still feel like a newcomer.

Hopewell made her feel welcome, much more than how she'd felt in her own hometown once Jon's dirty laundry had been aired.

Between that and Jon's shenanigans on the sale of the house, she'd felt like she'd been pushed right out of the place that she'd called home for so many years.

But tonight she didn't need to sit and mull over all of that stuff. Tonight she had plans. Her first guests since she and RayAnne had relocated.

She figured RayAnne's favorite dinner would be a safe bet for the kids. She'd fix a salad for Diane and herself with the fried chicken nugget pieces on top, and a glass of wine. Simple, yet satisfying.

The church lot was empty now, and it wouldn't take long to drive back to the farmhouse.

Her thoughts wandered. What would things look like next year at this time?

Would RayAnne be back in her old school?

Would she be helping with the Christmas program, dealing with the women who were always trying to push their personal agendas? Those same women who were part of the PTA and blew every little problem at the school into a big deal?

Back to normal didn't have nearly as much appeal now. Being away from it, even for this short while, had made her realize just how out of balance her life had been.

The only inviting images in her mind were those of The Book Bea, neighbors coming out of church, and friendly nods on Main Street.

When she got home, she went straight to work in the kitchen and had everything prepared right at six-thirty as she'd planned. She slipped the food in the warming tray of the new oven. That fancy appliance had been a splurge, but something she'd always wanted and so she'd put it on Jon's account and had it shipped before she moved out. Why should Jon be the only one getting what he wanted?

She set the table and then started a fire in the fireplace to chase the chill from the downstairs. Just as she slid the fireplace screen back into place, she heard a car pull up. Through the sheers in the living room she could see the dark-red minivan in the driveway.

Kids piled out of the car, doors slammed, and RayAnne led the charge to the front door.

Shrill screams of delight were a welcome sound. The house seemed too quiet when she was alone here. The bad part was that mini-dose of quiet she'd just had was just a little taste of what it was going to be like once Jon picked RayAnne up on Wednesday. It was going to be a long holiday. Thank goodness she had the store to keep her busy.

Sydney opened the front door and RayAnne, Jenny, and Zach raced right past her.

RayAnne did a u-turn and came back and hugged her.

"Did you have a good day?"

"Best time ever," RayAnne said. "We popped popcorn and watched Christmas movies. Jenny's so neat. We're like almost twins, or at least sisters. And her mom made us popcorn balls with the leftover popcorn." She held up a cellophane-wrapped wad of popcorn and what looked like sticky caramel.

"That looks delicious."

"It is. We tasted them."

Of course they had. Who could resist? "You're gonna share, right?"

"Heck, yeah! Later." RayAnne grabbed Jenny by the hand. "I want to show Jenny my room right now. How long before dinner, Mom?"

"It's ready. Are y'all hungry?"

"Yes!" All three of them yelled.

Diane walked inside. "I swear I fed them today. They just burn it off faster than I can fill their tanks."

Sydney laughed. "Trust me. I get it."

"Let's eat first," RayAnne reasoned. "Then can I show them my room?"

"Works for me." Sydney looked to Diane for confirmation.

"Absolutely. I'm counting on girl talk tonight," Diane agreed.

"Awesome. What are we having?" RayAnne looked concerned.

"Your favorite. Golden chicken nuggets, macaroni and cheese, and apple sauce."

"I love you, Mom!" RayAnne jumped up and down. "It's the best. Y'all are going to love this dinner. My favorite. Come on." RayAnne led the way.

Sydney closed the front door and followed them to the kitchen.

"Anything I can help with?" Diane asked.

"You can open the wine," Sydney said. "Everything else is ready."

It only took a few minutes to put dinner on the table. RayAnne proudly offered to say grace, and the kids devoured their dinner before Diane and Sydney even got through half of their salads.

"May we be excused?" RayAnne looked like a runner in the ready stance.

As soon as Sydney said *yes*, all three kids took off so fast she heard the chairs screech, and the footsteps hit the stairs almost in one long sound bite.

"Thanks for doing this tonight. It was a treat for me to not have to cook," Diane admitted.

"It's nice to have someone over. It's been an interesting adjustment the last couple of weeks."

"I bet," Diane said. "I mean coming from Atlanta to Hopewell is a big change. What brought you back?"

"It's a long story."

Diane sat back and took a sip of wine. "We've got a whole bottle. And if I can't drive, my sweet husband can pick us up."

"Tell me about him first."

"Tony? Oh gosh. Local boy. Football quarterback. This town lives for high school football, you know?"

"I remember."

"Did then. Still do. Tony was like royalty. We had a winning season our senior year. We'd been friends forever, but never dated or anything. Then it was like out of the blue he asked me to the spring formal. He said he'd known I was going to be his wife since the first day he laid eyes on me."

"He'd had his eye on you the whole time," Sydney mused. "That's so romantic."

"I was completely clueless he was even interested. The rest is pretty much history. Graduated. He took over his daddy's service station. We got married at the church. Babies. Happy ever after and then some."

"Sounds like a romance novel."

"I still think it's funny that I had no idea. He was kind of shy. How was I supposed to know?"

"Don't ask me. I don't have a good track record for what falling in *or out* of love looks like on a man."

"Ouch," Diane said. "Was it that bad?"

Sydney topped off both of their glasses. "The worst Valentine's Day you could imagine."

"No card?" Diane raised a finger in the air. "Worse. No candy. I love Valentine's Day chocolates."

"Oh there was a card all right. And chocolates too." She took a sip of wine. "Let's see if I can remember exactly what that card said. 'Dear Syd, Thanks for being my Valentine all of these years. I know you adore these chocolates. I'm sorry these will be the last you'll get from me. I've already packed my things. I'm in love with someone else. Forgive me. Jon.'"

"Back up the bus. He couldn't have."

Sydney raised her hand. "I swear."

"Did you suspect anything? Had y'all been having problems?"

"No. Well, clearly yes. But none that I knew of. And it was like the hits just kept coming day after day."

"You had to have been in shock."

"When I got up the nerve to tell people, they all

knew. People who were supposed to have been my friends knew Jon had been unfaithful, and yet not one of them had the guts to tell me. It was so humiliating."

"Maybe they didn't want to hurt you." Diane downed a gulp of wine and then sat up. "I take that back. I would have given him a piece of my mind for sure, and then told you. That's what friends do."

"Exactly."

"What's wrong with people?"

"I really was the last one to know. I swear it was like everyone was giving me that bless-her-heart, head-cocked-to-one-side, it's-such-a-shame look. I couldn't stand it."

"Oh, I know that look. It's the worst."

"It is, but it wasn't the worst. That came the next week when I saw Jon in town at our favorite restaurant, with our best friends, and his new girlfriend. She looked young enough to be my daughter."

"No."

"Yep. She wasn't *that* young, but it stung twice as bad to know that I'd been dumped for someone younger."

"We're not even that old. How long were y'all married?"

"I was married for twelve years, but apparently he was only married for ten of them."

"How's RayAnne doing through all of this? I mean she seems fine."

"She wanted to go live with him." Sydney's lip trembled. "I'm sorry." She swept at a tear. "It just kills me. Not only because I'm so mad with Jon, but because I love her so much."

"Of course you do. We're mothers. We live for our children."

"She was always a daddy's girl. He spoils her so

much. He'd always wanted a little boy, but she came out day one as scrappy as a little boy. And Jon does love her. I have to give him that."

"But she's here with you. So everything's fine."

"For now. He keeps luring her with expensive toys. I didn't have much choice but to move here. He sold the house out from under me. I couldn't buy him out of my half of the equity so there was nothing I could do. I begged him to wait until the summer to sell, but he's buying a fancy place out in Buckhead for her. He needed the money."

"I'm just numb," Diane said. "I'm sitting here in shock. How can someone who loved you enough to marry you and have a child do that?"

"I guess he either never really loved me to begin with, or something changed. I don't know."

"Well, thank goodness your grandparents' place was still here."

"It was the only asset I had that was just in my name."

Diane scanned the room. "This is a great old place."

Sydney laughed. "It's drafty and cold."

"It's got character."

"Yeah, it kind of does, and it's mine. When I told RayAnne we were moving she threw a fit and said I was taking her from her friends. Jon promised her trips, toys, and her friends. Hard to compete with."

"But she's here."

"I promised we'd reassess at the end of the school year. I was hoping I'd either be in a position to go back to Atlanta and make a decent living there, or she'd fall in love with Hopewell and we'd stay here."

"The right thing will happen. Things will turn out great."

"I just want to find a new normal. This has been such a hard year."

"Did you work back in Atlanta?"

"Never had a real job, but I did some freelance projects over the years. Mostly for Jon though. I'm a pretty good graphic artist. I was lucky to have enough samples to land a position with Peabody's."

"That's a really good place to work. You got lucky getting an opportunity with them. I have to admit I have a great marriage, but sometimes I do worry what would happen if something happened to Tony. I mean I put my whole life into being a good mother and wife. I guess I could run the shop and hire mechanics, but I'm just not sure how all that would work."

"I know what you mean. My attorney really thinks I should take alimony for a year to get on my feet, but I hate to do that. It's like Jon would then somehow still be responsible for me making it. I don't want him to help me, and I don't want him to pay his way out of feeling guilty, either."

"You got a job so fast. I think you'll be fine."

"I'm counting on it. I can't even think about it not going right. I'd just be a mess if I started worrying about that. Right now I just need to stay busy until I start my job the first week of January."

"Do you like working at The Book Bea?"

"Are you kidding? I love working there. I still love The Book Bea as much as I did when we were kids. I feel so different when I'm in that place. Like I'm supposed to be there. Like I'm good at something."

"Oh, don't shortchange yourself. I'm sure you're good at lots of things."

"I'm trying to find that part of me again. I feel like there's something better here for us." Sydney set her wineglass down. "What if RayAnne decides she wants to live with her dad? He's picking her up Wednesday, and I know there'll be a slew of expensive gifts. It's so hard to compete with that."

"It's not going to happen. She loves you. All little girls love their daddies, but when it comes down to it, she's right where she wants to be."

"I'm hoping the distance will help with us living here. He was taking her cool places with barely any notice. Now at least he'll have to make a plan. He was making me the bad guy every time I said no." Sydney stood. "Come on. Let's go sit in the living room."

Diane followed along behind Sydney. "I think you moving to Hopewell was a smart thing to do. This is a great place to raise children, and this community is filled with good people who will help you. Plus, I'm excited to have my old book buddy back."

"Me too."

"Reading naughty passages out of those romances." Diane covered her mouth as she laughed. "We were so bad." She sat down on the other end of the sofa.

"I'm sure Bea knew exactly what we were doing, too."

"She had to have known."

Diane tucked her feet underneath her. "How about the summer we had the *Charlotte's Web* book club and they had that pig in a pen out in front of The Book Bea?"

"I'd forgotten about that. That pig stank, and do you remember him eating the giant cardboard spider that was hanging on that fence?"

"You cried," Diane said with a laugh.

"I loved Charlotte," Sydney said. "It was devastating."

"Charlotte was a spider!"

"A really smart one. I still love that story." Sydney

hadn't even remembered that until just now. "Seems so long ago." She should buy that book for RayAnne.

"It was a long time ago," Diane said. "We were our girls' ages. Miss Bea doesn't do the bookworm reading thing in the summer anymore. I'm not sure why."

"She probably can't climb the ladder to put those big construction paper circles with each book we read on the soffit like she used to." Only Sydney knew that wasn't the reason there wouldn't be another one.

"True. That was one psychedelic bookworm."

Sydney had always picked pink for her circles. "More like a caterpillar if you think about it."

"You should start that again, but year round. It sure fired up our competitive nature. We both read like fiends trying to be the winner."

"Would sell more books, too," Sydney said.

Diane lowered her voice. "I don't know if she's told you anything, but the talk about town is that she's thinking of closing the place down."

"She did tell me."

Diane looked like the wind had been sucked from her sail. "I've been hearing the rumors. I just hate that. It seems like it's usually pretty busy, too. Anything we can buy locally we do. Doesn't matter if you can save money by going online. It's our way of supporting our own around here."

That explained a lot about why Bea's business stayed steady.

"The Book Bea closing would be so sad," Diane said.

"I haven't said anything to RayAnne, but I've been toying with the idea of maybe taking it over. Bea said she'd work out something with me. Like maybe we could work together for a year or something."

Diane sat up tall. "You totally should. I'll help you out while the kids are in school a few hours a day. For free even. Oh, you've got to do it."

"Buying The Book Bea would be really amazing, wouldn't it? That place holds such special memories for me. I'd love to be that for others."

Diane clasped her hands in front of her. "It would be so neat. I bet that store makes a nice little profit each year."

"After the way Jon left me, I want to be in control of my future. No way will I ever put myself in a position where I have to count on someone else."

"I don't blame you, but just because Jon was a jerk you can't be bitter about all men."

"I'm not. Men are fine. I just don't need one."

"Yeah, you tell me that in six months."

"It won't change."

"I hear ya." Diane stood up. "I better get the kids home and tuck them into bed."

"It's already nine o'clock. I'm sorry. I didn't even get to hear what all's been going on with you."

"No worries. We've got a lifetime to do it now that you're back." Diane walked over to the stairs. "Jenny, Zach, come on down. Time to go."

"Thanks so much for coming by tonight, and for all the help with RayAnne. I'd thought I'd be here to take care of things until after the holidays. Then this thing with Bea just happened."

"The Book Bea brought us back together, and RayAnne is no trouble at all." Diane waved Zach and Jenny down the stairs and then opened the front door. "Load it up." She wrapped her arms around Sydney. "I'm glad you're back. And Sydney, I'm sorry all of that happened to you."

"Thanks, Diane."

RayAnne came down the stairs and stood in the doorway waving as the minivan headlights swathed a path through the dark night.

"Dinner was awesome. They loved it. Thanks for fixing that tonight."

"My pleasure, treasure."

"Jenny and I had a such a good time, and her little brother is funny."

"I'm glad. I'd planned to help you start packing tonight, but I'm pretty tired. How about you?"

"Me too."

"We'll do it tomorrow night. But there's only three more days before your dad picks you up."

"I can't believe it's almost here. I was telling Jenny about my trip with Dad. She was so jealous. She's never been skiing. Think Dad would let her come with us sometime?"

She highly doubted that. "You should ask him," she said. Happy to put Jon in the bad guy seat for a change, especially since Jon had never agreed to travel around the holidays when they were married.

The fact that a broken family was the price of that trip had seemed to escape RayAnne completely.

Sydney tossed and turned most of the evening. Partly because even in flannel pajamas under a quilt the old farmhouse seemed to hold a damp chill. But more than that, her mind was still in overdrive with the possibilities of what her future could look like.

Giving up on sleep, she wrapped herself in the quilt and climbed out of bed. The wind whistled between the gaps in the old wooden sash windows. The clock showed

2:47. Every board creaked beneath her feet as she tried to quietly make her way down the hallway. She had such great memories about this house, but with each step and each gusty draft, she wondered how practical it was to live here. Even if it was paid for.

RayAnne was in a heap at the top of her bed as usual. Only her forehead poking out of the covers. The modern colors of the walls looked so out of place amid the fancy crown moldings, but RayAnne had picked out every paint chip, and when they'd gotten done, she'd said that it was even better than her room at their old house. Not an easy accomplishment.

Still, after ten years, each time she watched her daughter sleep her heart filled with so much love that even RayAnne's worst moods couldn't dim that light.

The little electric heater she'd bought for RayAnne's room hummed, working overtime even though it was thermostat controlled.

RayAnne slept quietly. No need to bother her.

She pulled the door closed to help keep the heat inside her room, then went downstairs.

The Book Bea buzzed her brain. The initial thought had been a bit of a fantasy, but now it was more like a need.

She wondered what price Bea would be looking to get for the place. Dipping into her savings so soon was going to be hard. She'd barely stepped out on her own, and this house definitely needed some fixing if they were going to stay.

She filled the teakettle with water and set it on the gas range, hovering near the warm flame. Just as the kettle began to whistle she tugged it from the burner and dropped in the chamomile tea sachets.

Maybe if she gave in to her thoughts for a little while

she'd finally find a way to catch some sleep before morning.

She plodded back out to the living room with her tea and restarted the fire. It would help if she could leave it burning all night, but she just wasn't comfortable leaving it unattended in the old wooden frame home. At least it would be warm when RayAnne came down in the morning.

She took a long wooden match from the container on the mantle and struck it hopefully. For the first time, she was able to catch the starter log on fire with the first match. Finally getting the hang of it, she put the box of matches away.

So, maybe she wasn't *Survivor* fire challenge good, but the first few times she'd used so many wooden matches to start the fire that it was like extra kindling scattered in the bottom. This was definitely progress.

She stood there warming her hands in front of the fire, glancing over at the floor-to-ceiling bookshelves that flanked the fireplace. Bottom shelves on both sides held the children's books that she and RayAnne couldn't let go of, along with all of her current books. Sydney's collection had easily filled most of the space on the other shelves, leaving only a few open spots for strategically placed colorful mementoes and decorative pieces that tied the room together.

She'd opted for all new furniture, purchased with the money she'd gotten from her old home's garage sale. It wasn't anywhere as nice as the furniture she and Jon had bought together, but it was hers. Fresh, comfortable, and not one memory came with it.

Sydney set her mug on a coaster on top of the square oak coffee table, then took her laptop from one of the baskets underneath. With a press of the power button, her computer came to life. She opened up her budget spread-sheet and started moving things around.

Working through the numbers and what-if scenarios wasn't really getting her anywhere without knowing what financial outlay purchasing the store would require. Her attorney's words kept coming back to her. He'd strongly encouraged her to accept at least a year of alimony to give her time to find a job.

She hadn't asked for it, but Jon had offered it. She knew that was just because he felt guilty. Did she really want to let him off the hook that easy? She had been dead set against freeing him from the guilt.

Besides, she didn't want to be one of those women who gouged her ex. Not that what he was offering would make any difference in his style of living. Jon would never feel *that* guilty.

Still, the idea of alimony rubbed her the wrong way. Her attorney had made her hold off on a definitive *no* until after the New Year.

For the first time, she was actually considering it.

On her third cup of tea the sun began to rise and the sky filled with yellows, pinks, and oranges. No sense in trying to fall asleep now. By the time she fell asleep it would be time to wake up again. She started searching the Internet for everything she could find about running a bookstore. There was even a southern independent booksellers group. She wondered if Bea was a member. Maybe not, since she seemed to still be in a pen-and-paper world. She started a new Favorites folder and began saving links of helpful tips.

RayAnne came downstairs in shorts and a long-sleeve t-shirt.

"Where's your robe? Aren't you freezing?" Sydney asked.

"I'm fine." She swung around the bannister and headed for the kitchen. "You been up long? It's still early."

"A little while."

RayAnne scrubbed a hand through her hair. "Something wrong?"

"No." Sydney lowered the screen on her laptop. She was dying to tell RayAnne about her ideas for The Book Bea, but the last thing she needed was Jon hearing about her idea before she'd even had a chance to really think it through. And she'd promised herself no matter what shenanigans he threw into the mix that she'd never bash him to her daughter, or ask her to keep something from him. "Why do you ask?"

"I don't know. Whenever I can't sleep you ask what's on my mind. Figured maybe something was bothering you."

It was moments like this that made her feel good about how she'd raised her daughter.

It was so hard to keep her ideas from RayAnne. But if RayAnne mentioned it to Jon, he'd break the confidence she was starting to regain.

She could hear him now. *What makes you think you can run a business? Small businesses are risky even in good times.*

And maybe he'd be right, but this wasn't his decision.

Eventually she'd have to discuss it with RayAnne if it really looked like an option, but they hadn't been in Hopewell very long. Could they even make this decision right now?

RayAnne came back into the living room with a bowl of milk and a box of cereal. "Can I turn on the TV?"

"Sure."

"How do you just sit here in the quiet?" RayAnne lifted the remote and aimed it, filling the room with her favorite morning show.

Unlike a lot of kids RayAnne's age, her daughter chose to watch a morning show for adults. The mixture of current events, news, weather, and entertainment kept her young daughter informed and gave her the chance to form her own opinions, apart from what Sydney shared. Of course, it also made for some interesting questions.

"My favorite song!" RayAnne leapt from the couch and got closer to the big screen.

The country singer filled the screen, nearly life size in their living room since Sydney had let RayAnne pick out the television. Sixty-five inches was the biggest they'd had and thank goodness this front room was so big. It was like a theatre in here.

RayAnne danced around the room to the popular song. There went Sydney's calm and balanced morning.

Rather than let it bother her, Sydney rolled with the moment. Flinging her quilt to the side, she danced alongside RayAnne to the upbeat country tune that was really just a remix of a song she'd grown up on.

"You know all the words, Mom!"

"I'm just too cool," Sydney said. A few energetic steps in the morning never hurt anyone.

With the last beat of the drum they both dropped to the couch. "That was crazy," RayAnne said, half out of breath.

"It was. Now eat up so we can hit the road. Don't want you to be late for school."

RayAnne grabbed her bowl and started shoveling

spoonfuls of cereal into her mouth as she tromped up the stairs.

Far from ladylike, but she wouldn't change a thing about her wonderfully unique daughter. RayAnne was the best thing Sydney could have ever done in her life.

Chapter Nine

Sydney dropped RayAnne off at school and then drove over to Main Street and parked in front of Cookie Doe. As soon as she opened the car door the air smelled of spicy gingerbread.

A man exiting the bakery with a cardboard box held the door for her. She slipped inside, eyeing the full case as she approached the counter.

"Good morning," the man behind the counter said. "You're back. I must be doing something right." He straightened his apron.

"Everything I've had has been good. I'd say you're doing it all right. I thought I'd pick up something to go with our morning tea down at the bookstore. What do you recommend?"

"First, I think we should introduce ourselves. I'm Dan. My wife Cookie is the one who does all the baking."

"Nice to meet you, Dan. I'm Sydney. I'm helping out down at The Book Bea through the holidays."

"I heard. Welcome to Hopewell." He rubbed his hands together and glanced into the case. "So, today, I recommend the scones. Fresh cranberry-orange with a citrusy drizzle on top."

"That does sound good. I'll take two."

He grabbed a pair of long-handled tongs and gently pulled two scones out of the case, then slid them into a white bag.

She pulled out her wallet.

"This one is on us. You'll have to come one afternoon so you can meet Cookie. She gets up in the middle of the night and does most of the prep and baking. I run the place in the daytime, but I know she'd love to meet you."

"Thanks, Dan. I'll do that."

With the bag in hand, she walked outside and hitched the collar of her jacket up around her neck.

She looked for RayAnne's bike in the window at Wheelies. It really was a pretty bicycle. When she'd been RayAnne's age all she'd had was her brother's hand-me-down mountain bike. She'd ask Bea to make one of her famous big bows to put on it for Christmas.

Wes had decorated Wheelies' window with wreaths hanging at different levels on long pieces of shiny bicycle chain. Each one was made out of a different size bike wheel or sprocket with sparkly ribbon and evergreen sprigs woven into its design.

The Book Bea was still dark when she got there, but it was early and that would give her time to brew tea before Bea arrived.

She let herself inside and turned the sign to OPEN. Bea's tradition of being open anytime she was there seemed like a good one. Why miss a sale just because of the time of day if she was there anyway?

Lights on, tea brewed, coffee made, and six Christmas CDs loaded into the stereo brought the place back to life again. At five minutes to nine the timer for the Christmas lights in the front window came on.

Even Monday morning seemed appealing here.

She stepped behind the counter and pre-cut several sheets of shiny wrapping paper about the right size for a book. That would save time when they were busy.

Her cell phone chimed. Diane was going to stop by later. Things felt so right.

The door chimes jingled. Her first customer of the day. She looked up to see the mayor walking toward her. "Good morning, Mayor. What can I do for you?"

"I'm so glad you're open early today. My wife saw that pop-up book in the display window and says we have to have one for the grandkids. Please tell me you have some left."

"Just so happens I do. I'll even wrap it for you." By the time the mayor walked out she had two more customers. The morning was busy and she felt like she was at the top of her game for a change, but she hadn't heard anything from Bea yet.

By eleven o'clock she was more than a little worried about Bea. Why hadn't she at least called? Sydney hadn't thought to ask Bea for her home phone number. She riffled through the papers at the counter, then in the office for something with a phone number on it. Sydney found an old set of loan papers that had an address and phone number on them. She dialed Bea, who finally answered on the fifth ring.

"Hi, Bea, it's Sydney. I was worried. Is everything okay?"

"Oh goodness. I meant to just lie down for a moment. I'm so sorry." Bea's voice was heavy and slow. "I must've fallen asleep."

"No, it's fine. I've got everything under control here. I just wanted to be sure there wasn't something wrong."

"I'm okay, dear. I can't believe I let you down."

"Don't you worry. I'm here to help however you need

me to. I opened up and we've had a really good morning. Even sold a couple more pop-up books because of the window display."

"Oh, Sydney. You *are* my angel. I knew someone would come along that would make things right. It was you all along. I'm so glad you came to Hopewell. Thank you."

"I'm excited we're having such a good morning after our jackpot day yesterday."

"I think The Book Bea is going to outlast me," Bea said sounding more awake and cheerful.

"Don't say that. Can I bring you something? What can I do?"

"You're doing it," Bea said. "You're such a help. I don't know how I thought I'd manage through the holidays."

"That's why you hired me. I'll help you. I want to do more than that. I want to help you keep the The Book Bea open indefinitely."

Silence.

"Are you okay?" Had she offended Bea? Maybe Bea didn't want to sell the store to her after all. Had she just been polite yesterday?

A quiet sniffle came across the line. "You are exactly what I've prayed for, Sydney. You don't know how happy it makes me to hear you say that. The right path is always there. That store has been mine. So pay attention."

Sydney hugged the phone tighter. The Book Bea felt like her true path.

"Sydney, I believe your future has found you here in Hopewell."

A swirl in Sydney's chest made her wonder if her heart had skipped a beat. "Bea, how will I really know when my future has found me? What if I choose the wrong path? What if moving RayAnne away from Jon was a bad idea?"

"Honey, your path will present itself. That's the way it works. You only have to be open to accepting it when it comes."

"Things just got crazy in Georgia. I kind of ran away from that situation rather than deal with it straight on. I'm not sure running away qualifies as finding your path."

"Sometimes that's the best we can do. It's going to be okay. You're on a good path." Bea spoke in a hushed tone. "Trust me, my angel. And what better time of year than Christmas for magical things to happen, and wishes to come true?"

This was really going to happen. Her hopeful heart pounded. She swallowed back the excitement. Until they talked money she didn't dare get her hopes up. She needed to stay calm, and be practical.

The front door opened, and another customer walked in. "We've got more customers. I'll check in on you later."

"I'll get myself together and be there soon. I really am sorry about this."

"Oh, Bea. It's no trouble at all. Stay home and rest. I've got this completely under control. I'll even call at the end of the day with all of the numbers and we can go over the ledger together in the morning if you're up to it." Bea didn't argue, so Sydney took that as a win. "Get some rest." Sydney hung up and went to help a customer who was balancing a hand basket and an armful of books. "Let me help you with that."

As soon as the customers cleared out Diane walked in. "What a morning. I meant to pop in on you early this morning."

"That's fine. Everything okay?"

"Oh yeah, Tony had a customer's car towed in from the interstate. Young college gal on her way up to Virginia to be with her folks. But it's not a quick fix. He called to see if I could give her a lift to the hotel."

"That was nice of you."

"Least we could do. Wouldn't it be awful to be stranded in a strange town?"

Sydney felt like she'd been stranded this whole year.

"I was telling Tony about you last night. He told me to tell you if you need any help at all to call us first. If he can't handle it, he probably knows someone who can."

"Thanks. So far, so good, but I'll definitely take him up on that."

"Good. He's a fixer. It's what he does. Full-time hero whether it's at the garage or for neighbors. It's what made me fall in love with him."

"I can't wait to meet him," Sydney said. There'd been a time when she'd thought Jon was quite the hero.

Diane pulled her scarf off and looked around. "No customers?"

"It's been pretty steady all day. This has been my first break. Coffee?"

"I'd love some."

They settled in the plush oversized chairs with their coffee. No flavored creamers, no lattes or cappuccinos, just regular old coffee. And free. She'd calculated in her budget that by not meeting with her old friends in Atlanta for the fancy-schmancy coffees they all favored she'd saved over eight hundred dollars already.

Diane recapped her day and filled Sydney in on some of the activities the school put on through the year that parents usually helped with.

"I almost forgot," Diane said. "Tony reminded me that I should've told you about the Ruritan Club Steak Dinner coming up next week. It's just ten bucks a plate. All the guys cook and wait on us. It's kind of neat for a change, besides I love seeing Tony in an apron."

Sydney almost spit her coffee trying to picture Jon serving in an apron. He'd never have gone for that—well, unless there was a deal to be landed by doing it. She really needed to figure out how to still like him while not loving him. He'd been the best part of her life for a long time. He'd treated her well, and had been an excellent provider. And as bad as it hurt that he'd cheated, for the first ten years of their marriage it was pretty darn great. One day she hoped she could forgive him. But right now it was still too tender.

"You'll meet a lot of the locals there. There are also several single guys in the Ruritan Club. A couple of them are pretty successful and good-looking, too."

"No thanks. I'm not even out of this marriage."

"Come to the dinner anyway. You can never have too many friends. Those boys know how to put on a good feed, and RayAnne will see a lot of the kids from school there, too."

"Okay, put us down for two tickets."

Diane's phone blasted "School's Out Forever." "Oh. Time to pick up the kids from school already. Man, this went too fast."

"It sure did." Sydney got up and got her purse and her BE RIGHT BACK sign from behind the counter. "I'm so glad you came by. I really needed some girl talk time. I feel like we've been friends forever."

"I know. I feel the same way."

Sydney stuck the handwritten sign on the door, locked up, and hoped things would be okay. More than one customer had said they were used to the hours being hit or miss, so it shouldn't be too much of a problem.

She and Diane walked out to their cars together and Sydney followed Diane to the school.

RayAnne and Jenny were standing at the curb when Sydney drove up. She wondered if RayAnne would still be in a sunny mood this afternoon or if she needed to brace herself for an arctic blast. To her pleasant surprise, RayAnne waved and bounded over to the car.

"Hi, Mom," she said, leaning over and giving her a kiss.

Sydney bunched her lips. "Should I be worried?"

RayAnne laughed. "No-oo."

"I hope you don't mind, but Bea isn't feeling well. We're going to go back to the store for a couple hours until closing time."

"That's cool."

"Great." She didn't dare question the attitude adjustment for fear of scaring it away.

"We were talking at lunch today," RayAnne said.

"We?"

"The girls. Jenny and them."

Sydney nodded.

"So, at lunch everyone was talking about Christmas trees and how their parents always do *all* the decorating."

Sydney had to admit the perfectionist in her always liked to take control of that, too. Did it really matter if all the ornaments were clumped in one place, or big balls were at the top and small ones at the bottom?

"I was thinking since we're not going to use our old artificial tree at our house, what if we put ours up at The Book Bea? It would look so pretty! I could invite the kids from school to come and we could all decorate it however we want. And since Dad won't be here until late

Wednesday, we could do it, like, right after school lets out for Christmas break on Wednesday. Please? Everybody thought it was such a cool idea."

Sydney parked in front of The Book Bea. Did she even need to ask Bea about this? She'd pretty much already given her carte blanche on the decorating. Plus, if the kids came to decorate that could bring in parents. Parents meant customers. Customers meant sales. No brainer.

"I think it's an amazing idea." She'd give Bea a quick call later to give her a heads up.

"I know." RayAnne got out of the car. "And you and I can hang our favorite ornaments on that tree, too. You know, so you won't feel sad while I'm gone."

Sydney walked around the car and stepped up on the sidewalk next to her daughter. "Sounds like we've got after-school plans on Wednesday. You can tell your friends at school tomorrow." She watched RayAnne. Not so much as a flinch when she referred to the girls at school as her friends. "We'll get the tree out of the garage tonight. We'll set it up tomorrow after school so it'll be ready for y'all."

RayAnne wrapped her arms around Sydney's waist. "Thank you. Thank you. Thank you. You're the best."

How had she been so lucky to have a daughter like this? "We can bake some cookies for everyone."

"And cupcakes. Can we make cupcakes?" RayAnne's eyes danced.

"Sure thing. With red and green sprinkles!"

RayAnne nodded. "And the green sherbet kind of punch. I love that. Plus it's Christmassy looking. That would be so awesome. Right?"

"Absolutely," Sydney said starting to get excited about it herself.

RayAnne ran ahead of Sydney up the walkway to the porch of The Book Bea.

"Figure out where you want to put the tree and we'll clear a spot for it before we leave."

Sydney took the BE RIGHT BACK sign down and stood there looking around. Bea's words echoed, "You don't have to be looking. Your path will present itself. That's the way it works. You only have to be open to accepting it when it comes."

She straightened the store, hoping to calm her wandering mind. She'd wanted so badly to talk details with Bea today, but that wasn't going to happen.

"Excuse me, it's Sydney, right?" The man's voice caught her off guard.

"Yes. Hi." She pushed her hair back behind her ear. "Sorry, I was miles away there for a second." She recognized him immediately from yesterday. One didn't just forget those arresting eyes. "Mac. Hi again."

"I didn't see Bea. Is she here?"

"No. She wasn't feeling well. Can I help you with something?"

"She orders books in for me from time to time. I teach history over at the high school."

"I used to love history. Could never remember the dates so I never got good grades in it, but I always liked the stories."

The young boy to his side spoke up. "He's the baseball coach, too."

Mac blushed. "My son. And biggest fan. Seth."

"Hi, Seth. My daughter is around here somewhere. Y'all are probably close to the same age."

Seth looked around.

Mac fumbled with a piece of paper. "I have all the

information on the books here. Titles. Author. ISBN. Do you think you could order one of each for me?"

"Sure." Sydney took the piece of paper and tried to act like she knew exactly what to do, although she was completely clueless about where Bea ordered her books. But she could certainly find out. "Happy to. If you want to leave me your number I can call you and let you know when they arrive."

Mac pulled an ink pen from his shirt pocket. "Great."

She handed him the list back.

He wrote down his name, an email address, and his phone number, then scrawled a line under it and handed it back to her.

"I'll take care of this," she said, feeling very much like maybe he was expecting her to say something else.

Seth spotted RayAnne and walked away.

Mac watched his son walk away. When he turned back his eyes connected with hers. "You're new to town, so I was wondering if I might be able to show you around sometime. Nothing fancy. Just, ya know, I thought I could introduce you to some people. Someone said you were a single parent. I am too. Not like a date. Just being neighborly. I mean it's not easy being a single parent. Or new to a town. I'm rambling."

She laughed nervously. "Yes, you are. And yes." *Oh my gosh*. She felt absolutely giddy.

"Yes?"

"We could do something some time." She pointed to Seth and RayAnne. "Looks like our kids are hitting it off already."

"Great. Then yes."

"Okay."

"So, I'll show you around."

"I guess I should tell you that I did just move to Hopewell, but I used to come here as a kid. My grandparents had a place on the edge of town. My grandmother brought me to The Book Bea all the time. I'd read more books over a summer than I could pack in a box to take home."

"And now you're back."

"Yeah. I'm back. Time for a change." Sydney's cell phone rang. She pulled it from the back pocket of her jeans and immediately silenced it when she saw Jon's name. This was not the time for him to be bugging her.

"It's a good town to raise a kid. Looks like you're already getting settled in with the job and all."

She smiled and nodded. Bea closing was not her news to tell, and wanting to buy the store might be, but it would be awfully embarrassing if she started telling people that and then couldn't afford to do it. So she said nothing.

"You probably know about the caroling night since you're helping Miss Bea."

"Yes. It sounds fabulous."

"Why don't you come along with us. We have a group of folks that go together every year. You know. Friends. Neighbors."

"I'll be helping Bea."

"I thought of that. I could find someone to cover here if Bea needs the help, but she usually handles it alone, so I think she'd be okay."

"And RayAnne leaves this Wednesday night to spend the holidays with her dad."

"Wow. The whole Christmas break? That must be hard."

"I don't know. It's my first one. But I'm dreading it."

"All the more reason to be with new friends then. You can't be alone at the holidays."

"That's what RayAnne said, too."

"Then you really can't say no. It's Christmas. The whole neighborly thing is kind of a requirement around here."

"I see." *Was he flirting with her?* she wondered.

"Too bad your daughter won't be in town. I wasn't sure what kinds of things a little girl would want to do, but I thought the caroling was a safe bet. Women, I know. Little girls, not my genre."

"Genre, huh?"

"Poor attempt at a bookstore joke?"

"I get it. Cute." She appreciated the effort. "Well, for the record, my little girl would probably rather be doing whatever your son likes to do. Catch frogs, jump over bike ramps. The child is fearless."

His laugh was warm, reminding her of better days.

He leaned against the counter. The stammering had stopped. He was nice. Easy to talk to. He crossed one boot over the other. Nice boots, too. Western. Probably alligator or snake, but pretty.

"So, then we don't have a date. And I'll see you for Christmas caroling, if not sooner. I'll pick you up here."

"Okay. It's not a date," she confirmed. Only it felt kind of like a date. Which was just weird, because even if Jon was living with his mistress their divorce wasn't final yet. There was still the custody stuff to settle, and there was just too much hanging over her head to deal with something like dating.

But friends was a whole different story. Bea had reminded her that she needed to open herself up to the right path, and what was the harm with people getting together for the holiday?

Over her shoulder she heard RayAnne call out. "This is it, Mom. This is the perfect place."

And RayAnne may have been talking about where she wanted to put the Christmas tree, but boy did those words carry so much more meaning at that very moment.

Mac felt like a fumbling teenager. As a teacher he talked to parents all the time. Why was talking to Sydney any different? And yet when he'd come face to face with her he was blabbering and stuttering like a hormonal fourteen-year-old hoping for a first kiss.

"Good," he said. "It'll be good."

"Yeah. I'm looking forward to it." She shrugged, and smiled tentatively.

He could feel her anxiety too. Was that good? "Me too. The kids always like it."

Seth raced over to his side. "Excuse me," he said.

"What do you need, buddy?" Mac asked.

"Her." He tipped his head toward Sydney.

"Oh? Me? Sure. What can I help you with?" Sydney asked.

"Um." Seth glanced toward his father and swallowed hard. "RayAnne was talking to her dad on the phone. She's real upset. Like crying." His face scrunched. "A lot. I think you'd better check on her."

Sydney's brows pulled tight. "Oh?" She made a slight movement as she processed the information. "Excuse me. Thank you, Seth."

"She's by the windows over there," he said.

Sydney made a brisk exit.

"What happened?" Mac asked.

"We were just talking about the Christmas tree and baseball and stuff. A bunch of kids are going to come tomorrow to decorate the tree. Sounds like a pretty cool idea. She plays ball, likes four-wheelers, and we were just talking. It was fine."

"The part where she started crying, Seth."

"Her phone rang, and it was her dad. She was all excited at first, but then everything went bad." He looked down at his shoes. "She kind of just sank to the floor in a puddle and started crying into the phone. I didn't know what to do."

"You did the right thing." He got that from his old man. Mac never could handle a woman crying, either. Not even happy tears. Didn't even matter what it was over, just tore him up. "Never gets easier. Girls crying, I mean."

"They were going to go on this big ski vacation for, like, the whole Christmas. She'd just been telling me about it when he called."

"That sounds pretty cool." Mac hadn't been skiing in years. He should take Seth. There was decent skiing just a couple hours west.

"I guess he cancelled. Something about Paris. I don't know. But she was messed up." His chest heaved, and his eyes got big. "Like really messed up."

Mac pulled his son close. At least Genna had never played those back-and-forth games with Seth's heart. He could only imagine what RayAnne was feeling. Her parents divided. He knew from her visit to him as Santa that she was struggling with it. Now this.

"Let's see if they need us," Mac said.

"Dad? Really?"

He put his hands on Seth's shoulders and turned him about face. "March. It's the right thing to do."

Seth made that noise, like a cat with a fur ball, which usually grated on Mac like nails to a chalkboard, but in this case he knew exactly how the kid felt. Not a fun thing to do.

Mac could hear RayAnne's air-gobbling sobs as they got closer. He glanced at Seth, whose expression said *Please don't make us do this*.

Mac stopped short as Sydney tried to calm RayAnne.

"What happened?" Her voice was soft and calming.

"Dad's . . ." She sucked in air. ". . . not coming."

"Of course he is."

"He's not." RayAnne shook her head. "He's taking Ashley to Paris instead."

"Maybe you misunderstood. Is it just a change in plans?"

"No. He's taking her there, and I can't come with him."

"Unbelievable." Sydney's head dropped back like one of those rock-em sock-em robots Mac had as a kid. Couldn't blame her. That had even kind of sucker punched him, and it wasn't his kid. Sydney pulled RayAnne into her arms. "I'm sorry, sweetie."

"He loves her more than me."

"That's not true. He's just not thinking. There's probably a good reason."

"Nah-ah. He said I can't go with them to Paris. I don't even know if they have skiing there anyway."

"That doesn't mean he's not coming to get you. Are you sure he's not coming?"

"He said he'd come on Christmas Day to see me."

Mac could see those momma bear instincts flaring in Sydney despite her gentle moves with RayAnne. Her jaw pulsed, and she didn't utter a single word. If there'd been a thought bubble over her head he could imagine the punctuation flying around in there like shrapnel.

"Go to the bathroom and put some cold paper towels on your face. You need to calm down. You're going to make yourself sick."

RayAnne pulled the sleeve of her t-shirt over her hand and dabbed at her tears.

"I'll make this right for you, sweetie." She hugged her tight again. "I love you so much."

"I love you, too, Mom." RayAnne sniffled and dragged herself to her feet. "I hate Ashley."

"Don't say that. We don't hate anyone. We may not like their choices, but that's not hate. Settle down."

RayAnne pulled away and went back toward the bathroom.

Sydney walked over to Mac and Seth. "Thanks for coming to get me, Seth."

"You're welcome. She's pretty upset." He dipped his head.

"Anything I can do?" Mac asked.

Sydney had a half-cocked grin. *Pffft.* "Not anything legal. I swear I don't know what has gotten into that man."

"I know it won't make up for her dad disappointing her, but Hopewell is a great place to spend Christmas," Mac said. "Let's plan some things."

Sydney pulled her arms tight across her chest. Why did it have to be so hard to protect her daughter's emotions? What if Mac let them down too? He wouldn't. He wasn't Jon. This was different. Friends. Just friends. "Yeah. Maybe we can do that."

Seth asked, "Do you think she's still going to want to put up that tree here in the store tomorrow?"

"We'll definitely do that."

Mac cuffed Seth's shoulder. "Great. We'll be here."

"Thanks," she said to Seth. "Thank you both."

"You've got my number," Mac said. "Not sure what I can do, but let me know if I can help."

Sydney attempted a smile, but her eyes had lost that sparkle.

"We're going to get out of here so you can close up shop." He hitched his chin toward the door to Seth, who looked relieved and led the way out at nearly a jog.

Mac opened the door then stopped and twisted the sign to CLOSED.

When he looked back Sydney was nodding a thank-you, and waving.

Mac and Seth didn't say a word all the way to the truck.

Seth's sneakers scuffed along the sidewalk. "That really sucked."

"Yes. It sure did."

"Seems like her dad would've known that would make her sad. I mean it's Christmas. That was like her present."

"You'd think."

Seth toyed with the bottom of his shirt. "It's not really the same as Mom, but I know how RayAnne feels."

"I wish I could fix it. For you. For her." He felt as helpless today as he had back when Genna left. "But you can't undo what someone else has already done. All we can do is make better memories to help dim the bad ones."

Seth shrugged, and Mac wanted to know what that meant. That it didn't matter? That it was okay? Or that those memories never dimmed no matter how hard they worked at making better ones? "She's really sad."

"This one is bigger than us, Seth." Mac looked over, hoping that Seth wouldn't carry the burden of RayAnne's disappointment.

Only Seth didn't look so convinced.

Chapter Ten

RayAnne was quiet all night and didn't feel like baking cupcakes after all, so they opted for snuggling in front of the television with popcorn. They fell asleep on the couch like a couple of college girls.

The next morning, after dropping RayAnne off at school, Sydney stopped by Cookie Doe to pick up some treats for the tree-trimming get-together. "Good morning."

"Good morning. You're back."

"I am. Those cranberry-orange scones were amazing."

"Thanks. Same thing this morning?"

She waved her hand. "Oh, no. I can't splurge on those calories that often. Today, I need a bunch of snacks for hungry ten- to twelve-year-olds who will be trimming a tree in the store this afternoon. Can you put an assortment together for me?"

"Sure. When do you need them?"

"Not until one o'clock."

"We've got cookies in the oven now, and we can make some bite-sized ones. Probably better for busy hands. And less waste. I'll walk them down around noon." He put his hands on the counter. "I need to pick up a couple gifts, anyway."

"Need me to pay you now?"

"No. I know where you work," he said with a hearty chuckle.

She pulled her purse back to her hip. "Thanks."

She turned to leave and he called her back. "Wait a second. Got something for you."

"What is that?" Sydney took the treat in the wax paper.

"It's a snowflake fortune cookie."

"I've never heard of that."

"That's because I kind of invented them. Whisper-thin ginger cookies woven into the shape of a snowflake with just enough of a dusting of powdered sugar while they're still warm to make them look like the snow just fell. Oh, and inside, there's a Christmas wish for you. Some are just generic, but there are a handful of special ones."

"Which is this?"

"No way of knowing, but somehow the right wish *always* lands in the right hands. You let me know if that's the case."

"That's a lot of work. Thanks. What do I owe you for this?"

"My gift to you."

"Thanks, Dan." She tucked the cookie into her purse and walked down the block to the market to pick up a half-gallon of lime sherbet and some liters of ginger ale to make punch. She tossed a sleeve of paper cups and napkins into her cart, and she was done with her morning list of to-dos.

Sydney balanced the groceries on her hip as she twisted the handle on the door to The Book Bea and backed inside. An instrumental Christmas tune filled the air. It sounded a little like "Momma Kissing Santa Claus" had gone Caribbean, complete with steel drums.

"Oh goodness. What all do you have there, dear?" Bea rushed over to help.

"Thanks." She let Bea take the light bag. "The stuff for punch for this afternoon. And the bakery is bringing down some cookies later."

"Wonderful! I was so excited when I got your message."

"I've got our pre-lit artificial tree in the car. I'll go out and get that if you don't mind putting this in the freezer for me." She handed off the sherbet and then placed the ginger ale down near where the tree would be set up.

"I can help you with the tree."

"No ma'am. I've got it. It's not heavy." Sydney made two trips to her car. One to get the large decanter for the punch and one for the tree.

She set up the tree while Bea tended to the few customers who wandered in.

Just as she straightened the red and white fur-trimmed tree skirt around the bottom of the faux pine, a pair of black boots stepped up next to her.

On her knees, she followed the well-shod legs up. "Mac? Hi." She got up as gracefully as she could and swept at the dust from her hind parts. "Thought I might never hear from you again."

"Why?"

"The tears. Drama. Sorry for all of that."

"Wasn't your doing. How is RayAnne?"

"Hurt." She pushed her bangs to the side. Then glanced at her hands, hoping she hadn't just smudged dirt on her face.

"Can't blame her. But the tree trimming is still on?"

"Yep. We're going make the best of things. Of course, I didn't have a thing planned for Christmas since I thought she'd be gone. I'm kind of scrambling now. Shouldn't you be at school?"

"Had to pick up an order at the bakery. Someone's covering my class. Just thought I'd drop in and see if you were here, and you know, how RayAnne was and everything."

"Thanks. That was nice."

"Seth's looking forward to the tree trimming, so we'll be back this afternoon. Anything we can bring?"

"Nope. I think we've got it pretty well covered. Each of the kids is bringing an ornament or two. Should be relatively easy going."

"Sounds good. Are you by chance off Friday afternoon?"

"Actually, I am. But I'm sure Bea can help you with whatever you need. She says it's always quiet on Friday afternoons in here. Insisted that be one of my days off."

"No. Actually, that's perfect. I have an idea for Friday. We'd like to invite you and RayAnne to come over for dinner with us. Can we talk about that this afternoon?"

Friday night? "Sure. We can talk about it." She sure couldn't say she was working, she'd already said it was her day off. It was dinner. With kids. And technically, she hadn't even said *yes*.

"Good. See you later." Mac walked out and she couldn't take her eyes off of him all the way down the sidewalk.

Bea was staring at her with that left brow arched so high it was like a finger pointing her way. "*Uhhh-huh.* Did I overhear something about a dinner?"

"Just with our kids. Don't read anything into it. Besides, I didn't say yes."

"You will," Bea said.

Sydney laughed. But it was a nervous laugh, and it sounded odd even to herself.

"He's a nice man, and we all need friends. There's one thing I'd like you to remember. No matter what. The happier you are with yourself, the happier your daughter will be. Be the example of a strong, independent woman without ever saying a word." Bea tilted her chin up, then threw her arm up in the air in a flourish. "So have some fun."

True. It wasn't like there was a rule that she had to be in a relationship or even date. Just dinner. Kids. Easy.

"Oh. I almost forgot," Sydney said. "The mayor came in the other day. He said they've been pre-selling tickets to the big caroling night this year and that you need to double your batch of goodies. And he wants you to save one special for him."

"My famous chocolate-dipped pretzel rods." A hearty laugh filled the room. "I've been making them for years. Doesn't even require any baking. Just melting chocolate. I never was a good cook. My poor husband lost about twenty pounds the first year we were married because nothing I made was edible."

"That can't be true."

"It is. I just never got the knack for it. He did all the cooking. Now I just heat stuff up."

"You'll have to come to dinner at my house then. RayAnne and I would love that. I'll even send you home with leftovers to heat up."

"Be careful. I'll take you up on that."

"I hope you will."

"If he wants me to make a double batch, then I'll have to order more pretzels, and plastic bags to wrap them in." She shuffled through some papers on the counter. "Here it is. I'll call them and get them on their way. We're almost out of time. I'm going to have to get moving on those."

"Do you need help?"

Bea hesitated.

"Just say yes," Sydney said. "Make it easy on yourself. We're happy to help."

"That would be wonderful. They are easy as pie to make. Quite fun actually, but it does take time. And lots of counter space."

"I happen to have tons of counter space and a huge island in my kitchen at the farm house. We can do it there."

"Great. I'll ship the rest of these supplies directly to your house then."

"Deal." Sydney went about getting ready for the kids. She draped a long tablecloth over an eight-foot folding table for the snacks, and set out the cups and napkins.

She picked up her purse from where she'd left it near the tree and carried it over behind the counter. "Oh yeah. Almost forgot. The sweet man at Cookie Doe gave me one of these today." She held up the whisper-thin cookie. It was so delicate looking that she was afraid it might break.

"His famous snowflake fortune cookies."

"Want a bite?" She held the cookie between her fingers. "I'll share."

"No, but I do want to know what your wish says."

Sydney broke off a small piece of the snowflake and popped it into her mouth. "Wow. That's the best ginger crisp I've ever had. You sure you don't want a bite?"

"No thank you." She wove her pointer finger over the cookie, toward a slip of paper folded in the center.

"Probably just says 'Merry Christmas' or something. Cute idea though."

"Let's hear it."

Sydney pinched the corner of the paper with her fingers and pulled it out. "Oh. It's not just a greeting. It says, 'You're starting a new chapter on your journey. Don't question gifts of the heart.'"

"I knew you'd have a real fortune in your cookie. Just knew it." Bea looked smug. "He only has a handful with real fortunes in them. They are quite special. And they usually come true. I think this means you'll fall in love."

"Are you saying you think he gave me this one on purpose?"

"Oh, no. He has no way of knowing which is which. He makes those cookies up in huge batches. Ships most of them out all over the country. Internet business and all of that."

"I wonder what it means?" Maybe it was about her taking over The Book Bea. Or that Hopewell was the place she'd always been meant to be.

"You ask me, it's saying that those boots you saw under the tree a little while ago are going to be part of your future."

"Oh, stop it. That's just silly."

"Is it?" Bea removed her glasses and let them drop to her chest on the beaded chain.

"Yes. It's a random cookie. And a guy who is just being nice and happens to probably feel sorry for me because he was here when my jerk of an almost-ex-husband let my daughter down."

"We'll see. I'll let it go for now, but mark my words, there's more to this story."

Sydney didn't argue. She knew when there was no point to.

"But there is something else I want to talk about," Bea said.

"What's that?"

"I'd like to talk in detail about the store numbers with you. I've got all of the ledgers here. If you still would like to consider taking over the store, I think we could start with a thirty-day trial. For January. That way if it's not what you expect you can back out and there are no hard feelings."

"I won't want to back out. I think the only problem will be whether I can make it work financially. I mean this place . . ." She spread her arms and took it all in once again. "It's a dream. Who wouldn't want to run it?"

Bea's laugh was hearty. "Not many people have the same love for books that we do, I'm afraid. It's special."

"I'm almost afraid to let myself get too excited. I mean, just the inventory alone is worth . . . oh gosh it's going to add up quickly. I don't know what makes me think I'm going to be able to afford it. I would want to talk to RayAnne too. I don't want to mislead you, Bea."

"I promise you, if this place is in your heart, we'll find a way for you to afford it."

Sydney wasn't quite sure what to say, or even what that meant, but her heart was filling with hope. "How am I ever going to thank you for this opportunity?"

"You're going to run this store and let people know and love you like they have me all of these years."

"Those are awfully big shoes to fill."

"Nonsense. You are already making your touches known. Today is a perfect example."

"Well, then we better get a move on and get ready for the kids who are coming to decorate the tree. We'll work through all of this later. We have plenty of time to get through the details before the first of the year," Sydney said, but now she was more anxious than ever.

Suddenly she felt a renewed excitement that she hadn't

felt in years. She'd have to do both, work the job at Peabody's and help out at the bookstore for a while. At least until they had everything figured out. The idea of someday owning The Book Bea felt so right.

This might end up the best Christmas ever.

Sydney envisioned a fancy advent calendar, only instead of tiny chocolate Santas leading to Christmas Day, it had Hershey's Kisses, her favorite, in each window until the day The Book Bea would be hers.

Decorating the tree today was going to be even more special now for so many reasons.

Chapter Eleven

After school, Mac and Seth made short work of getting the Christmas decorations down from the attic in the garage by tying a heavy-duty tarp at the top of the attic stairs and securing it at a gentle angle to one of the four-wheeler's handlebars. Box by box Mac sent the dusty boxes down the makeshift chute, and Seth stacked them to the side.

"Last one," Mac called down.

"Okay, I'm going to take the two big boxes of ornaments in the house to find some to take with us."

"Untie the tarp first."

"Yes, sir."

Mac made one last sweep through the attic to be sure he hadn't missed anything, then untied the tarp from his end. He climbed down the folding attic ladder, then raised it until the door closed with a gentle slap.

He smacked the dust off the knees of his jeans and went inside to wash his hands. Seth was probably making a mess of those ornaments. Mac could hear tissue paper being wadded and glass tapping against glass. He wanted to call out for him to be careful, but sometimes you just had to let things happen. This was one of those times.

"How's it going in here?" Mac walked over and sat on the couch. He bent over, his forearms on his knees, watching as Seth pulled out ornaments. He had a small pile to his side. "Are those the ones you're thinking of taking?"

"Yeah. Is that okay?"

"Whatever you like." Mac looked at the winner pile that Seth had set aside. An ornament painted like a baseball with Seth's name and jersey number on it, two multicolored glass balls, a glittery snowman wearing a top hat, and a sled made out of popsicle sticks that Mac's mom had made for Seth when he was little.

"I think I'll take three. I don't know how many people are coming. It would be nice if the tree looked really good. Might cheer RayAnne up."

"That's true." Mac sat for a moment, giving Seth time to decide what he wanted to do. "You know, you could take that whole pile with you. We can just take three in, but if you think the tree needs more you can get the rest out of the truck. How does that sound?"

"That's a really good plan."

"Are you ready to go?" Mac felt like he'd just been given the best gift in the world. He didn't mean to rush Seth, but a small part of Mac was a little afraid that this switch in Seth's enthusiasm about something Christmassy might go away as quickly as it had shown up.

Seth piled the ornaments into a plastic shopping bag, then ran into the kitchen and grabbed his favorite baseball cap off of the bar. "I'm ready."

"Then, let's do this."

As they rode to town, Seth turned in his seat. "Can I ask you something, Dad?"

"Of course."

"If Mom never left us, but you got divorced like RayAnne's parents, would I get to still live with you?"

Wasn't like Mac hadn't thought about that before. "That's a pretty big question. I really don't know the answer to that. Most courts think children should be with their mothers. So I'm not sure what would've happened. What I can tell you is as sad as it makes me about the way things happened for us, I am really thankful that you're here with me. I wouldn't want it any other way."

"Me too, Dad." Seth nodded. "It's messed up how things like that work."

Or don't work. And that his son knew enough to worry about that at all bothered him the most. Genna had been a wild one when they'd met, but that had also been part of her allure. He'd never fully understand why she'd decided to abandon them the way she had.

Her excuse had been simply that she wasn't happy.

And then she was gone.

He'd been hurt, but his love for Seth was much stronger than the hurt in his heart. He'd pushed his own hurt to the side to care for his son, and to never let him see how torn apart he was. He'd never let Seth down.

Seth was the reason why Mac had been so careful about dating, too. There was no way he'd put Seth's feelings at risk ever again. He may not be able to fix the past, but he had full control over the future.

Mac circled the block to find a parking spot. From outside he could feel the hive of activity in the bookstore. It looked like most of the kids from school had shown up to contribute to the special Book Bea tree.

He and Seth walked in and got sucked right into the youthful energy that hummed at the left end of the store around the Christmas tree.

Kids snacked and others circled the Christmas tree hanging ornaments. Seth immediately raised his hand in a high-five to Mac, which surprised Mac. He'd seen Seth and Haley do that the last few days.

"This is good." Seth disappeared into the throng of people with his ornaments, leaving Mac standing there alone.

Mac hadn't heard this much racket in the store ever. It reminded him of his college days at the bars back at UNC.

Mac veered off toward the register on the opposite side of the store from the kids. He scanned the room looking for Sydney.

Her laugh caught his attention. He loved the sound of her laugh. He turned to see her standing next to a rack of holiday puzzles chatting. Her hands told a story without having to hear a word she was saying.

"Hi, Mac," Bea said from just behind him.

"Bea? Hi," She'd caught him off guard, and she had that look in her eye, like she knew he'd been watching Sydney. Caught in the act of staring. Awkward.

"She's been such a blessing to have around."

He tried to act nonchalant. He looked back over his shoulder, but she'd moved on. "Sydney? Yeah, I bet it's great to have some help during the holidays this year."

"She's more than that. Very special lady. Not the kind that lets you down." Bea just smiled and leisurely moved on.

Was that supposed to be some kind of message or something? Mac wondered. Everyone knew about Genna. In the beginning he had so much help that he could barely do anything on his own. He'd finally had to ask people to stop so he could figure it out on his own.

But that had been a long time ago, and people seemed to respect Mac for his relationship with his son.

A tap on his shoulder made him break free from Bea's insinuation. He turned around and Sydney stood there with a cup of green punch in one hand and a cookie in the other. Actually, it wasn't just any cookie. It was one of Cookie Doe's famous snowflake fortune cookies.

"Hey, there. For me?"

She nodded.

"Thanks. I'd say the tree trimming event is a huge success."

She rose on her toes, leaning in, and talking loud over the noise. "It's a hit! You missed Bea singing 'I Saw Mommy Kissing Santa Claus' a little while ago. She was a hoot. Even got RayAnne up there with her."

"Sorry I missed that. How's RayAnne today?"

Sydney lowered her gaze. "Jon is such a jerk."

"Was it as bad as RayAnne thought?"

"He's a coward. We traded emails. He's already on his way to Paris with his girlfriend."

Mac sipped the punch. He didn't want to fan this flame, but he agreed with her. The guy seemed like a jerk.

"He's going to come on Christmas Day to see her."

"Wow. So from a two-week skiing vacation to a one-afternoon visit. That's a heck of a trade off."

"On the bright side, RayAnne will be here for the Christmas caroling, and honestly I would have missed her like crazy." She looked around at the crowd filling the store. "I never would've made the commitment to help Bea if I'd known RayAnne was going to be home, but I can't let her down now. I'll do my best to make it a special holiday for RayAnne. I'll get creative. Thank goodness she seems to like hanging out here at the store with me."

"She can come and spend the day with us whenever she likes. Just let me know. I can pick her up from home or here. Won't be a problem. She and Seth are becoming good friends."

"Thanks. One of the other girls' moms is willing to help, too."

"Just speak up, Sydney. People around here stand by each other. It's one of the best perks of living in a small town."

"You're right. I'm not used to that," she said. But she sure did like the sound of it.

"It won't take long. I have a feeling you'll fit right in."

She looked him in the eye. A slight smile played on her lips. "I'm lucky to be here."

He felt like he was the lucky one right now. "How much longer is this going to go on?"

"Supposed to close at five, but it's almost that now. I thought we'd let it run until about six. A lot more people showed up than I expected. It's been a really strong sales night, too."

"Good. I'm guessing RayAnne will be the talk of the school after break."

"It was good timing for something positive to happen for her. I've had the opportunity to meet some of the parents. I think they're enjoying it as much as the kids are."

"How does the tree look?"

"It's a complete and utter beautiful mess," she said. "I wouldn't change a thing."

Bea imposed herself on the two. "Have you seen the tree, Mac?"

"No, not yet. I might just wait and see it tomorrow when there's no crowd."

Bea's hearty laugh carried over all of the noise. "Crowds aren't everyone's thing," she said. "My Henry was the same way."

"A good man."

"The best," Bea said. "You know we're going to be working on a huge batch of my special chocolate-dipped pretzels at Sydney's house Monday night. You and Seth should come. The mayor is asking us to double the number we usually make. We could use the help."

"We'd be happy to help," Mac said. "I'd heard that the pre-sales were going gangbusters."

"Yes, that's why we need more treats." Bea's hands flounced around as she spoke. "Many hands, light work, and all of that."

"If you don't mind," he added, glancing over at Sydney. "Since it's at your house." Did Sydney just give Bea a passing stink eye? "You don't mind, do you?" he asked Sydney.

"Of course not. Bea's right. So much quicker with more help."

"Good. And we still need to talk about the details for Friday," he added.

"Friday?" Bea patted them both on the arms. "Y'all just get to talking that through. I'm going to go check on something." She left with a skip in her step and a smirk.

"Sorry," Sydney said. "She's relentless."

"No worries. That's just Bea." He shifted his weight, wanting to talk about Friday but feeling nervous all of a sudden in the busy room. He cleared his throat. "It's so loud in here. Want to step outside so we don't have to shout at each other?"

Sydney motioned him to follow her to the front porch. "When you walk outside, you can really tell how loud it is in there." She opened her mouth and worked her jaw, trying to pop her ears.

Mac said, "I think the louder the kids got, the more they cranked up the music. After three hours, it's probably at full volume."

Blue sky gave way to a soft purple evening as the sun set. "It's getting dark so early these days." She leaned against the rail looking out over Main Street. "It's pretty though."

"I was thinking maybe y'all could come over around three on Friday. We can have an early dinner. Nothing fancy. I'll cook on the grill or something."

"That would be nice. What can I bring?"

"Not a thing. I could come and pick y'all up, or—"

"Don't be silly. I can drive over. I'm learning my way around town pretty quickly."

"Okay, then three." He pulled a card out of his shirt pocket. "Here's my address. The weather is supposed to be clear. So I was thinking an early supper, and then we can horse around a little on the back property. I've got a couple of four-wheelers we can ride."

His tension rose at her hesitation. Was she getting ready to back out?

"And before you say you're too busy or make up an excuse, or anything besides yes, it's just a couple parents hanging out for a nice meal and letting their kids burn off some energy."

"If I said no to that RayAnne would absolutely disown me for the rest of her life. She loves that kind of stuff. She's been dying for a four-wheeler. Not that it's going to happen."

He did know. But it was Santa intel. Could he tell her that? "Well, then you can't say no."

"As a mom I might have to."

"Why?"

"I worry about her safety. Those things are danger-ous."

"They can be. You're absolutely right. But I've got safety equipment, and rules. That should alleviate your worry. At least a little."

"Not really," she said. "Worry. It's what we do about our kids. It's love."

"You're right. How about I let you set extra ground rules if you want. You can be the honorary queen of my back yard. Am I begging?"

"Getting close," she laughed. "How can I pass up be-ing the queen?"

"You can't. It's your duty to the people."

"Well, then I guess we're in." She lifted her hand in one of those royal elbow-wrist waves. "But if I get scared we have a signal to stop without me looking like the bad guy. Deal?"

She had a sassy side to her that intrigued him. "Deal."

"Excuse me. Let me say goodbye to these folks."

He watched her as parents began to usher their kids out of The Book Bea to head home and start their winter break. Seth was talking to RayAnne over by the Christ-mas tree. He was glad they were getting along so well. Maybe Seth could make RayAnne's adjustment in Hopewell a little easier. Mac had lived here his whole life, so he'd never experienced changing schools, but he'd certainly seen the struggles his students had gone through when they transferred in mid-year.

Seth walked up and tapped his arm. "You ready to go home, Dad?"

"Sure. Yeah. Just waiting on you."

Seth was so amped up after the tree trimming at The Book Bea that Mac had almost headed to the tree lot right then and there. If it hadn't been his night to play Santa, he would have. Instead, they went straight home and shoved all of the furniture to one side to make room for the Christmas tree that they didn't even have yet.

Now the living room was pretty much a mess. Boxes of Christmas decorations and the couch were shoved against one wall. It sort of looked like the Abominable Snowman from Rudolph had taken their house and given it a good shake like a snow globe.

Small price to pay for Christmas joy.

Someone knocked at the door, and Seth leapt to his feet. "That must be Haley."

"Is it that time already?" Mac had completely lost track of time. He needed to get a move on or he'd be late.

"Hi, Mac." Haley looked around the room, looking a little horrified. "Wow, y'all have been busy."

And from her tone, not in a good way. "Looks like way more work than it is. We're excellent mess makers," Mac teased.

"I see that. They teach you that in college?"

"If they did I'd have gone for my Masters in it."

"I'm just a natural at it," Seth added.

"Got his old man's sense of humor, too," Mac said. "Guess I better hit the road."

Mac grabbed his coat and drove to Santa's Village. He had just enough time to pick out a Christmas tree for their house before he took his shift as Santa for the evening. He found a tall blue spruce that had that perfect shape, the one that spelled Christmas in his mind. He paid for the tree and then carried it over to his truck.

Still smelling like pine, he walked through the Village to the dressing rooms. As he passed excited children clinging to their parents' hands, he thought of RayAnne and the disappointment he'd watched unfold beneath her eyes. It was those types of Santa moments that tugged on his heart in a whole different way.

Once he got that red suit on and took his seat in that chair, he was Santa. He never tired of the children's hope-filled wishes.

The line was already long when he walked by on his way to his dressing room, but Rebecca had everything in order by the time he took his spot in the big chair.

> **Rebecca:** It's crazy tonight. Biggest night ever.
> Here we go. ❄
> **Rebecca:** First five.
> Tommy and his sister, Kate
> Sandy
> Lizzy and Libby—twins
> **Santa:** 👩

"Ho-ho-ho. Tommy?" Mac arched his brow, and as soon as the magic twinkled in little Tommy's eyes, all felt right.

And two hours later, there was still a line as far as he could see, even though Rebecca had texted him to let him know that she'd stopped allowing more people in line thirty minutes prior.

When Mac looked at the new text from Rebecca his heart tightened. The last name on the next group of five read

> SETH (yes, yours.)

How had Haley talked Seth into a Santa visit? Something he'd tried to do himself for years.

He scanned the line of children waiting and saw his boy standing there. He could barely hold back the joy in his heart.

Mac took a longer than normal pause before the next kid. He needed to give them each his all even though his stomach was in knots.

Would Seth recognize him beneath the getup?

This sure wasn't the way he wanted him to find out about this part-time annual gig.

Would Seth feel betrayed? There was no time to call in a replacement, and if Mac pretended to be sick to avoid the risk, he'd let all of the children still in line down. He could never do that.

He gave Rebecca a nod, and one by one he went through the line until Seth was next.

Rebecca led Seth to Mac, only Haley was still no-where in sight.

He and Rebecca had worked together long enough that an inconspicuous motion was full communication. And the little nod and hand motion she'd just sent him said that Seth was here alone.

Mac's paternal side flared, but it wrestled with his holiday heart to stay in character.

Mac gave his best *ho-ho-ho* and motioned Seth closer. Hoping that the hair, the beard, the glasses, and the fat red suit might be enough to keep Seth from recognizing him, he kept his head tipped slightly away.

"Haven't seen you in a very long time. You've been on my nice list every year, though."

"Yes, sir. I try." Seth didn't sit on his lap. Instead he lounged against the giant chair, leaning his body away from Santa and constantly scanning the crowd. "Pretty sure I'm getting ready to get kicked off of that nice list, though."

Did Seth recognize him?

"Ho-ho-ho. Now, maybe we should talk about that."

"Have to tell you," Seth said staring down at his shoes. "I don't believe in Santa. I mean I've been trying to figure out if you're real or not. I'm pretty sure you're not. I mean, it's nearly impossible. But I don't know what else to do, so just in case you are . . . I could use some help."

"I see."

"My mom left me and my dad a long time ago."

"Yes." The pit in Mac's stomach squeezed, leaving only enough space for guilt to seep in. He felt like he was eavesdropping on his son's private thoughts.

"It's okay," Seth said. "We're men. We got it. We're good. But there's a new girl. Her dad really let her down. Never saw anybody so sad in all my life. Could you do something nice for her? She's ten. Her name is RayAnne. And she likes baseball and four-wheelers. Like me, but a girl. Her dad keeps messing up. She's not so lucky lately. Can you help her?" Seth shrugged and scanned the line. He turned his gaze away. "This is probably stupid. Maybe a cool present would help."

"That's real thoughtful of you, so—" Mac caught the slip. He'd nearly said *son.* "—Seth. Sometimes things don't fix feelings though. You know that, right?"

"Yes, sir. I do. But you didn't see her. We have to do something to be sure her Christmas is good. I've been sad about Christmas for a lot of years since my mom left. I don't want her to be like that."

Hold it together, Mac thought. All he wanted to do right now was hold Seth in his arms. He took a moment, trying to steady his voice. "I understand. I'm sure we can find a way to make sure your friend knows that she's loved and that she has a good Christmas. You just gave her the best gift of all though."

"Me? No, I haven't done anything."

"You care enough to ask for help. That's big. Extra special. She's very lucky to have a friend like you."

"We're not friends yet. I just met her. But I get her. And my dad, well, he's really good. He'd never leave me."

"She may not know it yet. But you are, indeed, a very special friend to her." Mac had never been more proud of Seth. This was the kind of caring that you couldn't teach. "What is it that you want for Christmas?"

"I pretty much got everything I need. You don't have to fake this Santa stuff with me."

"I'm not."

Seth stared at him so long that Mac was certain he'd recognize him.

Instead, Seth drew in a breath. "A new computer game, maybe. But Dad and me do a lot of stuff. I'm good. Oh, and the lady that is living next door. Haley. Be sure her husband gets home soon. Maybe drop off some socks for her. She's always wearing crazy, cool socks. She's really nice."

"Look at my elf." Mac said, pointing to Rebecca. "Do I know crazy socks or what? I got that covered, no problem. I'll get her to pick them out."

"Cool."

"You're a very good boy. Can I ask you why you thought you'd be on the naughty list?"

His cheeks reddened. "I snuck out. Rode my bike here. My dad doesn't know. And Haley thinks I'm sleeping."

Mac's emotions were torn between pride and concern. The bottom line was Seth was okay, and his heart was in the right place. If this wasn't the Christmas spirit, he didn't know what was.

He leaned forward, his voice feeling shaky. "That's serious, Seth. You realize that was dangerous, too."

"I know." He hung his head. "Especially if you're not real. But I had to take the chance. Dad said it was bigger than us. I didn't know what else to do."

How the heck was he supposed to handle this?

"Tell you what. I'll take care of those requests. Even leave you on the nice list, but we're going to arrange for a ride home for you."

"I'm not supposed to ride with strangers."

"You're not supposed to ride your bike out of the neighborhood, either." Mac hoped he hadn't just blown his own cover.

Seth's mouth dropped open, then snapped shut.

"It'll be okay. I'll write you a Santa pass for this one time. But you have to promise that it will never happen again."

"I promise."

"Let's get a picture."

"I don't have any money, and my dad would kill me if he knew."

"This one is just for me. To put in my personal things."

"Okay."

Rebecca took the picture.

"You go stand right next to that door, and wait. I'm going to have my lead elf, Rebecca, help with your ride home.

Seth walked down and stood next to the exit while Mac spoke with Rebecca and explained the situation.

"You're kidding me!" Rebecca said, wide-eyed. "I've got it covered. I'll get Wes from Wheelies to take him home. He's printing the pictures tonight, but I can do that. Don't worry. We'll make sure he gets home safe."

Mac worked his way through the rest of the kids, then he and Rebecca turned off the lights for the night. He drove home with the Christmas tree in the back of his truck, feeling like he may have just gotten the best Christmas present any parent could ever receive. Sure, Seth broke a rule. A pretty darn serious one, but Mac had done his share of that as a kid, too.

When Mac let himself into the house, Haley was watching a movie in his living room. He wondered if Seth had come clean with her.

"Hey," Mac said.

Deep lines creased in her forehead. "Hi there. He told me everything. Are you speaking to me?" she whispered.

"Of course." Mac laid his keys down.

She nodded. "He's upstairs. For real this time. He apologized to me for sneaking out. Begged me not to tell you." She whispered. "But then you're Santa. You know everything."

Mac breathed in deeply. "Yeah. The reasons were all good. But damn he could have been hurt. Not cool. He did it for the right reasons, though. It was sweet. A little girl he knows, her father cancelled their Christmas plans. He was there. She was sobbing. Heavy scene."

"Ouch."

"Apparently it hit a little close to home for Seth. It's been years since Genna left."

"He did mention a little something about that."

"I'm doing the best I can."

"You're a great dad. It's not about you, Mac. It's about Seth, and he's getting to the age where he realizes his life is different than most of his friends'. Probably even more noticeable in a small town."

"How am I supposed to handle all of this? I feel like I should do something as a parent, but I'm also proud of him. He was only thinking of others. And this is the first year since Genna left that he's shown any interest in the holiday." As upset as he was that Seth would take a risk like sneaking out and going all the way across town, he also knew he'd never forget this moment. The indication of what kind of man he was raising, the kindness in his son's heart, was something he didn't want to mar, either.

"Let me talk to him next time I see him," Haley said. "We've really created a bond over the last few weeks. I can help you get your message across without you having to give yourself up in the process."

"Thanks. Yeah. I appreciate it."

Haley went out the side door and crossed the lawn to her parents' house.

Mac watched until she was safely inside, then closed the door and locked it. He walked out into the garage. There were so many things out there that he and Seth did together. Sports, tools, half-done projects.

He rustled around the garage until he found the bucket he used for the Christmas tree each year. He carried it outside to the spigot to fill it; water splashed and lapped at its sides.

It was a clear night. The stars twinkled, and the night felt still. Once the bucket was full he put it next to the house, then dragged the tree from the bed of his truck. A burst of pine scent filled the air as he picked up the tree and put it in the bucket to hydrate until they were ready to take it inside.

The tradition of piling gifts under the Christmas tree would probably never go away. Glossy paper, dazzling ribbon, and the excitement of the hidden surprise, but to Mac the shining moments were the intangible ones. The ones you had to hold close to your heart because there was no other way to take a snapshot of those memories— like the smell of pine after carrying the tree.

School was officially out for Christmas break, so Mac and Seth both slept in, then spent most of the morning going through boxes of lights. They tested each strand, tossed anything broken, and made a list of items they needed to replace so they could zip into town to get them.

Mac had thought going to town to pick up three strands of lights was going to be a quick and easy task. Unfortunately, technology had changed all that. Finding just a regular old plain strand of Christmas lights to match what he already owned had been darn near impossible amid the LEDs, and mini, micro-mini, icicle, and chasing lights.

That sure made him feel old. And he wasn't.

He and Seth finally settled on buying enough new lights to fill the whole tree so they'd all match. They drove home singing along to Christmas tunes.

Mac had just finished putting the tree in the stand when there was a knock on the front door.

Seth ran to answer it.

"Hey there," Haley's voice came in from the hall. "Now that is one amazing tree," Haley said, nodding with approval.

"Dad always picks out the best ones. Do you and your husband get a live tree or have a fake one?" Seth asked.

"This would've been our first Christmas together. So

I don't know yet. We're going to celebrate when he gets home, but there won't be any real trees available then, so I'm pretty sure we'll have an artificial one this year. But next year I think we'll buy a real one together. I like the real thing."

"Me too," Seth said. "They smell good."

Mac tightened the anchors into either side of the tree until it was standing straight, then crawled back out from underneath.

"Can you get a pitcher of water for the tree, Seth?"

"Sure, Dad."

Haley watched Seth until he turned into the kitchen. "I just wanted to check to see how things were going after last night."

"He doesn't know that I know, if that's what you mean."

"Good. I think that's the best plan. He's a good kid. Don't worry."

Mac glanced down the hall. "I'm a dad. It's what we do." At that moment Sydney's concerns echoed in his mind. *"Worry. It's what we do about our kids. It's love,"* she'd said to him.

Haley ran her hand through her hair. "I promise you he will not slip by me again. I really feel awful about this."

"You know I don't blame you for that."

"I know, but I do feel bad about it. I've always wanted children, but maybe I'm not cut out for it."

"You're going to make a great mother one day."

He realized now that playing Santa to RayAnne's four-wheeler dreams might not be the best way to be helpful to Sydney. Being a parent wasn't easy even when everything went right. Adding to her stress was not his plan. He'd tread lightly about the four-wheeler this afternoon. If Sydney wasn't comfortable, he would find something else to do besides hot dog it on the ATVs. There were other options.

He pictured Sydney riding on the back of his ATV, hanging on and laughing when he went too fast. Had the invitation ever really been about RayAnne, or more about having a chance to see Sydney again? He wasn't sure.

He'd better figure it out quickly, because they'd be here in less than an hour.

Chapter Twelve

Sydney walked into The Book Bea, but instead of a greeting she was met by a glare from Bea and a snippety, "What are you doing here? It's your day off, and today's the big day."

"The big day?"

"You're meeting Mac."

"Oh stop it."

"You need to get gussied up for the most handsome available man in all of Hopewell. That takes time."

"Bea. You know it's just an early supper with our kids. Not really a gussy-up type of thing."

"What I know is that you need someone to remind you how fantastic you are. You're a beautiful, smart, vibrant young woman. You should be appreciated for that."

"You appreciate me plenty for a lifetime."

"That is not the kind of admiration I meant and you know it. And he's a good one. I have an intuition about people."

"He seems very nice. I do have a question about him, though."

"I have most of the answers around this town." She lifted her chin. "What is it you want to know?"

"It's just not often you see a father with custody of his child. Which seems to be the case with Mac. What's the story there?"

"Oh, yes." Bea rubbed her aching fingers. "That's not your usual story. His wife was younger than him. She was a wild one, but boy he loved her. They hadn't been married long when she got pregnant. He was so excited. Handing out cigars the day they found out it was going to be a boy. She never seemed as excited as he was about it, but then she was pretty sick through the pregnancy, too, if I remember correctly."

Sydney thought back to when she'd been pregnant with RayAnne. She'd had one of those horrible, sickly first trimesters, too. It was torture.

"Once the baby was born she spent more time out on the town than home. She really didn't have a very nice reputation, if you know what I mean. Mac was home taking care of the baby most of the time. He was pretty much a single parent even when she was around."

"So they divorced?"

"No. She left. Well, yes, Mac finally got the divorce as irreconcilable differences. It wasn't easy, though. She up and left on Christmas. He had to track her down to get the divorce. She just abandoned them both and never came back."

"Not even for a visit?"

"Nope. She moved on to something new and never looked back. No communication at all, from what I hear. Quite bizarre. The girl had absolutely zero maternal instincts."

"Wow, and I thought my situation was bad. Just goes to show you things can always be worse."

"It depends on your perspective. Mac was sad. He adored Genna. Worked two jobs just to spoil her. He was so happy, I think it really came to him as a big surprise."

"That's too bad."

"But I think once he got over the initial shock, it was also a huge relief for him to not live with that frustration. No one wants to be with someone who doesn't want them."

Sydney couldn't agree more.

"Where is RayAnne this morning?"

"She's spending the day with a friend from school. So I have the morning to myself."

"She's making friends already," Bea said. "I knew she would." Bea eyed her cautiously. "Are you okay? You seem a little melancholy today."

"I guess. It really bothered me when I heard Jon was taking his girlfriend to Paris. That had been my dream trip. He'd never wanted to go. I'm not the jealous type. At least I never thought I was, but boy did that hit me wrong."

"That's not jealousy. That's disappointment. Very different."

"Is it really?"

"Of course it is. And you'll get Paris. Your own kind of Paris, and it will be more special than any trip you and Jon could've gone on."

"You are the most optimistic woman I've ever known. I hope you're right. But right now what I need is to get some stocking stuffers. I hadn't planned on RayAnne being home for Christmas. I've got work to do to piece the holiday back together."

"Well, you know the inventory almost better than I do. Take whatever you want. On the house."

"No. I won't do that. This is a business. We can't give away the store. Was that a test?" She shot Bea a glance.

"No. But if it had been you'd have passed. Not that I'm surprised."

She left The Book Bea with a bag full of stocking stuffers, but she had no idea how she was going to get the farmhouse looking festive before RayAnne got home. Especially since their Christmas tree was now sitting in the middle of The Book Bea.

She tried Jon's cell phone again on her drive home. He'd avoided her calls ever since the big letdown. Why he'd felt the need to call RayAnne's phone just because she didn't answer still boggled her mind. Wasn't like his news couldn't have waited another day.

Her call to Jon went to voice mail again.

When she got home, she went up into the attic to find all their Christmas stuff. Stockings, ornaments, and wreaths.

The first stocking she lifted out of the box was Jon's. She was so tempted to throw his in the trash. Instead, she shoved it down into the bottom of the box. Out of sight.

She found hers and RayAnne's. Hugging them to her chest, she remembered the weekend they'd stayed at that little island off the coast of Georgia a few summers ago. She could only spend so many hours in the hot sun on the beach while Jon golfed, so she and RayAnne had taken advantage of a workshop at a little Christmas store. For twenty-five dollars a piece they'd spent two afternoons working on personalized Christmas stockings. They'd cut, whipstitched, appliqued, glued, and bedazzled one for each of them and then one for Jon, too. It had been a wonderful mother-daughter project. She wondered if the store was still there.

The things she'd picked up this morning filled RayAnne's stocking with just enough room for a few sweet treats and fruit—an apple, an orange, and a banana, just like Sydney's mom had done for her when she was that age—it would be perfect. She'd bought herself two novels and some drawer sachets to fill her own stocking from Santa. She'd been a good girl, too, after all.

Feeling good about getting that done while RayAnne was gone, Sydney dumped the gifts back into the bag and hid it away in the top of the closet under the stairwell.

Then she looked for the wreath boxes. She'd brought only three of them from the old house in Atlanta. Each year everyone in their old neighborhood had tried to outdo each other with their door wreaths. Not just for Christmas either, but year round. These three had been her favorites.

She spread the boxes out on the couch and took the tops off of them. Their house in Atlanta had been quite different from this one. The two-story brick house had twice the space, too. Not the nicest in the neighborhood, but all she'd cared about was that it was in the best school district in the entire city.

Although each of these wreaths was quite beautiful, none of them seemed right for this house. Or this year. A fresh start was in order. She hated to dismantle the high-dollar wreaths, but she was sure she could combine some of the pieces to come up with something a little more in line with the cozy rural setting that wouldn't cost her a dime.

She went upstairs, where she'd turned the extra bedroom into a craft room for her and RayAnne to work in.

She got her glue gun, scissors, and some floral wire, then went downstairs to see what she could create.

She spent the next hour cutting, gluing, and tucking the pieces together until she had a whole new creation in front of her.

Sydney stepped back and looked at her handiwork.

The fancy pheasant feathers had looked a little too highfa-lutin in the copper and gold wreath, but by combining them with traditional pine cones and poinsettias, she'd been able to give the wreath a rustic feel that was perfect for this house. Something she thought RayAnne would like, too.

She carried it to the front door and hung the wreath from a rusty nail that had probably been there since she was just a baby.

She walked out to the middle of the yard to see how it looked. Bright and warm, it would give RayAnne a nice Christmassy welcome home when Diane brought her back. She glanced at her watch. That wouldn't be long, either. She went back inside and wove a length of green pine garland through the stair railing and then followed that with a string of lights. She plugged the lights in. It instantly made the room look more festive.

She went upstairs and changed into a pair of black jeans, hiking boots, and a plaid western shirt. Her red sweatshirt was downstairs. It was definitely a layers kind of day outside, although the sun was warm if she could stay out of the breeze.

Better safe than sorry, she gathered their jackets and put them by the door.

She sprawled out on the couch to read. She was turn-ing the page to start a new chapter when the doorbell rang, startling her out of her reading daze.

RayAnne must've forgotten her key in the excite-ment this morning. She jumped up and ran over to the door, expecting RayAnne, but instead it was the mail carrier.

"I have a registered letter for you, ma'am." He scanned the code on the thick envelope and then handed her his computer device. "Sign here."

She used the stylus to sign, although if anyone could recognize that as her signature it would be a miracle. "Thanks." She shut the door behind her.

Trepidation filled her.

She turned the envelope over in her hand. If the fine quality of the envelope hadn't been hint enough, then the Atlanta lawyer's address was a sure thing. Her lawyer.

Divorce papers. Jon was on a flat-out roll, spreading disappointment among the Ragsdale girls equally this Christmas. He'd finally signed the papers.

She laid her hand on the chair near the door and lowered herself, feeling as if someone had just punched her in the gut. She'd been the one to push for the quick divorce, and now that she had exactly what she had asked for, it hurt. It hurt a lot.

The timing couldn't have been worse. One more reminder she'd be spending this Christmas alone. Then again, maybe the timing was right. A reminder to move forward and quit looking back.

Like Bea had said, she needed to open herself up to new opportunities. Professionally and personally.

She slipped her finger under the edge of the envelope and pulled out the papers. Just like that. One person decides, and it can all be washed away like it never happened.

She stuffed the papers back into the envelope. She'd been mourning the loss of her relationship since February, so there weren't any tears. Just that black heaviness in her heart.

It was over. And there wasn't a single word to describe how she felt. She wasn't Mrs. Ragsdale anymore. She wasn't a wife. Just a mom, and there was no reason to feel guilty for spending time with Mac when this relationship was behind her. But then why did she feel so awkward about it?

Mac was a nice guy. They were friends. Two single parents making memories with their kids over the holidays. No harm in that.

With that freshly planted in her mind, she heard Diane's car pull into the driveway. She placed the envelope in the drawer of the table next to the door. She didn't need to bring RayAnne's mood down with the news. Better they should have some fun before letting Jon land another disappointment on RayAnne.

If she dared be honest with herself, she wasn't ready to speak the words aloud, either.

Mac paced the living room, waiting for Sydney and RayAnne to arrive. Wasn't like he hadn't invited tons of people to the house over the years, but for some reason this felt a little different. He looked out the front window again.

How many times had he looked already?

He walked past the Christmas tree again, and adjusted a couple of the lights to fill a bare spot. Music? Should he put music on? Would that seem like he was trying too hard? It was just a friendly get together. They'd said so. It's not a date unless both of you say it is, and he hadn't and she'd clarified it, so there was no problem.

"We should put Christmas music on, Dad."

Smartest kid ever. "You're right," Mac said. "Why don't you do that?"

"Okay." Seth plopped down on the couch and started thumbing through his phone for music.

"You can play my Christmas music," Mac said.

"The CDs and old plastic records? Get real, Dad."

"They're vinyl, not plastic."

"They're totally lame," Seth said.

Mac's collection took up two shelves of the bookcase. He still wasn't a fan of the whole download music craze.

A moment later Seth had his phone playing Christmas music through the house speakers.

A car pulled into the driveway.

"They're here." Seth ran for the door.

Mac counted to four and then walked that way, trying not to look too eager. He stepped out onto the front porch just as they were walking up.

"This place is cool," RayAnne said. "I've never known anyone who lived in a log house before."

Sydney smiled as she walked toward him, balancing a covered dish.

"No problem finding the place?"

"Nope. Pretty drive out this way."

He'd lived in this house for six years now. His dream home. Simple in style. Kind of like him. The wraparound porch had been the most important feature. Well, aside from the extra garage space he'd had the builder integrate into the design. That had meant giving up the porch on the east side of the house, but how much porch did one man really need anyway? That had been an easy decision.

Out here there weren't many neighbors, but the ones he had were of the kind from generations ago, when people helped people just because they lived nearby.

It had been a while since he'd considered what the first impression would be like to an outsider visiting.

"It's great. I thought the farmhouse was quiet," Sydney said as she stepped up onto the porch.

"You didn't have to bring anything."

"Are you kidding me? I'm a southern girl. We do not arrive without a proper host gift."

He took the dish from her and started to lift the lid. "May I?"

"Absolutely. It's homemade fudge."

"It smells good. Should I do a quality check?" He reached in and took a small piece off of the top row. "Chocolate peanut butter? How did you know that's my favorite?" He chewed slowly, letting the sweet chocolate fill his mouth. He swallowed, then took one more piece. "I may have to hide this from Seth so I won't have to share. If you're going to bring these kinds of host gifts I'm going to have to go ahead and invite you back now."

She tossed her hair back as she laughed, and followed him inside. "Glad you like it."

"I do, come on in."

She followed behind him, and Seth and RayAnne came in right behind her.

"Real tree?"

"Is there any other kind?"

"It smells so good." She stepped into the living room, her eyes trailing all the way to the ceiling. "Not an inch to spare."

"Takes precision selection skills to do that."

Seth interjected, "That and sometimes a chainsaw. Last year we made three wreaths out of all the limbs Dad had to trim off to fit the tree in the house."

"Years of practice does improve my precision."

"So I hear. Do I smell spaghetti?" She took a second sniff in the air. "Maybe garlic bread?"

"Lasagna."

"Homemade?"

"My grandmother's recipe. It's the best. I'm warning you now, you're going to be begging me to cook for you again."

"Really? You're pretty sure of yourself."

She seemed comfortable, and that put him at ease, too. "My lasagna skills are even better than my tree selection skills."

"And a lot more useful throughout the year. I do love lasagna."

"And way easier to eat than spaghetti. Although I have a good recipe for that, too."

"Should've known from that olive skin that you had some Italian in you."

"Italian, Portuguese, and a dash of French."

"Ooh la la. Hope I get to try the French cuisine sometime."

"That can be arranged. Ever been to Paris?" He regretted it as soon as the words spilled out of his mouth. "Sorry. That's probably a sore subject with your ex headed there. Wasn't thinking." He picked up a bottle of wine. "Can I pour you a glass of wine?"

"Maybe later. It's fine. No, I've never been, but have always wanted to. Except for the eight-hour flight, I can't imagine anywhere more perfect to go. It's totally on my bucket list. The food. The wine. The art. Everything. I picture it breathtaking and amazing."

"It is. I'll have to tell you all about my time there one day."

"You've been? Do you speak French? Not knowing the language might be a little daunting."

"I speak it well enough to get around. I'll tell you all about it some time. But for now, I think we have enough daylight to spend some time outdoors. Work up an appetite and then eat. Unless y'all are really hungry now."

"I can wait. How about y'all?" Sydney turned to see

Seth and RayAnne yammering over by the tree like they'd been buddies forever. They hadn't even heard her. "Y'all want to eat now or later?"

"We can wait until later," Seth and RayAnne said in chorus.

"Sounds like we all agree," Sydney said.

Mac moved closer to Sydney. "I thought we'd head outside and do some four-wheeling. How do you feel about that?"

"RayAnne already saw them when we drove up. She'd kill me if I said no."

"I'd take the hit on that," he said. "She can be mad at me. If you're not comfortable, we don't have to ride."

"No. That's not fair. We'll be extra careful?" She looked up, her eyes catching his. "My rules, right?"

"Scout's honor."

"Let's see how it goes. I still have kingdom rights. Right?"

He did a sweeping bow. "Queen Sydney, would you like to lead the way outside?"

She sauntered forward, then Seth leapt ahead.

"Follow me," Seth said. He and RayAnne ran ahead and jumped onto the seats of the two four-wheelers parked in front of the house. Bantering about their favorite baseball teams, they looked like old friends.

Mac stepped in front of the two ATVs and clapped his hands together. "Okay, y'all ready for the plan?"

"Yeah!" Seth and RayAnne shouted out.

Sydney clapped and walked over next to the four-wheeler where RayAnne was sitting.

"Have you ever ridden before?" He looked at RayAnne and then over at Sydney.

"Yes!" RayAnne's eyes danced wide. "My dad taught

me. I can shift and everything, but Dad rides me on the back of his a lot, too."

"Not me," Sydney offered.

"Are we going to ride?" RayAnne threw her hands onto the handle grips.

"Alrighty. First things first. Seth, you go grab a couple gloves and a ball. You and RayAnne can play a little catch while I take Miss Sydney out on her very first four-wheeler ride."

RayAnne slung her leg over the seat to get off and stood next to the bike. "Man."

"You'll get your turn, RayAnne. If I can convince your mom here that you'll be safe," Mac said.

RayAnne whooped. "This is going to be so funny. Mom, you're gonna scream like a girl."

"Hey. I *am* a girl, and proud of it, I might add."

"She's *such* a girl," RayAnne said, nudging Seth.

"Be nice. Nothing wrong with girls being girly." Mac gave Seth a nod.

"Come on, Ray," Seth said. "We can watch and toss from over there." He handed her one of the ball gloves.

"Okay." She took it and jogged ahead then pounded her fist into the glove. "Over here."

Seth tossed the ball to her and RayAnne caught it and slung it back.

"Seriously?" Sydney looked slightly worried. "You want me to ride on this thing?"

"I'd never ask you to let your daughter do something you weren't comfortable with. So, let's just take this a step at a time. You'll ride with me. If that's okay, I'll show you how to drive one yourself. After that, we'll decide."

"Oh great and if I say no I'll be the bad guy."

"No. If you say no, we'll just play around until it gets dark and we have no choice but to put them up before they get a turn. Deal?"

"I like the way you think, Mac."

"Thought you might." He handed her a helmet. "Put this on." He got on the ATV and started it, then took the helmet swinging from the handlebars and pulled it onto his head and strapped it under his chin. The only reason he wore one at all was to set an example for Seth. It was one thing to get a little crazy as an adult, a whole other thing when it came to kids.

She pulled her hair into a ponytail and swirled it into a topknot, then tugged on the helmet.

He patted the seat and pointed to a peg on the rear where she could get a leg up. She pulled herself up and over and then leaned forward, holding him tight.

"Ready?" Mac said over his shoulder.

"I don't know."

Her cheek rested against his back, and her arms felt as rigid as a stack of hardcover books. He took off slowly, hoping not to scare her. Then he picked up speed, carefully selecting the smooth parts of the trail back to the gate.

By the time he pulled to a stop she'd let up her grip a little. "What do you think?"

"It's fun."

"Wait here." He climbed off the ATV and walked over to the gate and opened it.

"You ready?"

She nodded, so he climbed back on and took off through the gate. She laughed and squealed, but in a fun way. He rode up to the path that led to the highest point on the land and then stopped. From here he could see the entire parcel, all the way over to his house. "Great view, huh?"

"Yes." She took off her helmet, sending her hair tumbling back over her shoulders. "Wow, it's pretty up here."

"My favorite spot."

"I bet it would be perfect for a picnic here in the spring."

"Oh yeah, the field is full of wildflowers then. And everything is so green. Not much color this time of year."

"Still pretty. And peaceful."

He didn't rush her. It was nice to share this place with someone who appreciated its beauty. All Seth saw was a place to ride fast, slide, and do doughnuts.

"This would be the perfect place to watch a meteor shower in the night sky. I bet it's pitch black here at night."

"It is. Seth and I camped out here a couple times. Can't see your hand in front of your face at night unless there's a full moon out."

"Wow. You know, the Ursids meteor showers are supposed to be visible starting next Tuesday through Christmas Day. With a dark spot like this I bet we could catch a glimpse of a few. Maybe the kids would like to do that?"

"Sounds like a plan. We could come out earlier, maybe make some s'mores and drink hot chocolate. If there's chocolate involved, Seth is a sure in."

"RayAnne, too. Think about it. Let me know if you can work it into y'all's schedule."

"I don't have to think about it. I think we should just plan on it."

"I'd like that." She put her hands in her back pockets and lifted her chin to the sky. "I love it out here, but I guess we should head back."

She walked over and started to climb up behind him. "Oh, no ma'am."

"What do you mean, no?" She took a step back.

His jaw set, and he shook his head matter-of-factly. "I'm not giving you a ride back."

"You're going to make me walk?"

"No." He got off the ATV. "You're going to drive me."

"Oh, no." She took a giant step back. "That's not going to happen."

"Sure it is." He patted the seat. "Hop on up."

"I don't know how."

"I'll help you."

"We should get back to the kids. I'll just ride behind you again. Let's get back to the house."

"That's where we're headed. Don't worry; my neighbor is right next door. They're always keeping a watch over things, and Seth is a responsible kid. We've got time."

She bit down on her lower lip. "You might regret this."

"Hope not." He waited until she got into position and then slid behind her. "I'm a great teacher. Got a degree and everything."

She laughed and when she did her helmet tipped back and banged against his. "Oh, no. I'm sorry." And darn if she didn't bump him again.

"Hope your driving is better than your multitasking."

She laughed, her shoulders rising and falling as she did. "Real funny."

"Okay, so here's all you've got to do." He ran through the do's, don'ts, and how tos.

Sydney started the motor and tried to ease out the clutch.

And after half a dozen popped clutches and missed gears she had the hang of it and was speeding back down the path much faster than he'd taken her. "You're a natural," he yelled.

She lifted her hand and gave him a thumbs up. "You're an ace teacher. Let's head back so you can give RayAnne a ride."

"You're on!" He rested one hand on the crook of her waist. From here he could just see the side of her face beneath the bulky helmet, but it couldn't hide that smile. It looked like freedom and joy, and that made him happy.

The look on RayAnne's face when her mom came screaming around the corner toward the house was priceless. Her eyes were as wide as one of those anime manga characters'. She and Seth ran over to the driveway, slapping high-fives along the way.

"I can't believe you taught my mom how to drive," RayAnne said. "No way."

"I'm pretty good." Sydney took her helmet off and held it close to her chest. "I do drive a car. Give me some credit."

"You gonna take me for a ride?" she asked.

"No. I'm going to let Mac do that. I'm not *that* good yet."

"Oh, yeah, but you let me put *my* life in your hands?" Mac teased.

"Kind of like driver's ed." Sydney got off and gave her helmet to RayAnne. "Have fun, kiddo."

Mac scooted up, and RayAnne climbed on back with a thousand-watt smile.

"Seth, are you going to ride along?"

"Heck yeah." Seth grabbed his helmet and strapped it

on. He patted it twice on the top, and Mac echoed the movement. Then Mac revved his motor, making RayAnne squeal before they ever took off. Seth hit the throttle and led the way.

When Mac came back he pulled his four-wheeler straight into the garage and parked it. He was helping push Seth's into its spot when Sydney walked out of the house. She didn't have her jacket on this time. The sleeves of her shirt were turned up, and she looked like she'd just stepped out of a country western outfitters catalog. Fresh, fit, and filling every curve in those jeans.

RayAnne raced across the garage and hugged her mom around the waist. "This has been the best day ever. Thanks."

"Wait until you taste Mac's lasagna," Sydney said.

"You snuck a taste?" Mac raised a brow.

"How could I resist?"

"It's hard," Seth said. "Dad's lasagna is the best."

"Hope you don't mind, but I went ahead and set the table. Everything is ready. I thought y'all might come back starved."

"Mind?" Mac shook his head. "Hardly. Let's hit it, gang."

They all went into the house and washed up before gathering at the table. Sydney had managed to round up everything to set the table and even made a little impromptu centerpiece with Mac's grandmother's white milk glass bowl filled with Christmas ornaments, probably from one of the boxes sitting in the garage.

It looked like a real family dinner table.

As Seth and RayAnne took their seats, Mac helped Sydney get the garlic cheese bread out of the oven.

"Man that smells good," Sydney said. "Major garlicky."

Mac set the pan on the counter and tossed the oven mitts to the side. "Major good. Thanks for getting it ready."

"Least I could do. You had everything prepared." She slid the bread into the basket Mac held, and then they took their seats at the table.

Mac cleared his throat, and Seth already had his hands pressed together and eyes closed.

Sydney and RayAnne followed suit.

"Dear Lord," Mac said. "We've gathered to share good times, good conversation, and good food with our new friends, for which we thank you for all. Amen."

"Amen."

Conversation lulled as everyone dug in and even went back for seconds of lasagna.

With tummies full and everyone tired from being out in the fresh air, they moved to the living room and sat by the Christmas tree.

"So, Monday night we're at your place to do the chocolate-dipped pretzels for Bea?" Mac asked.

"Yes. Everything was ordered and is supposed to arrive at my place Monday. So unless there's a shipping snafu we should be in good shape."

"We'll be there."

"Wouldn't want you to drive all that way just to turn around. I could call you when I get home and make sure we have everything we need," Sydney said.

"It's not that far. In fact, if I take the old gravel road it's less than a mile between us."

"It was a lot farther than a mile for me to get here," Sydney said with a chuckle. "Men and their measuring systems."

He smirked but didn't comment on that. "There's a gravel road on the other side of your property next to the big oak tree. A yellow pole gate is at the road there, but I don't think I've ever seen it closed," Mac said.

"Yeah, Mom. It's on the left side of the house. You know."

"I have seen that. It leads here?"

Mac nodded, and pointed out the window. "Sure does. Just on the other side of my neighbor's house there. It used to be a service road when all of these farms shared tobacco and cotton farming cooperative rights. The county keeps it clear because the power lines cut through there."

"I had no idea. So I guess we're almost neighbors," Sydney said.

"As the crow flies, we are."

"That's funny. What does that mean?" RayAnne asked.

Seth nudged her. "Means we have to drive on roads but birds can fly in straight lines. So as the crow flies is the shortest distance between the two places."

"I should be a bird," RayAnne said.

"A cuckoo bird," Seth said and snickered.

Mac flashed Seth a look.

"I was just kidding. You know it, right, Ray?"

RayAnne turned to Mac. "Don't worry. I'll get him back Monday when y'all come to make pretzels at our house."

"We don't have to make the pretzels," Sydney said. "Thank goodness. We just have to dip them in chocolate and decorate them."

"Miss Bea's chocolate pretzels are the best," Seth said. "They have candies on them and stuff. It sounds totally gross, but they are so good. Everybody gets one when we do the caroling thing."

"I don't really get what that whole caroling thing is all

about. Everyone at school has been talking about it, though," RayAnne said.

"You just have to be there. You'll see. It sounds lame, but it's pretty cool."

Seth actually sounded enthusiastic about it. Mac had considered letting Seth off the hook on the caroling this year, since he'd always complained about it in the past. If a little of RayAnne's Christmas joy was influencing Seth's interest in the holiday, that was okay by him.

"Let me give you my number in case anything happens on Monday that we need to adjust the schedule for," Mac said. "Got your phone handy?"

She leaned over and took her phone out of her purse.

He took it and typed in his number. "There you go."

She pressed the button and his phone rang.

"We're all set." It was a whole lot easier to get a phone number these days than back when he'd been on the dating scene.

"I think it's time we headed out," Sydney said, getting up.

"I'll walk y'all out." Mac grabbed his jean jacket and followed them outside.

RayAnne climbed into the passenger seat. "Thank you so much, Mr. Mac. I had such a blast."

"You're welcome." He waited until RayAnne closed the door. "I didn't want to say it without checking with you first, but it'd be great to do it again. I think she and Seth had a lot of fun together."

Sydney's smile was easy. "I think that might be okay."

"I had fun too," he said.

"Coming here was the best part of my day. It couldn't have happened at a better time. The morning started off pretty bad."

"How so?"

She glanced back toward her car. RayAnne was messing with the radio dial. "Got my divorce papers today," she said in a hushed voice.

"Ouch. Even if it's your decision those are hard times. Boy do I know it. Sorry."

"I wasn't looking for your sympathy. Coming here just made today that much better. So, thank you."

She'd made his day, too. In ways he hadn't expected.

Chapter Thirteen

On Monday afternoon, Sydney drove home at lunchtime to be sure the boxes of pretzels and additional supplies had arrived and they had everything they needed for that night. Bea had loaded her up with two shopping bags of plastic containers full of what she called the "delightful parts," which she later learned were different colored sprinkles, colored sugars, coconut, teeny chocolate chips, and toffee bits.

She opened the door and took the inventory to the kitchen, then went back and wobbled the big box on its edges to get it through the door. Sliding it down the hall, she got it to the kitchen, where they'd be setting up for the decorating tonight.

The kitchen was her favorite part of this old house. Even the outdated harvest gold was growing on her after she and RayAnne decided to do the room up right in an old-fashioned sunflower theme. The huge island in the middle would give them plenty of space to set up an assembly line of sorts. Hopefully, it would be a fun project for the kids.

Sydney unloaded the box, stacking all the pretzels at one end of the countertop. After doing a little research she'd determined the slow cooker might be the best way to melt the chocolate and allow multiple people to dip and decorate at the same time. Four mason jars would fit perfectly into her slow cooker in a water bath that would keep the consistency of the melted chocolate just right. Plus, they could do some in white chocolate and some in milk chocolate that way.

She texted Mac.

> Sydney: We're on for tonight.
> Mac: Looking forward to it.
> Sydney: 7?
> Mac: See you then. ☺

It was a little after six when Bea showed up. She'd insisted on driving herself over despite Sydney's objections, stating that she'd driven in this town for so many years she could do it blindfolded.

That thought was a little scary.

"This place looks so inviting," Bea said as she walked inside. "You've really added your personal touch to things."

"Thank you," Sydney said. "Still a work in progress, but we're starting to get settled in, wouldn't you say, RayAnne?"

"For sure," RayAnne said from behind Bea. "And thank goodness Hopewell isn't nearly as boring as I thought it would be."

Relief flooded through Sydney. She'd hoped RayAnne was taking a shine to this town. Maybe things really were going to be okay here.

Bea followed along to the kitchen, then paused at the island. "Looks like you have a real system set up here, Sydney. It's like a factory. Not sure why I'm surprised."

"This is a boatload of pretzels," RayAnne said.

"Good thing Mom always has a plan, or else it would take forever to dip all of these into chocolate."

Light danced in Bea's eyes. "It most certainly is a boatload," she said. "I've been doing them myself for years. Takes me a long, long time. I sure appreciate y'all helping me this year. It's been hard enough to make the number I'd been doing every year. With double to get done, I don't think I could handle it by myself." Bea perched herself on the high-backed stool at the very end of the island.

"I think we've got everything set up." Sydney dipped a knife into the chocolate and gave it a stir.

Bea peered into the jars. "I should have told you to pick up some good, old-fashioned shortening. Sometimes you have to thin the chocolate down a little."

"Not a problem. I have some." Sydney got it from the pantry and set it on the counter in case they needed it later.

The doorbell rang. "They're here." Sydney straightened her shirt before turning.

Bea grinned. "Yes, they are."

Sydney flipped the hand towel she was carrying into Bea's lap. "You're incorrigible. And a hopeless romantic."

"Sue me," Bea yelled behind her. "Why can't you be the new owner of The Book Bea, and in love with the most handsome man in my town?"

"The Book Bea? No problem. I'm going to make you so proud. The other? That's just silly talk."

"No, it's not. I have a feeling you could make Mac pretty happy, too."

Sydney half-ran to the front door, then stopped and took in a long, slow breath. She exhaled to the count of three, then opened the door. Only there wasn't anyone there. Well, maybe there was, but mostly there was just . . . pine. Lots of pine.

"Who . . . what? Hello?" she said.

A child's laugh came from the other side of the tree.

RayAnne came around the corner. "Whoa? What is that?"

"I'm not quite sure, but I believe a tree is trying to sell us something," Sydney said.

"Surprise," Seth said, pulling branches aside and poking his head through.

"What is all of this?" Sydney asked.

Mac lifted the tree and carried it inside. "A hostess gift."

"A potholder would have sufficed," Sydney said.

Seth slipped inside. "Where should we put it?"

"This is so exciting," Bea said, clapping her hands.

"By the window, I guess," Sydney said. Wasn't that where Christmas trees were supposed to go? Part of the fun was neighbors seeing your tree lit up from the road as they passed by.

Mac wrestled the fat tree through the door.

"I can move that chair." She rushed over and scooted it across the shiny oak floor. "I can't believe you did this. You really brought me a tree?"

"If I recall correctly your tree is at The Book Bea. I—we thought it would be nice if you had one here, too."

"Y'all rock," RayAnne said. "Man it smells so good."

"Not better than chocolate," Seth said. "Is that the chocolate for Miss Bea's decorated pretzels that I smell?" RayAnne grabbed Seth by the hand and dragged him to the kitchen.

Sydney stepped out of the way. "Oh, gosh, I don't have a tree stand for a live tree."

"Don't need one. This one is a live tree. In dirt. I'll help you plant it out front after the holidays."

Her throat gave a squeeze at his thoughtfulness. Had anyone done something this thoughtful for her? Ever? "Oh my gosh. It must weigh a ton." She hopped out of the way as he moved through the hallway into the living room, toting the tree.

"Put it down anywhere," she said. "We can just scooch it into place."

Muscles rippled against the sleeves of his shirt. Not a huge surprise. She'd felt them when she'd clung to him as they rode the other night, but he had a lumberjack ruggedness to him tonight.

He stepped in front of the window, checked behind himself to find the center, then lowered the tree with a thud.

"Merry Christmas, from us to y'all." He took off his leather work gloves and tucked them into his back pocket. "I guess now we all scrub up and start decorating pretzel rods."

"Thanks, Mac. It feels very Christmassy in here now."

Mac stepped back, admiring the tree. "You might need to unleash those kids on this tree. I bet they'd have it decorated in fifteen minutes flat."

"They were like a Cat 5 tornado on the one at the bookstore, weren't they?"

"Pretty much," he agreed. "Now about those treats."

"Yes. Come on back." Sydney led them back to the kitchen and Mac stopped mid-step. "Was Willy Wonka's chocolate factory this elaborate? I don't think so. Probably smelled a lot like this though. Man, this is going to be quite a production." He eyed Bea. "What have I gotten myself into?

"I've got a plan." Sydney pointed to the sink. "You boys go wash up and when you're done I've got plastic gloves for all of us. Need aprons?"

Mac spun around and shook his head. "No, ma'am. We've got play clothes on. We're not afraid of a little chocolate."

"Suit yourself. Don't blame me if you ruin your outfit."

Mac gave Seth a playful slap. "Outfits?"

Seth rolled his eyes and shrugged.

"Whatever," Sydney said. "You know what I mean. Chocolate is hard to get out of clothes. Nothing wrong with wearing an apron."

"Oh, that would be front-page news around here," Bea laughed. "Our big, rugged baseball coach in an apron. We could raise a lot of money for this town using that as blackmail."

"It'll never get that far." Mac scrubbed his hands at the sink, then dried his hands on a paper towel. He turned and scanned the room.

"Trashcan is over there," Sydney said pointing across the room.

Mac tossed the paper towel across the room, high over Bea's head, right into the trash bin.

Sydney spun around to him. "Okay, now you're just showing off."

"Pretty much," Mac said.

Seth rolled his eyes. "He does that all the time. Everywhere."

"No throwing in the house," Sydney said in her sternest mom voice. "That goes for all of you."

"Awww, man." Mac smirked. "I can't get a hall pass since I brought you a Christmas tree? I mean that's way better than some lousy flowers."

"He's got a point," Bea said. "And it's a live tree."

"Fine. I'm going to lose this one, aren't I?"

"I'll let you throw in my house," Mac said.

"Are we ready to get down to business?" Bea asked.

A resounding *yes* couldn't have been more in sync if it had been rehearsed.

"Okay," Bea said. "Sydney has us set up like a manufacturing plant here. We've got stations. We'll each have a job. We're going to need dippity dunkers, pretzel-doodlers, and wrap-and-packums." Bea counted on her fingers. "Did I get that right?"

"Yes. RayAnne and Seth, I was thinking you two could be the pretzel-doodlers. Mac and I will do the dippity dunking. Mac, we just dunk the pretzel rods into the Mason jar, then tap-tap-tap the excess off—that's very important—then place them on the wax paper for the doodlers to do their thing.

"Tap-tap-tap," Mac repeated, mimicking her hand movements. "Just three times. Not four? Not two?"

"Precisely," she teased.

"Got it." Mac gave a quick and exaggerated nod.

"RayAnne and Seth. We'll start with one of the vats of goodies. Your choice, and do that one kind of decorating until those are gone. Then we'll switch to another. Sound good?" Bea said.

"Yes, ma'am." Seth leaned forward on the counter. "Man, there's good stuff. I think I want to do the confetti-looking sprinkle dots first."

"I'm doing the tiny candy snowflakes." RayAnne pulled her container toward her.

"I think we're ready," Sydney said. "Everybody put your plastic gloves on."

"Let's do this." Mac picked up a pretzel rod and made like an airplane from the counter, ending with a nosedive into the melted chocolate. "Tap-tap-tap." Then he placed it on the wax paper for the kids to decorate.

Pretzels were dunking and decorations were flying, but the work was surprisingly fast.

"These are the prettiest treats ever!" Bea said with delight.

At nine o'clock they had only a few dozen more to go, but Bea was slowing down. "Bea, why don't you lie down? You can spend the night here if you like. I have plenty of room."

"I'm fine, but I think I will go on home. Looks like you'll be finished up here shortly anyway."

"Sure." Sydney came around the island, and just as Bea stood she gave a wobble and grabbed for the counter. "Are you okay?"

"Just a little dizzy for a split second there."

Mac rushed to her side. "Let's get you in a regular chair." He helped her into the living room and she sat quietly. "I don't think you should drive. I can take you home, or you can stay here tonight."

"But—"

Mac tilted his head. "Please let me drive you. I really think this is best."

"How will I get my car in the morning?"

"I'll stop by in the morning, and I'll follow Sydney in your car. Not a problem at all."

"I really think I'll be fine if I just sit here a moment." But Bea's voice wasn't nearly as confident as her words.

Sydney reached for her hand. It was clammy, filling Sydney with concern. "Would you like me to call a doctor?"

"No. No need." Bea waved them off. "Quit fussing. I'm just old. We poop out sometimes. I'll be here when you're ready to leave."

While Mac and Sydney were tending to Bea, the kids had taken it upon themselves to shift jobs to keep the assembly line going, and they were on the last three pretzels. "Thanks, guys. You really stepped up. I appreciate that."

"We're a good team," RayAnne said.

"Think we can team up on a quick cleanup?" Sydney asked.

"Sure," Mac answered before anyone could answer otherwise. "Where are the trash bags?"

RayAnne jumped down from her stool and got one from the pantry.

"Thank you." Mac shook the bag with a snap, then started sweeping salt and sprinkles from the island countertop.

RayAnne and Seth wiped down the counters, and Sydney put lids on the mason jars that still had chocolate in them. She then dumped the water from the slow cooker into the sink.

"All that's left to do is wrap the last ones in plastic as soon as they dry enough. I can handle that," Sydney said.

"Seth, I think that was our cue to go."

"I'm ready," Seth said. "It was fun, but that was hard work. I'm tired."

"Thanks for helping." RayAnne said goodbye and then ran up the stairs. She'd probably be asleep before Mac walked Bea out to the car. "You okay to ride home, Bea?" asked Sydney.

"Yes. I'm fine. Thank you all so much for helping me with everything. I am truly so grateful." Bea scooted up in the chair, put her hands behind her and pushed herself up. She looked steadier but Sydney was still a little worried about her.

Bea hugged Sydney, whispering, "You were serious about The Book Bea tonight, right?"

"Yes, ma'am."

Bea glanced over at Mac, and Sydney knew what that look insinuated. She gave Bea a nudge and a "stop-it" look. Bea giggled like the instigator that she was. "You two say your goodbyes, I'm going to just get a little head start."

"Wait a second. Let me walk you to your car," Mac said.

"No. Seth can help me. Can't you, son?" Bea held her hand out, and Seth took it.

"Yes, ma'am."

"You raised a nice young man," Sydney said to Mac. "I'm really proud of him."

"You should be. I enjoyed tonight. Thank you so much for coming."

"Still want to do that stargazing and s'mores later this week?"

He remembered, she thought. "Yes! I'd really love that. Just tell me when."

"We'll make a plan in the morning when I come over. What time? Nine-ish?"

"Yeah, that's fine." She wished he didn't have to leave. She was tired, too, but a little quiet adult conversation would feel nice about now.

She stood at the door watching him walk out to the truck and then help Bea get in. He was gentle and patient with her, and as he backed out of the driveway he blinked his lights off and on in a little goodbye.

She shut the door behind her. She'd forgotten to thank him again for the tree. But then how many times do you thank someone? It was such a nice gesture. One that would live on, too. Probably longer than any of them.

Knowing Bea's car was out front made her a little sad. Bea didn't have anyone to help her. Was she really okay to be driving and living alone? The mayor had said she'd been unable to keep store hours lately. And she'd been very unsteady tonight. Her heart clenched.

Why was it that things so special were also fragile? Memories. Marriages. Friends. The Book Bea. And Bea.

Chapter Fourteen

Sydney relaxed into the happiness that warmed her. Yes, making over five hundred chocolate-dipped pretzels was a job, but it had been a labor of love with Bea, RayAnne, Mac, and Seth. She peeked in on RayAnne, who was fast asleep.

Her daughter looked so peaceful there, sleeping in the room that had once been hers. She tipped her chin to the heavens and prayed. *Thank you, Gram and Pop. If you hadn't left this house to me, I really don't know what I would've done. I'm doing my best to stand on my own two feet.*

Suddenly the fatigue fell away, leaving her mind clear.

The distance between Hopewell and Atlanta had evened the playing field for her and Jon with RayAnne. Sure, he'd disappointed RayAnne again and, in typical Jon style, left the clean-up of his mess to Sydney, but at least he couldn't pop in unexpectedly with some elaborate plan or gift to smooth things over. That man thought he could buy happiness.

Sydney was too awake to go to bed now, so she went downstairs, feeling blessed to have made new friends so quickly and to have found the holiday job at The Book Bea.

It really didn't matter if the store was hers or not. She'd be perfectly happy helping Bea run the place. Her mind raced with ideas.

She got her laptop and sat down on the couch. A few Google searches later, Sydney had found some pretty easy tools to put her ideas to work.

She'd probably regret it by the afternoon if she didn't get to bed right now, but as she pointed and clicked and watched her idea come alive right in front of her, it was just too exciting to set aside.

A few hours later she sat on the couch, looking at the brand new website she'd just created for The Book Bea.

Pride. Excitement. Feeling like a part of something. It all felt amazing. She'd used the picture she'd taken of the sign at The Book Bea that first day that she'd rediscovered the store as the banner at the top of the page.

She clicked through the website again. Excitement danced inside of her, and she couldn't wait to show Bea.

She added a page for events. Bea no longer had activities or book signings in the store, something she could easily change.

Some for kids, and some for adults. Crafts and seasonal activities would bring variety to the book focus of the store. It wasn't about the money so much as folks getting together. Keeping The Book Bea the center of activity in the small town.

In the newsletter signup she added a birthday field so they could build a birthday list. Sending birthday e-cards out to folks was a great way to keep a connection.

"Good morning, Mom," RayAnne said as she clomped down the stairs.

Sydney turned to see that her daughter wasn't only awake, but already dressed. "What time is it?"

"Eight-twenty. Jenny's mom is picking me up at eight-thirty. Remember?"

She'd totally forgotten about RayAnne's plans this morning. If she'd remembered she'd have woken her up. Her little girl was growing up. She'd gotten up on her own.

Sydney lowered her laptop. She'd love to show RayAnne the website, but with Mac on his way in less than thirty minutes to follow her over to Bea's she had to get a move on herself.

RayAnne stood at the front window watching for her ride. "They're here!"

Sydney gave RayAnne a kiss on the cheek as she sent her out the door. "Have a great day." She dashed upstairs, stripping down as she made the last few steps into the bathroom.

She took a quick shower, pulled her hair into a braid, and dabbed on a little bit of makeup.

Dressed in black jeans, western boots, and a black top, she was feeling very Johnny Cashish, except for the strand of pearls around her neck. She grabbed her black denim jacket from the closet and pulled it on, checking herself in the mirror. Turning the cuffs back on her jacket as she walked downstairs, she heard Mac's truck rumble into the driveway.

Sydney opened the front door and waited for Mac to come up.

"Good morning."

"You're looking pretty this morning," he said.

"Thanks," Sydney said. "Do you mind helping me get all of these pretzel treats to The Book Bea this morning?"

"Not at all."

And she wasn't going to mind watching him hoist heavy boxes. Seeing him carry that tree last night wasn't going to be a memory she easily shook, either.

She grabbed her laptop and tucked it into her tote bag next to the door, then strode back to the kitchen.

Their boots clicked off a beat against the old wooden floor.

"It's chilly in here," he said.

"It's so hard to heat. This place is drafty."

"Old houses. They've got charm, and built so much better than the ones they toss up in two weeks tops nowadays, but they aren't very energy efficient."

"If I'm going to stay I'm going to have to insulate and get new windows. If not, I could just sell this place the way it is."

"Sell? So this is just temporary for you?"

Was it? A couple of weeks ago her answer would have been *yes*. Definitely *yes*. That she and RayAnne were here during a time of change in their lives. That she was just here to build her résumé and break ties to Jon at the same time. That she might love to live here, but she'd pretty much promised RayAnne a say in their final plan, and RayAnne liked it back in Atlanta.

But now, that wasn't as easy of a question to answer. "Maybe semi-permanent is more like it. Things got complicated back home. I needed a soft landing place. This seemed to fit the bill." She looked around. "It's paid for. Holds great memories. So many great summers."

"We probably crossed paths at some point." Mac paused. "Although I can't believe I wouldn't remember meeting you."

"I spent a lot of time here close to the farm with Gram and Pop, except the weekly venture into town for groceries and stuff. That's when we'd go to The Book Bea."

"That place holds a lot of memories for a lot of us."

And I can be the one who carries that on with Bea, Sydney thought. She picked up two totes of the colorful pretzel treats and indicated another box on the floor. "Can you get that for me?"

"No problem." He lifted the box and carried it out to the truck.

She set the bags in the floorboard of his truck.

"We all set?"

"Yes." She flipped Bea's keys in her hand. "Follow me," she said, then jogged over to Bea's car and got behind the wheel. The car was clean, no wonder though. The circa nineteen seventy–something vehicle only had 14,212 miles on it.

Mac pulled out of the driveway and waited on the side of the road.

She pulled the huge car out and maneuvered through town to Bea's house.

She waved, and he rolled down the window. "I'll be just a minute. I want to check on her real quick."

"Take your time."

She felt his eyes on her as she walked up the path to Bea's house.

Bea opened the door just as Sydney began to knock. Still in her bathrobe, she said, "Good morning, Sydney."

Sydney dangled the keys. "Brought your car back. How are you feeling this morning?"

"I'm fine, dear." She squeezed Sydney's hand. "Thank you so much for last night. This will be the best batch of treats yet. Made with love and fellowship—the most important ingredients."

"We all had a good time."

"We did. I've got some things I want to take care of this morning. I'll be in a little later today."

"If you're not up to it, you know that I can cover things. I don't mind at all."

"Oh, I know you can. You remind me of myself the year my husband died. I had to find my own strength, and when I did I was stronger than ever. I'd been so afraid, but the freedom I found in my independence turned out to be a gift." She smiled gently. "I'll be in after I get my running around done."

"Okay, well, no hurry. But . . . ," Sydney said. "I have something to show you when you get there."

"What is it?"

"A surprise. For you. Well, for you and The Book Bea."

Bea's face lit up. "I can't wait."

"Me neither. I was up all night. I hope you love it." She hugged Bea and then jogged over to Mac's truck.

Chapter Fifteen

It was only a couple of blocks from Bea's house to the bookstore. Mac helped Sydney unload the treats, and then he drove her back to her house so she'd have her car.

"Thanks for the lift." Sydney pulled the handle and opened the truck door to get out.

"You're welcome." He leaned his arms across the steering wheel. "I'm off today. I was wondering if I could take you to lunch."

The smile hit her lips immediately. Not cool and aloof at all, but she couldn't help it. Mac made her feel good. A nice change. "I don't know when Bea will be coming in. She said she had a meeting."

"How about lunch in the store? If you're busy, it'll be a working lunch. If not, it'll be a picnic. With bees instead of ants." Mac looked hopeful.

"Was that a lame attempt at a joke? Bees? Like The Book Bea?"

"Guilty."

She liked the way he made her laugh. What was the harm in having lunch? She'd been up all night and missed breakfast. She'd need the pick-me-up by mid-day, and she liked spending time with Mac, but she wasn't ready for anything serious no matter what those butterflies in her stomach were up to. "You know, lunch would be really nice. But it's not a date. Right?"

"Whatever you say." He waited until she got into her car before he pulled out of her driveway. When they got to the intersection he turned right to go home, and she turned left to go to work.

"Neighbors. As the crow flies," Sydney said, remembering their conversation from the other day. It was good to have neighbors close by that she could count on.

It was a slow morning in the store. Customers came in like a perfectly timed relay, one at a time, which was fine by her.

At noon Mac walked in carrying a big brown paper bag.

The way his smile spread to those little creases next to his eyes made her stomach tighten unexpectedly.

"Hey there. Hope you're hungry."

"I am. I'd been thinking that I was so hungry I could eat a horse, but judging by the size of that bag, I'm afraid that might be what you brought. Please tell me I'm wrong."

"You'll know soon enough." He looked around. "Customers?"

"Not right now."

"Bingo." He took her hand in his.

A tingle chased its way to her fingertips. "Where are you taking me?"

He tipped his head and just smiled as he led her through the bookshelves down the fiction aisle. She had to take two steps to each of his long strides. He led her past the local North Carolina author display to the back of the store and then back up the next aisle toward the front, stopping next to the Christmas tree.

"I think you took the long way."

"The scenic route."

"Are we there yet?"

"Yes, Ms. Impatient. I think we are." He set down the bag and reached inside. A blue tablecloth peeked out of the top of the bag. He gave it a quick tug and spread it out on the floor. "For you, madam," he said laying on a heavy French accent. "How do you like our picnic spot?"

"I think it's perfect." The gesture was sweet and a little quirky, but she was loving the effort. She sat down on the floor and pulled her feet underneath her. The lights on the decorated Christmas tree and the pretty tablecloth made for a cozy picnic spot. Mac sat down next to her, then dipped his hand down into the bag again.

"Pour toi." He lifted a square box with a satiny red bow out of the bag and handed it to her.

"For me?" She held it in both hands, wondering what could possibly be inside. She gave it a little shake.

He nodded.

She didn't have anything for him, and that made it a little awkward with it being Christmas and all. The box was heavy for its size. "Should I open it now?"

"Kind of hoped you would."

"You didn't have to do this."

"Don't thank me yet. You haven't opened it. You might not even like it."

"I will." She thumbed her nose at him playfully, and then slid the ribbon from the box. Inside, nestled in a shiny layer of silver tissue paper, was a single Christmas ornament.

She lifted it out by the fancy swirly metal hanger affixed to the top. A Santa. She dangled it from her fingers, taking in the intricate details of the impressive wooden carving. The brilliant colors enhanced the fine craftsmanship.

"It's a French Santa," he said.

Santa's eyes twinkled like the ones that Americans had come to know and love, but this Santa wore a jaunty beret and had fleur-de-lis on his robe rather than the traditional red and white fur-lined jacket. He held a staff with the Eiffel Tower on top and a tray with champagne and cheese. "It's beautiful." And even that felt inadequate to describe the unique piece of art in her hands.

"You said you wanted to go to France. I thought of you when I saw this."

She turned and hung the ornament on the tree. "I love it. Mac, you really didn't have to do that."

He lifted a finger. "That's not all."

Digging back into that paper bag he pulled out a placemat and laid it out between them. Then he slowly started unloading the contents of the bag. First a crunchy French baguette, fresh baked if she had to guess by the warm aroma wafting up between them. Then he unwrapped a small plate of cheeses and fruit, and another with sliced chicken.

"You've really thought of everything."

Then he took two champagne glasses out of the bag. These were hand painted, one jolly old St. Nick, the other Mrs. Claus. "Can you hold these?"

"Sure." She held them by the stems as he produced a bottle of champagne from the endless goodies in that bag.

"Wow, you really went all out."

"It's been a long time since I invited a lady on a picnic. Did I go overboard?"

"Yes, and I'm loving it."

At that moment the cork on the champagne bottle made its release with a sharp pop.

"Nice!" She tipped the glasses toward him and he poured.

She glanced toward the door. "Customers are liable to get the wrong idea about me if I'm drinking while I work."

"I'll just tuck the bottle back in the bag in case any customers come in, and we can stick the glasses away on a shelf and pretend it's another fancy display like you did for the front window."

"You have an answer to everything."

"To good excuses to have fun." He raised his glass. "And new friends."

She tapped her glass to his. "And Christmas in Hopewell."

They both took a sip. "Can I take that to mean Hopewell is agreeing with you?"

"Very much so."

"That's great." He sliced the bread and handed her a piece. "I'm enjoying you being around."

That sent a shiver of excitement through her. It had been a long time since anyone had gone to this much trouble for her. It was a romantic gesture straight out of a Hallmark movie. Who wouldn't love being treated like this? Hopewell was good, but Mac made it even more special. "That's sweet. Everyone has been so nice. I wanted so badly for it to be a good experience, but I'd be lying if I didn't say I was scared."

"And . . ."

"And it's been more than I could have imagined. The old house is drafty, but we're doing just fine. And although RayAnne was pretty mad at me for pulling her out of her school, I feel like things are starting to get back to how they were between us. On the things that matter anyway. I'm feeling very blessed."

"Hopewell is good like that. A peaceful place. I know after Genna left us, I wasn't sure what the heck I was supposed to do. But when I screwed up, or struggled to figure things out, someone was always there to help us. I don't think you find those kinds of places much anymore. It's slower here. People still make time to help neighbors."

"I think people are just too busy to stop and notice you need a hand. I like the slower pace." She spread some cheese on her bread and then took a bite. "So good."

"Wait until you get the chance to eat real French bread. In France."

"Maybe someday. But for now this is pretty good. Thanks for doing this. I love my afternoon in France."

"Almost forgot." He pulled his phone out and swiped and tapped his fingers on the screen. French tango music began to play. "Ambience." He made a little sandwich out of the chicken and bread and took a bite, then washed it down with champagne.

"I don't know what you and RayAnne have planned for Christmas Day, but I've got the folks from next door coming over, and a couple of teachers from school that I work with. Nothing really fancy. But it's nice. You know a big group on the holidays always feels so good. Y'all should come over."

"RayAnne should be with her dad that afternoon. Last I heard. He seems to keep changing the times around."

"Then you should come."

"Yeah, I'll see how it all works out. I could bring something."

"Oh, not necessary. I've got it covered. More than plenty for everyone. Just bring yourself." He held her gaze. "Don't overthink it."

She laughed. "How did you know?"

"Because I've been overthinking everything even though we'd already made it clear that it wasn't a date. I finally had to convince myself that it was okay to just take it a day at a time. Think you can deal with that too? No promises. No pressure."

"My life is complicated. I have to be sure I put RayAnne first in all of my decisions. She's been through so much, through no fault of her own. Maybe it's not realistic, but part of me feels like I need to make up for Jon's mistakes. Mine, too."

"It's not that simple."

"It's the best I can do."

"Oh, I know," he said. "Trust me. The last thing I want to do is mess up the rhythms that Seth and I have going on. But steady as she goes? Well, that's not really living either, is it?"

She breathed in. She wished it was that simple. She and RayAnne didn't even have a rhythm to break yet. Jon moved on, maybe she should, but there was more to consider.

"Just roll with it," he said.

She lifted the champagne to her lips, hoping for a little liquid courage. Did he notice her hand shaking?

"We're good. Right?" A crease formed across his forehead.

She lifted a shoulder. "Of course. We're good." Maybe he had noticed.

They finished off the food and she helped him clean up. "Thank you so much. That was fun." She folded the tablecloth for him and tucked it back into the top of his bag.

The front door swung open. "Hellooo," Bea called out, her head swiveling across the store, then landing squarely on the two of them. "Good to see you, Mac. And my sweet angel, Sydney."

"Hey, Bea." Sydney was so happy to see Bea looking like she felt better that afternoon.

Bea pulled the scarf from her head and hung it on the coat tree. "Help me with my coat, will you?"

Mac stepped forward, removed her coat, and hung it up for her.

"Are you checking on the books you ordered?" Bea asked.

"No," Mac said with a nervous glance in Sydney's direction. "I brought a little picnic lunch to your hard-working helper here. I'd offer you some but we pretty much annihilated it all."

"You did?" Bea pulled her lips together in a mischievous grin. "I'm glad I missed it. Sounds romantic."

Sydney's teeth clamped down, resisting the urge to deny it. She was so thankful when the door burst open and a mother and four children ran inside in an over-enthusiastic roar. "Get back here." The mother looked haggard and over it. "I'm so sorry," she said, sweeping her hair from her face.

"It's fine," Sydney said. "Mac, thank you. It was such a nice lunch. I'm going to go help our customers."

Sydney race-walked over to the children's section and helped the woman wrangle her kids. One quick glance back told her that Mac wasn't as quick to leave. He stood talking to Bea. He had a way about him that made her feel like everything really might be okay. Or maybe that was just the wishful, trusting, romantic-hearted Sydney who had had her heart broken. Could she really risk that again? Could they be just friends? Was that what she really wanted?

When Sydney walked over to ring up the next purchase, Bea was seated in the chair behind the counter, reviewing the ledger. Apparently the going rate for kid wrangling was to the tune of . . . she hit the total button on the big antique register. "One hundred and three dollars and forty-two cents."

"Thank you so much for helping me. I swear sometimes these four just run me ragged." The woman counted out a stack of twenties.

Sydney counted back her change. "My pleasure. I only have one and she wears me out all the time. Don't know how you do it."

"You were so helpful."

"We can wrap those for you if you like," Bea offered.

"No. I've got that. Wrapping gifts is what I do when they go to bed. It's like therapy. All that paper, tape and ribbon. I love it."

"Well, you have a Merry Christmas. I hope we'll see you again." Sydney loved this job. It was so much more than just selling books.

The woman took a twenty from her billfold and passed it to Sydney. "Merry Christmas."

"Oh, I couldn't," she said.

"Please. It'll make my day."

Sydney took the twenty-dollar bill and tucked it into her pocket. "Thank you. Very much. My daughter and I will do something fun with this and think of you and your family."

"That's wonderful." The woman wove her arm through the handles of the bag of books, and then gathered up the herd of kids. "Bye."

Sydney heard the woman calling out names all the way down the sidewalk.

"Glad I had just the one."

Bea said, "Did you ever think you wanted more children?"

"Oh yeah. Always wanted a boy and a girl, but Jon wasn't willing to try again."

"Jon had a lot of rules," Bea said.

Sydney settled her weight against the fat arm of the chair. "I never noticed it while we were married. I wonder why that is? It's been easy to notice now. In hindsight."

"Some relationships are just like that. One person does all the deciding and the other compromises. I was lucky. My Henry and I both compromised."

"That's nice." She wondered whether, if she'd been a better negotiator, she might have had a different relationship with Jon. But leaving her parents' house to go to college, and then straight to getting married to Jon, there'd been little chance of that. He'd always led the way. Made the decisions.

It didn't matter, though, because it was over now. Some little part of her was always looking for some logic to what had happened. There just wasn't any.

"RayAnne didn't come with you today?"

"No. She's with her school friends again. She's going to join them for the caroling, too."

"You should join them. It's a wonderful experience."

"No. I want to be here to help you. Besides, RayAnne will probably have more fun without me."

"True. They grow up so fast these days. Does she still believe in Santa?"

"I wasn't sure until we went to Santa's Village on Saturday. That Santa's either the real deal, or that water bottle he was slugging from was filled with vodka, because I've never seen a Santa enjoy his job that much."

"That's right. You went on Saturday, didn't you? He's our very best Santa Claus." Bea laughed. "I hadn't put that together until just now."

"Put what together?"

"Oh nothing, just that it's so nice that RayAnne is making new traditions here in Hopewell. And that you are, too," Bea said.

"RayAnne came down from her visit with Santa convinced he was the real one, which surprised me. I'd been preparing myself for this to be the year she realized it was a hoax."

"I think most kids will believe as long as we let them. It's peer pressure that usually breaks the magic. Speaking of magic, you and Mac seem to be becoming pretty good friends too. I sense a little bit of magic there."

"No. Just friends. That picnic today was really thoughtful, though." Her heart fluttered as she reflected on the gift, the champagne, the food. Paris might have to really step up to beat that. "I'll be right back." She went over to the tree and rescued the ornament Mac had given her. She couldn't risk it getting broken or lost. She brought it back over and showed it to Bea. "Isn't this pretty?"

Bea lifted her glasses and looked closely. "Ahhh. Père Noël. Father Christmas. Where did you find that?"

She twisted it in her fingers to face her. "Mac gave it to me. I don't know where he got it."

"Exquisite. I'm sure he got it in one of the shops over at Santa's Village. They have all kinds of unique stuff over there."

"We didn't get a chance to walk through every shop when we were there."

"Oh, you have to. And go at night when it's all lit up."

Sydney placed the ornament in the top of her purse.

"I think he's smitten with you, dear."

"That's ridiculous. I barely know him."

"Doesn't seem ridiculous to me. I knew the first time I spoke to Henry there was going to be something special there. I didn't know exactly what it was going to be, but you can't discount those kinds of connections. Certainly, you've felt it. I could feel it from across your kitchen the other night."

"Oh, stop it, Bea. That's crazy."

"If there's one thing this old gal can recognize, it's a connection. I'd call it love, but I'll wait and see."

"The ink is barely dry on my divorce papers."

"So what? You afraid you'll hurt Jon's feelings?" Bea got up out of her chair. "The way I see it, you've got two years of catching up to do, Sydney."

Sydney stood there feeling a little dumbstruck as she watched Bea slowly make her way over to the teapot.

Catching up to do? That made it sound like a race. She was certainly not in a hurry to make another mistake.

"I can hear you overthinking it from all the way over here," Bea called out.

Wasn't the first time Bea had made a comment that made Sydney think that the old woman was a mind reader.

"Wouldn't kill you to have a good time, ya know. Let Hopewell breathe new life into you. Take some chances."

"Thanks for the advice, but I'm just fine. And I've got plenty to do that's fun. I love helping you here in this shop."

"Why are you so afraid to move on?" Tea threatened to go splish-splashing over the side of the delicate tea-cup with every wobbly step she made back over to the register.

"Because I'm a mom. My focus is exactly where it's supposed to be right now. And I'm happy." Sydney could see the doubt in Bea's eyes. "Don't look at me like that."

"You can have it all. I did. Well, not the blessing of a daughter like RayAnne. But the rest. Just do me a favor. Trust your heart."

"No one has it all."

Bea raised a brow. "Not true, my dear. Maybe you should ask Santa for exactly what you want." She low-ered herself into the chair and sipped the tea.

Sydney couldn't picture herself acting like those two women the other day that had made fools of themselves going to sit on Santa's lap. That was the last thing she was going to do.

"I'm going to have my hands full here, that is, if you're still going to work with me on taking over The Book Bea when you're ready."

"I'm counting on that, dear."

"I was up all last night thinking about it."

"Really? I'd have thought you might have been thinking about Mac all night."

"You never give up. Seriously. Let's switch subjects. I made something for you last night. Let me show you." She grabbed her laptop from the cabinet under the regis-ter where she kept her purse and placed it on top. "I made a website. The Book Bea is now officially on the Internet."

Bea leaned in closer. "How did you do that?"

"Stayed up all night last night working on it. Come look."

Bea placed her tea aside and stood. She stared at the screen, her mouth moving as she read the words. "You did this? In one night?"

"I did."

"That was so fast. Where did you get the money to do that?"

"Didn't cost much at all. I did it myself."

"I'm impressed."

"And look. We can start putting the community things that we host here on the calendar."

"I'll be darned." Bea folded her arms. "Can people look at that from their little phones? Everyone is always tapping on those things."

"They sure can." Sydney got her phone out of her purse and brought up the website. She handed the phone to Bea. "See?"

"My goodness. I knew you were going to take The Book Bea to the next level."

"You like it?"

"Like it? No." Bea shook her head. "I don't like it at all. I love it. This is wonderful. Exactly what we need."

"You really don't mind?"

"No, darling. I'm thrilled that you are ready to make this store your own. It's time. Actually, it's long overdue. I've been waiting for you to come along."

Sydney wasn't quite sure what that meant, but before she could ask, the chimes overhead caught her attention and the mayor walked inside, followed by the UPS man.

The mayor raised a hand in the air. "Ahh, so good to see you both here today. I'm just doing a quick and personal check with each of the merchants to be sure they're ready for the big night."

"We're ready," Bea said proudly.

"You should have plenty of song sheets, but we'll know up at the front end of the line if things are running low. We have a plan, so don't worry. Someone will be around with more if needed." The mayor checked a list on a small spiral notebook. "And the first carolers will come through at seven o'clock." He took a CD out of a small box he'd been carrying. "O Christmas Tree. This one is yours."

Sydney took the CD. "Thanks. I think we've got everything we need then."

"Excellent."

"I'm going to sign for the package. Excuse me," Sydney said as she listened from within earshot of them.

He rubbed his gloved hand under his chin. "Now, the new gal did tell you we needed more treats, didn't she? I really should have checked with you sooner."

"Of course she did. You can count on Sydney just as much as you count on me, Mayor. We're two peas in a pod. We finished up all of the treats Monday night. Had quite a little factory assembly line going. Want yours now?"

"Could I?" he rubbed his hands together. "Yours are my favorite."

"I have a feeling this is the best batch yet. Sydney is pretty amazing. She's going to do great things with my store."

"I'm glad you have some help that you trust."

Bea walked over to the boxes of chocolate-covered pretzels and pulled out one with light-blue sugar sprinkles over white chocolate. "Here you go. Matches those pretty blue Sinatra eyes of yours," Bea said.

"Thanks. My daughter says my eyes are like Bret Michaels', but Sinatra works, too."

"Either way, you have the prettiest eyes I've ever seen. Only reason I ever vote for you, to be honest."

"Bea, you did not just say that," Sydney walked up behind them. "That's not true, Mayor. She's always singing your praises."

Bea laughed. "Keeping him humble. It's what we old gals do."

The mayor unwrapped the pretzel stick and took a bite. "Mmmm. She's right. Sydney, these are even better than normal. My goodness. What's the secret?"

"Teamwork," Sydney said with a smile. "And true friends."

Chapter Sixteen

Tuesday night Sydney set up social media accounts for The Book Bea. She friended and linked up with every name she could remember from her interactions around town and the store so far, and by morning The Book Bea had almost fifty "likes" on the brand-new Facebook page, and just as many followers on the other social media sites.

"That was fast." Satisfaction filled her. Even just a week ago she had no idea that she could spend a little bit of time to help someone else and feel so much in return. This social media stuff was second nature to folks back home, but it was a whole new ball game in Hopewell.

She pulled her knees up on the couch and continued to post pictures she'd taken while the gang was there making Bea's famous pretzel treats. The assembly line looked pretty impressive, and darn if her mouth wasn't watering just a little at all that sugary sweet goodness. The colorful edible adornments looked festive, and Bea looked vibrant. Sydney opened the app and added the Christmas caroling event to the calendar page of The-BookBea.com website.

"What ya doing, Mom?" RayAnne was wearing her red pajamas with the white snowflakes on them.

"Updating the website I made for The Book Bea."

"You really like that place. It makes you happy, doesn't it?"

Sydney paused. "Yes. I guess it does."

RayAnne stood quietly, then nodded slowly. "That Santa has some tricks up his sleeve I think." RayAnne walked over and gave Sydney a hug. "I love you."

"Are you trying to butter me up for a last-minute addition to your wish list?"

"No. I'm just happy because you're happy."

"Thanks, sweetie."

"Jenny called and asked if her mom can pick me up here before you go to work. She has to go drop something off to her husband and will be right near here. I told her yes, is that okay?"

"Sure. I hope you're helping out while you're over there. You're spending a lot of time together."

"I am. Her mom likes us being around. Plus Zach plays with us. I think it helps."

"Good." RayAnne had always wanted a little brother, so Sydney wasn't all that surprised that she'd taken to Zach so quickly.

"It's like having a bigger family. It's fun."

"Yeah," Sydney said. "I always thought a big family would be fun, too."

"Thanks for letting me hang out with them. Do you think we could go shopping this week and get presents for them?"

"Sure. That's really thoughtful of you. There were some cute shops in Santa's Village. Maybe we go back there and take a look around first. Whatever makes you happy."

"I am happy, Mom. This has turned out to be my best Christmas break yet. I want you to be happy, too," RayAnne said. "I told Santa that."

"RayAnne? Why did you tell Santa that? What makes you think I'm not happy?"

"Because I know. I'm a kid, but I know."

"You don't need to worry about me, kiddo. I've got you, and you make me happy. And Santa has plenty to worry about without you telling him about me." How embarrassing. "That visit was supposed to be about your wish list."

"I know," RayAnne said. "I told Santa if Dad's not getting me a four-wheeler he could get me one."

Sydney was relieved to hear the car pull up in the driveway just then so she wouldn't have to discuss that darned four-wheeler again. They'd had fun with Mac and Seth, but having one around all the time would make her a nervous wreck.

She walked out to the minivan with RayAnne. Diane rolled the window down, while RayAnne raced around to the other side to get in. "Do you want me to bring RayAnne back before the caroling tonight? I was thinking she could just stay with us today, if that's okay with you."

"I'm beginning to feel bad. You're doing so much."

"Oh, don't be silly. You'd do the same for me. It's how we do things around here. It takes a village and all that." Diane leaned out the window. "Trust me, it's been so nice to have RayAnne around to keep mine busy. I'm getting a ton done."

Jenny poked her head between the seats. "We're going to practice carols today."

"See?" Diane said with delight in her eyes.

"You sure?"

"Absolutely. We'll see you tonight."

And if teamwork was Sydney Ragsdale's secret weapon for making Bea's famous chocolate-covered pretzel rods, it was just the right ingredient for Wednesday night when the caroling started, too.

She'd brought a thick warm quilt from home and a heating pad to fix up one of the rocking chairs on the porch for Bea. Traditions at The Book Bea were important, and now she was a part of that.

Bea deserved a front row seat to this show, and from there she could point folks to the music sheets, too.

By a quarter to seven Sydney had helped Bea get everything arranged for the event.

Bea sat down in the rocking chair. "This is toasty. You are spoiling me, Sydney."

"I thought you'd be more comfortable."

Bea rocked. "Henry would love that this is still going on. He was as big a sucker for a good tradition as I am. Are you watching from up there, Henry?"

And there it was again. Like Bea had read her mind about the importance of tradition.

Sydney paced, unsure of what the night would hold. Being a part of The Book Bea for the event tonight held its own special charm. She was making a memory that would last forever.

At seven o'clock on the dot voices rose into the air, drifting up the block. The crisp night was filled with song and something sweet in the air. Maybe it was just the huge inventory of chocolate-dipped pretzels, but somehow it seemed different than just that. Her heart tapped out a beat, kind of a little "Joy to the World," as she anticipated their first group of carolers venturing up the walkway to The Book Bea tonight.

The air was nippy. If it were just a little bit colder

they may have seen a few flurries, but so far the temperature was hovering closer to forty.

The Book Bea was the fifth caroling stop. From here she could hear the groups singing each song. That wouldn't be the case once carolers started showing up on their doorstep. Then she'd hear "O Christmas Tree" over and over again, which was just fine by her, too.

Hopewell held a gentle spirit and she was so thankful she'd been brave enough to try to start over here. Her heart felt light and peaceful.

A group of carolers chatted as they walked up the pathway toward her. The leader of the group wore a long black coat, a top hat, and a striped scarf like he'd time-travelled right out of *A Christmas Carol*.

He stepped up to the porch. "Madam?"

"Here you go." Bea passed him a stack of song sheets.

He promptly passed them out to everyone in the group. Bea reached for Sydney's hand and squeezed it. The man in the top hat gave Bea a nod, and she pressed the button on the old CD player. A boom box really. Could you even buy those things anymore? The town of Hopewell probably had a monopoly on the last of them.

The music began and he led his group in the prettiest rendition of "O Christmas Tree" Sydney had ever heard. Young voices, old voices, some totally off-key and some mixing up the words even though they were reading them off the sheet, but together it was nothing short of heavenly.

Afterward, Sydney carried the large basket of treats to the base of the stairs and handed out the goodies, wishing each caroler a Merry Christmas.

"Awesome," a young boy said as he high-fived another kid. "Told you they'd have them."

A tall man with salt-and-pepper hair who had to be at

least forty took his and saluted Bea. "You're still the love of my life," he said.

"You go on," Bea said with a laugh.

It was obvious from the comments and from the delight in the face of each caroler that they really had been waiting all year for Miss Bea's famous chocolate-covered pretzel rods.

It had been so much fun making them, but Sydney was even more proud to be a part of the special holiday memory now.

She carried the basket back up the stairs and sat on the porch rail across from Bea. "Wow. That was *so* pretty." She ran a hand up her arm. "Gave me chills."

"And with no practice. Just joyful hearts."

"Christmas joy. I guess it's like fairy dust."

"You need to see the whole thing. Experience it. I'll be fine right here. Trust me, those folks will climb those steps to get my treats." Bea let out a hearty laugh. "If we hadn't made them they might have done a sit-in until we did."

"I think you're right."

"We have plenty. This thing runs on its own. Why don't you catch up with the next group?"

"I don't want to leave you here alone. This is our memory."

"And we've had it, dear. Now, don't be silly. I can handle it. And this town has taken care of me my whole life. I'll be fine. Always have been."

"Thank you, but no. I'm enjoying staying with you right here on this porch," Sydney said.

Bea grumbled, but didn't push.

The groups moved through quickly. In five minutes they were there and gone and the next group passed them on the walkway up. Bea got up and went inside, bringing a cup of hot cocoa for herself and Sydney when she came back out.

"Perfect," Sydney said taking a mug from her. "Thank you."

It wasn't until about the tenth group, close to an hour into the evening, that she spotted RayAnne.

"Hi, Mom!" RayAnne yelled as she walked up the sidewalk flanked by her new BFF Jenny. Right beside them Seth hung close. She found herself hoping Mac was there, and her heart squeezed when she saw him walking toward her. He was near the back, talking with the mayor.

The leader of this group did exactly the same thing as all the others had done. Not even one switch up. Sydney stood on the porch next to Bea, and just when she expected the leader to give Bea the signal, something else happened.

The mayor walked up on the porch. "As mayor of this town I'm mandating . . ." And he turned to Sydney, "that you join this group and enjoy the rest of the route. I'll be filling in here." He took the basket from her and then shushed her toward the stairs.

Sydney looked at Bea, who was smiling with that one eyebrow arched like a black cat on Halloween. "You did this?"

Bea shrugged. "He's the mayor."

The entire group of carolers cheered.

Sydney couldn't argue with that, and it did sound fun. She went down and stepped next to RayAnne, who had a small penlight lit over the song sheet.

Mac handed Sydney her own pen light. "Got one of these for you."

"Was this your doing?" She turned and looked up at him, but he twisted her shoulders forward and the music started. They sang, and as beautiful as that music sounded from the front porch of that old mansion, it felt even bigger and more pure from right here in the middle of it. Their words seem to lift straight up, filling the sky and the heavens. Her nose tickled and eyes teared as she sang with all her heart. Those pretty blue lights in the window display that she and RayAnne had worked on together were like tiny blue stars, lights on a runway leading them home.

With the last note of the song, Bea stood, walked to the rail, and blew her a kiss. RayAnne nudged her and pointed at Bea. Sydney blew her a kiss back, and Mac placed his hand on Sydney's shoulder.

The mayor walked down the steps with the basket of treats and everyone swarmed in to get theirs.

"Here, Mom." RayAnne handed Sydney a plastic handled bag, already partially filled with stuff.

"What's this?"

"They gave them to everyone. We got you one, too."

"We?"

RayAnne grinned. "Mac told us you'd be joining us. We got you one so you'd have something to carry your treats and song sheets in."

Sydney turned and looked at Mac. "I feel like there's been a conspiracy going on behind my back."

The mayor handed Sydney a chocolate-covered pretzel rod. "The merchants that don't have a singing stop sponsor those bags. Gives everyone a chance to participate."

"Great idea. Are you sure you're not just trying to put me out of my job so you can get more pretzels?"

He stomped his foot. "You found me out."

"Got my eye on you, Mayor." She reached up and gave him a hug. "Thank you."

"Don't get all mushy. Your group's going to leave you."

Sydney turned to see most of the group heading down the sidewalk toward the street. Except for Mac, who was waiting just a few steps away.

She skipped to his side, and he took her hand in his.

They caught up with the group. Sydney hadn't held hands with anyone in years, but it felt right tonight with Mac. He didn't let go of her hand until they began to sing and he pulled her from his side to the front of him. Her holding the music and him shining the penlight over her shoulder as they sang "Joy to the World." His voice was deep. Powerful. Together they sounded good.

The next stop was in front of the day care center, and Sydney could hardly sing "Rudolph the Red-Nosed Reindeer" from laughing as the kids, and Mac, all did hand gestures and the silly add-on lyric version of the song.

When they got to the end of the route, Sydney wasn't ready for the night to end.

"I'm so glad you got to come, Mom." RayAnne wrapped her arms around Sydney's waist. "So much fun. I love this town."

"Can't believe I almost missed it," Sydney said.

"We wouldn't let that happen," Mac said.

Seth hung close by. "Dad is like the most Christmas guy in the world. But this night is really cool. I told you, Ray. Didn't I?" He tugged on her ponytail.

"Hey, don't start something." But RayAnne was laughing, and although the nickname Ray had been one that Jon had always called her, Sydney found it endearing that she and Seth had formed such a great friendship so quickly.

Jenny's mom walked over. "You don't mind if RayAnne

and Seth go with us over to Santa's Village afterward for the light walk, do you?"

"How can I say no?" Sydney said.

Jenny and RayAnne bounced, clearly eavesdropping on the whole conversation.

"Thanks, Mom!" RayAnne said.

"We have the best moms ever," Jenny said.

"Seth's supposed to spend the night with Jeff Masterson tonight," Mac told Diane.

"I can drop him off over there for you when we're done."

"And Sydney," Diane said with a twinkle in her eye, "Let RayAnne stay over with Jenny. I'll bring her by the bookstore tomorrow afternoon once everyone gets up and going."

"Did you two plan this?" Sydney accused, only half-joking.

Diane shook her head. "No, but I'm liking what I see."

Sydney wagged a finger toward their kids. "After being up late tonight, they'll both be too tuckered out to watch the meteor showers tomorrow tonight."

"Now, would that really be so bad?" He squeezed her hand. "Don't think I'd mind starwatching with you alone."

She couldn't argue with him on that. Tonight had already been pretty fantastic. She wasn't sure how much better things could get.

"I'll walk you back to The Book Bea." He wrapped his arm around her shoulder. She felt small and warm in his embrace. They didn't say a word, just strolled back to the store in silence.

When they turned up the walkway to the bookstore,

the mayor was coming toward them. "Just locked up," he said.

"Thank you. Sorry, I should have come right back."

"No, don't be silly. It was my pleasure. I pulled everything just inside the door so Bea could head on home."

"You really made my evening. Thank you, Mayor, for insisting I participate."

"I knew you'd love it, and it's my duty as mayor of this town to be sure the good ones fall in love with Hopewell and stick around." He clicked his teeth and winked. "Merry Christmas, Sydney. Welcome to Hopewell."

Welcome to Hopewell. That sure sounded good. She leaned closer to Mac. "This is a pretty special place."

"The Book Bea?" He wrapped his arm more tightly across her shoulder.

"That too. I meant Hopewell." She stepped out from under his arm and climbed the stairs, stopping on the top step.

He climbed one more and pulled her close to him. Nose to nose. "Right now, I'm pretty sure you're the most special part of this town."

"I'm scared," she whispered.

"Don't be. I won't let anything bad happen to you." He kissed her. Just a sweet dab on the lips, and then he tilted his head forward, keeping her close.

His breath warmed her skin as she relaxed into his embrace. He lifted his hand and tipped her chin, then covered her mouth with his, gently but without falter, and she knew right then that she didn't need to be afraid.

"I had a great time with you tonight. Last night. The other day." He swept a hand through his hair. "I didn't expect this. Wasn't looking for it, but Sydney, this feels real to me. I know you're going through some rough stuff, but is it just me or . . ."

"I feel it too," she whispered.

Chapter Seventeen

Sydney had a sleepless night. She hadn't had a kiss like that in . . . well, she wasn't quite sure she'd ever had a kiss like that. She touched her lips, remembering every moment of last night as she drove to work the next morning. What she wouldn't give for another kiss like that. And tonight they'd be surprising the kids with the outing under the stars.

Yes, Hopewell was turning out to be very good for her.

She parked in front of The Book Bea and went inside.

"Sorry I missed you at the end of the night, dear." Bea was dressed in a cheerful red jacket with appliqued silver bells down the front with real jingle bells at the bottom of each one. She sounded like one of those holiday bell ringers as she walked through the store.

"I'm sure you were tired." Sydney felt more like she should thank Bea for not being there when Mac walked her back. If she had been, there certainly would not have been a kiss on the front porch.

"I wanted you to have the full experience. You'll have many years to host it going forward."

"It was amazing from the porch, but you were right. Actually making the walk and experiencing every stop along the way, every song, every*one* was better than I ever imagined."

"Yes. I know." Bea's eyes sparkled.

"So, I'm not really clear on how all that happened. Were you and the mayor in cahoots the whole time?"

"Cahoots? That sounds a wee bit manipulative. It wasn't like that. But I've gotten to know you in our short friendship and if it's one thing I know it's that you can be a little hard headed."

"That didn't take you long."

"Well, take it as a compliment. I'm the same way."

"Did Mac know, by chance?"

"We may have discussed it."

Sydney tried to hold back the smile. Had he adjusted his schedule to be there because of her?

"He seems really quite fond of you. Of course, I already knew that." Bea cocked her head. "What is that look for?"

"Nothing." Sydney turned her back to Bea.

"Oh, no, missy. You can turn right around."

Sydney turned around, but she couldn't play innocent. She was bursting at the seams to tell someone. "Mac walked me back to the store after we finished caroling last night."

"That is not a walk back to the store grin." Bea folded her arms. "You like him, don't you?"

"He's really nice. We've had fun together."

"And?"

"And he kissed me last night."

Bea's face lit up. She grabbed Sydney's hand. "I knew it. I knew it. I knew it. I could just tell the first time I saw y'all in the same room together. He is a nice man, Sydney. One of the best I've ever known. How was the kiss?"

"Nice." She looked up to the ceiling to get out of Bea's zone. She was like a master interrogator. "Okay, it was very nice."

"This is wonderful news. The best."

"It was just a kiss. No promises for anything, but it sure did take me by surprise. I can't believe I put myself out there like that. Must have been the Christmas lights."

"You did do a very nice job on them," Bea said. "Nicest display The Book Bea has ever had. So when will you see Mac again?"

"We'd planned on getting together tonight to watch the meteor showers with the kids from behind his house. We were going to surprise them with s'mores. That was before the kiss. I sure hope it's not going to be awkward."

"Of course it won't be awkward. And isn't that a romantic evening."

"Well, not with our kids along it won't be."

"It'll still be special. You're special, and I want you to take the rest of the time off from the bookstore to enjoy the holidays."

"I can't do that. Won't do it. I already made a commitment to you that I'd help you through the holidays."

"I'm well aware of that, and I thank you, but that was before we decided that you're going to take over the store. It was also when you thought your daughter was going to be out of town."

"But—"

Bea held up her hand. "I've got it all figured out. I'll go through it with you soon. For now, take the break. Please. For me. My final request as the owner of this bookstore before we shift it over to you. And trust me, you and RayAnne belong here in this town."

Sydney felt like she should resist, but she didn't want to. She loved it here. "Thank you, Bea."

"By the way," Bea said. "The books we ordered for Mac came in. You should take them to him."

"Yeah. I can take them tonight."

"Or you could take them now."

"Why would I do that?"

"So you can see him, without the kids. Do I have to tell you everything?"

"Apparently so. I'm a little out of practice." Sydney took the books and flipped through them.

"Put those books in a bag. Go back to the washroom and give your hair a little pouf and put on some fresh lipstick. Then deliver them to our customer. I insist."

"He's going to see right through that."

"Don't be silly. He's going to be flattered. Do it."

She dipped her head into her hands. "I don't know. I'll feel so silly."

"Trust me. You have to make a little effort. He clearly did by showing up last night and walking you back."

"Fine." Sydney went to the back and freshened up. When she came back out, Bea was standing by the door holding one of her special The Book Bea shopping bags.

"That shade of lipstick is perfect. Perks you right up. He's going to be delighted." Bea gave her a kiss on the cheek. "Oops. Wait. I left a smudge." Bea brushed the magenta kiss into Sydney's cheek, then kissed the other side and did the same. "Better."

"Ugh," Sydney turned to leave.

"Love will certainly spin you in circles won't it?"

"Why do you say that?" But Sydney knew exactly what Bea meant when she turned and saw her holding out the shopping bag.

"Almost forgot something, didn't you?" Bea laughed.

Sydney took the bag and drove to Mac's house with nervous anticipation about surprising him. She wouldn't stay long, just enough to deliver the books and be sure he knew she was looking forward to tonight. They hadn't finalized a time, so they could discuss that. Short. Simple. Just showing a little interest.

She ran her finger across her bottom lip. She could still feel every emotion that went through her when he'd kissed her. His pickup truck was parked in the driveway, so she pulled in behind him. She checked her makeup in the rearview mirror then got out of the car and walked up to the front door. Switching the bag to her other hand, she wiped the sweat from her palm on her pants, and then knocked.

Excitement spun in her stomach as she waited. Why was she so darn nervous?

She heard footsteps, and her knees weakened as the door handle twisted.

A young woman answered the door.

"Oh, hi." Sydney paused, glanced over her shoulder at Mac's truck then stammered, "I . . . Is Mac here?" Her mouth felt as dry as if someone had just hooked her to one of those slobber suckers the dentist uses.

"He's in the shower. Do you want to wait? Or perhaps I can help you?"

Sydney noticed the rings on the woman's left hand. She wanted to heave, but for a whole different reason now. Anything to give her instant relief from what she was feeling right now. "No. Yes. You can help me." She shoved the bag toward the woman's gut. "I was just delivering these books he ordered from The Book Bea."

"Oh, great. I'll be sure he gets them. Does he owe you anything?" The diamond band on the woman's left ring finger dazzled in the sunlight.

Was he having an affair with a married woman? That made him just as bad as Jon. Didn't anyone believe in the sanctity of marriage anymore?

"No." Sydney raised her hand. "Oh, no. He absolutely does not owe me a thing." She walked to her car as fast as her feet would take her without breaking into a run. She twisted the key and shifted into reverse.

Only where the heck was she going to go now?

If she went back to the bookstore she'd have to tell Bea that the guy she kissed last night had a girlfriend. A young one, probably the same age as her other replacement. Oh, no, ma'am. She should've known. She knew better.

How could Bea not have known? Bea said she knew everything about everyone.

Sydney took a deep breath, trying to chase away the threatening tears. If she started crying she might never stop, and that would be a mess. Nothing had happened. Wasn't like she was in love or they had made a promise. It was one lousy kiss. Okay, one toe-curling, amazing kiss, but clearly a mistake. She just needed to get her head together and let it go. She could totally do that. She did not come to this town looking for love. All she wanted to do was raise her daughter and do right by her.

She looked over her shoulder as she eased down the long driveway until a rap on her window made her jam her foot on the brake. She spun around. Mac?

He pulled on the door handle, but the door was locked.

She put the car in park and rolled down the window.

"Hey, glad I didn't miss you."

"Why?"

He looked confused. "Because I was just getting ready to leave and . . . Are you okay?"

"Fine."

"Fine?" Mac lifted a hand to his mouth. "Yeah. Fine is never good. What is wrong?"

"Why don't you tell me?"

"Because I don't know?" Mac's brows pulled together.

"Who was that?"

He paused, looking like he didn't know which way to turn, and then his face relaxed. "Oh, Haley? She lives next door. She takes care of Seth for me sometimes. There's nothing . . . You didn't think? She's a friend. A married friend. I can introduce her to you."

"No. Please, no." The feeling came back into Sydney's hands where she'd been clenching them in anger. She had felt like she was hearing that news from Jon all over again. But that feeling was quickly being replaced with embarrassment. The flush in her cheeks was hot, and her hands were sweating. "I'm so stupid."

"You really thought that?" He stepped back and folded his arms. "Sydney, how could you think so little of me?"

"I'm sorry. I . . ." She felt the tears. Frustration really, but she couldn't help it. "I'm broken goods, Mac. This probably isn't a good idea."

"Syd, no. Please. Don't leave like this."

"I think I need some time."

"But tonight. You'll be here tonight, right?"

"We don't have to. The kids will be tired."

"Come on, Sydney. Give it a chance. Seven."

She put the car in reverse. "Just give me some time."

He stepped away from the car, and she backed out.

She wasn't ready to go back to the bookstore yet. She needed a little time to catch her breath first. Why did she jump to that conclusion? What was wrong with her?

She pulled into Santa's Village. Maybe the crowd and festivities would help her get outside of the negative thoughts looping through her brain.

Parents rushed excited kids into the long line to make their last requests of Santa, while others hurried around checking the last few things off their holiday shopping list.

The line at the wrapping station was long today.

She ordered a hot chocolate and dropped a dollar in the donation bucket, then ordered four cookies and ate every last one of them. Funny how a massive dose of sugar could soothe a person.

Finally she was pretty certain that she could face the conversation with Bea in a mature way, and she planned to avoid Mac's calls. Forever. She got up and went back to her car.

She was halfway to her car when she saw Mac's truck.

She ducked behind a minivan, praying he hadn't seen her when he drove by. Had he come looking for her?

She pretended to tie her shoelace and stayed tucked between the cars until she was certain Mac had to be at the other end of the parking lot.

She peeked around the minivan to look.

There was no sign of Mac's big crew cab pickup truck. And you couldn't hide those very easily.

"Are you okay, ma'am?" A security guard towered above her.

"Yes. My shoe. It came untied." She stood up straight and offered an awkward smile. "Thanks."

She made off in a hurry for her car, holding her breath until she got inside and started it. Her tires spit gravel as she gunned the engine and headed back to The Book Bea.

If Mac had followed her to Santa's Village looking for her, would he show up at The Book Bea? She wasn't ready to talk to him. Embarrassed and second-guessing her recent choices when it came to Mac, she parked behind the shop where the tenants parked. Maybe he'd think she wasn't there. She slipped inside the back door.

"Sydney! You were gone a long while. I was hoping I might not see you again today." Bea was looking as proud as a momma bird watching her fledglings take flight. "What took so long? Or do I even need to ask?"

"I stopped at Santa's Village."

"Oh?" She looked disappointed. "You did? With Mac?"

Sydney busied herself straightening the display near the door. "This table is our best sales tool. I swear I refill it every day."

"Yes. Always has been the best spot in the store." Bea walked over to the table and stood next to her. "Sydney, did something happen?"

"You know, I should've known better than to let down my guard. That's all. Nothing is the matter. It was one stupid kiss. I let it go to my head. It didn't mean a darn thing, and I don't have any business jumping into a casual anything with a man anyway. I have a daughter to raise."

"But Mac's a great guy."

"I think all men are closer to the same than we think." Her gut twisted, leaving her sick to her stomach. How had she let her guard down? "I will not let what happened with Jon happen to me again."

"Oh, Sydney. I don't know Jon, but from what you've shared I'd say those two boys are as different as night and day."

"Not really. They both have secrets."

"You found out." Bea let out a breath, as if it had been hard to keep the secret.

"Yes. I did. When I dropped in unannounced." The words Bea had just said were just starting to sink in. "Wait a minute. You knew? And you were okay with him keeping it a secret from me?"

"Okay, so it might be a little weird, but it's not like it's a bad thing."

"How can you say that?"

"So the man dresses up like Santa Claus every year. He brings so much joy to people. I personally think it's quite charming."

"Santa?"

"Yes, Santa. Mac is the best Santa at Santa's Village. The one you took RayAnne to see. Isn't that what you were talking about?"

"He is?" She stacked the books with a little more oomph than was necessary. RayAnne had told him about the four-wheeler. Was that why he'd invited them over to ride? How embarrassing to have your kid tell Santa that your mother isn't happy.

What did Mac think of her? Was that kiss all just him feeling sorry for her? Or did he think he was the real Santa granting wishes for her daughter? And which was worse? "It doesn't matter. That's not what I was talking about." She stopped and turned. "I wish you'd told me about the Santa thing."

"Does it make a difference?"

"No. Of course not, but Bea, a woman answered the door. A young woman, wearing a wedding ring, and I immediately jumped to the conclusion that he was dating her. She was so young. Like Jon's new girlfriend."

"Did you two straighten it out?"

"We did. But I was so humiliated for thinking that. It

wasn't fair. Bea, I'm broken after what happened to me. How will I ever trust anyone? I'm not ready for all of this."

"You will. Y'all have hit it off, and you're enjoying doing new things, too. Like that four-wheeler ride. You said yourself it was more fun than you'd had in a long time. And RayAnne loved it."

Sydney's jaw set. "The four-wheeler. I don't think that was a coincidence. RayAnne told Santa she wanted one. He knew exactly what he was doing, and I don't like being manipulated like that."

Bea didn't respond.

"I don't know this guy at all. I will not make that mistake again."

"What about your date tonight?"

"If he calls, I'm busy."

"You can't just ignore him. This is a small town."

"I can ignore him for now." And when the dust settled she'd just politely never mention their time together or that kiss . . . ever again.

Chapter Eighteen

Sydney spent the day going through the motions, but her mind was still replaying her time with Mac. How disappointing. Maybe she'd had her one true shot at love. Jon. So what if it hadn't lasted a lifetime and ended in disaster? She had more than some people ever had. She shouldn't have let down her guard. She knew better. Absolutely knew better. She'd said as much before he kissed her.

But could she blame him? The blame was on her. She could've, should've, stepped away.

He'd called twice and both times she'd sent the call to voice mail.

Diane had dropped RayAnne off, but RayAnne was so tired from her day with Jenny that she'd quietly sat in one of the chairs and read all day.

Sydney had kept one eye on the front door of The Book Bea all afternoon. She was as nervous as a squirrel trying to cross a road every time the door opened. She hoped he wouldn't show up here. She couldn't face him.

At 5:59 she had everything ready to close up shop and skedaddle. She didn't waste a minute twisting the key in the lock and hauling butt to her car with RayAnne in tow.

She'd made it through the day without having to see Mac again. She'd take that one small victory.

Her phone rang on the way home.

"Want me to get that?" RayAnne asked.

"No." Sydney slapped her hand on the phone. It was probably Mac and she was not about to have that phone call in front of her daughter. "I'll check it when I get home. Nothing is that important." She patted RayAnne on the leg. "Love you, kiddo."

"Love you too, Mom."

"How about we splurge and make pizza tonight?"

"Pepperoni?"

"Sure thing."

"What time are we going to Seth's to watch meteors tonight?"

Sydney hesitated. They'd talked about that in front of the kids the other night. She'd hoped RayAnne had forgotten. The s'mores were going to be a surprise, but the visit wasn't. "We're not going."

"Why not?" RayAnne's face scrunched up, her lips bunched like the pouty ten-year-old who'd moved here a couple weeks ago. Not a welcome sight to have back. "It was going to be so cool."

She hadn't prepared for this discussion. "Something came up. Had to cancel." Not a complete lie, even if she did elude to it being Mac's fault.

"Man," RayAnne flopped against the seat. "That's not fair. I thought we might get to ride the four-wheelers again."

"We'll do something here. It'll be fun."

RayAnne didn't say another word all the way home.

Sydney's phone rang again.

"Voice mail?" RayAnne asked.

Sydney nodded.

"It might be Mr. Mac saying we're still on for tonight."

"I don't think so. It's probably someone selling something. Voice mail will pick up." She turned over her phone to hide the number and kept her hand over it. She immediately regretted the big fat lie. It was most likely Mac. But she couldn't talk to him right now. She pushed the vent away from her. She didn't need the heat blowing on her with the hot flush that was pushing up her cheeks.

She was so glad when they got home. That car had felt eerily quiet as she sat there stewing in the fib.

They went inside and Sydney snuck a look at her phone as RayAnne raced upstairs. She was right. It had been Mac.

Sydney sucked in a breath when she saw the live tree in her living room. It had been a nice gesture. For what it was worth. At least the room smelled nice. She dropped her keys on the entry table and went to the kitchen to start dinner.

"RayAnne," Sydney called upstairs. "You going to come down and help me fix the pizza?"

"Coming. Just a minute." A few moments later RayAnne came into the kitchen. "Seth said his dad didn't say anything about tonight being cancelled."

"Here, you do the cheese."

"Cool. The cheesier the better."

Sydney picked up her phone and texted Mac.

Sydney: Have to cancel tonight.
Mac: Was looking forward to it. Tomorrow?

Sydney started to respond but decided less was more in this case. She put her phone on the counter, and then helped RayAnne slide the pizza into the oven.

"I'll set the timer. How long?" RayAnne stood poised over the timer.

"Set it for twelve minutes and then we'll check."

She twisted the knob, then threw her hands in the air. "Done."

Sydney's phone rang.

RayAnne peered over the phone.

Dread filled Sydney, knowing it would be Mac.

"It's Daddy!"

Somehow Jon didn't seem as bad tonight.

"Can I answer it?"

"Sure."

RayAnne answered the phone with a happy squeal. She danced around the kitchen as she ran down every detail in their lives since the last time she'd spoken to him. "I miss you lots, Daddy. Can't wait until Christmas Day. For Santa and for you. Mostly you."

RayAnne's enthusiasm bubbled. Sydney loved the sound of her daughter's laugh, even though it did hurt just a teensy bit to hear her gush over Jon.

"Why?" RayAnne said.

Sydney felt the vibe in the room change. As she turned she saw the crestfallen look on her daughter's face. *Oh no. Jon, don't do this again,* she thought.

"But you said we would still have fun on Christmas. It's Christmas, Daddy." RayAnne's eyes teared. "I don't care about the trip. Come here and stay with us then."

Sydney wanted to snatch the phone from her hand, but she held herself in check. She couldn't rescue RayAnne from Jon's actions, and giving him a piece of her mind would only sink her to his level.

"But I miss you, Daddy."

Sydney raised her hands to her face. It was so hard to stand by listening to this.

"No. That's not fair. You don't love me." RayAnne dropped the phone on the counter and raced from the room.

Sydney stood there for a moment. Just staring.

"RayAnne?"

Sydney could hear Jon's voice. But RayAnne wasn't there to respond. Her tennis shoes pounded against each stair tread to her room, then a door slammed.

Sydney picked up the phone. "Jon? Are you there?"

"What'd she do? I was talking to her."

"What did *she* do? I was standing here. She was listening to you. What did you do now?"

"I just told her we'd need a rain check. I'm going to take her skiing one weekend in January, and we'll do spring break."

"You canceled?"

"I didn't cancel. A rain check. You know, just same thing, different day."

"For Christmas? A rain check? Goodness gracious, Jon. She's not a box of cereal that's on sale."

"What's the big deal? I'm shipping her a gift."

Better not be a four-wheeler. "It's not about the presents, Jon. She misses you."

"I miss her too, but there's a lot going on here." He cleared his throat. "I'm transferring some extra money into your account for her for a gift. Get her what she wants."

"You can't buy your way out of this, Jon. This is her school break, and she's been talking about nothing but this trip with you for weeks. You let her down with the ski trip, and now you're not going to make it for one lousy day. Frankly, I'm sick of hearing about it, and it's not about me. This is not fair."

"Well, it can't be helped."

The timer sounded. She snatched the door to the oven with so much force that it nearly closed by itself. "What could be so important that you have to let your daughter down? On Christmas?" She grabbed the hand towel and slid the pizza pan onto the counter.

"Don't I deserve to be happy? Look, I'm not going to get hung up on by her and then have to listen to you, too. I don't have to explain my actions to you."

"You're right. You don't, and I don't even want to hear your lame excuse anyway. You don't just rain check your daughter. But I'm not shopping for you, and I'm not explaining for you. You are going to have to dig yourself out of this for once. And trust me, you've really done it this time. This is not the kind of disappointment that passes quickly. You better be ready to carry it for a long time."

"Don't preach at me," he said. "I don't deserve it."

"Don't even start trying to turn this on me. You deserve to put your daughter first . . . for once. Have your midlife crisis, but do that on your time."

"Well, I guess I might as well tell you. You'll hear it from RayAnne soon enough. I just told her. I'm going to be a father again. We're pregnant."

Syd lowered the phone and realized she probably looked exactly like RayAnne had. Just standing there, mouth slightly open, blinking. She ended the call and turned off her phone.

Sydney walked into the living room and sat down on the couch. Numb. That's pretty much how she felt. Not mad. Not sad. Not even worried. Just tired. Over it.

And she didn't have it in her to go upstairs and console RayAnne, because frankly she couldn't say anything nice or helpful when it came to Jon right now. And bashing him was a promise to herself she refused to break. She'd let RayAnne cry it out and come down when she was ready.

Sydney would cry it out too, if she had a tear left in her for him, but she was pretty sure that after tonight she'd shed the last tear for Jon Ragsdale that she ever would.

She curled up on the couch. Hugging the throw pillow, she pulled her knees up, wishing the world could fall away and she'd wake up three months later in Hopewell with all of this behind her. She closed her eyes and tried to dream of better days.

She woke up more exhausted than when she'd laid down. She was so tired of covering for Jon. She pulled herself up from the couch and checked the time. It had been two hours since that phone call. Enough time to let RayAnne feel what she was going to feel. She made two cups of hot chocolate and went upstairs.

With a double-tap on RayAnne's door with the edge of one of the mugs, she called, "Hey, honey. We need to talk about your plans with your dad." She stood there waiting to hear the stomping of a disappointed pre-teen, but there was nothing but quiet. She'd probably cried herself to sleep.

"Love you, RayAnne," she said quietly through the door.

Chapter Nineteen

Mac was thankful for the Santa suit gear tonight. Finally the weather was cooperating and acting like December. From here he could see the bubble-snow being sprayed from the hayloft of the reindeer barn, and it really did look like snow when the temperature was right.

He welcomed the next child in line with open arms. The little boy ran up and into his arms at full speed. Mac grabbed him in the air like a line drive and then swung him up onto his knee in one swoop. He didn't even get a good *ho-ho-ho* out and the boy was rattling down a list that, if he wasn't mistaken, may have been in alphabetical order.

He was pretty sure this was the fourth time in a week he'd seen this one, too. The line was extra long tonight. That always happened as Christmas Eve approached. Last-minute additions to the visits they'd made prior, or the children who'd skipped coming sooner because they weren't sure if it was still cool to believe. He loved it when they gave in to believe another year, just in case.

A steady stream of kids poured through their line. Just as the next kid was about to step past the rope to wait for his turn, Rebecca clotheslined him and ran up the steps toward Mac.

She never came up to him. They always texted any information that was needed. Had his phone died? He reached for it, but the display was still lit.

She didn't even wait for the boy on his knee to take a breath, just leaned in and cupped her hand to his ear.

"It's an emergency. It's Seth." She shoved a phone into his hand and he never heard what she was saying to the little boy as she helped him down from Mac's lap and guided him back to his mom.

Mac got up out of the chair and stepped behind the giant Santa throne.

"Seth? What is it?" But all Mac could make out from the other end of the phone were the words

DAD.

ACCIDENT.

HELP.

"Calm down, son. I can't understand you." But his heart was pounding. "Where are you?"

"Home. Back at the big turn. It's bad. Dad. You have to come."

Rebecca was back at his side, worry etching her young face.

"Are you okay? Is that the four-wheeler I hear?"

"Yes. It's Ray. You have to help me. I can't get her up."

"Ray? RayAnne? What's she doing there?"

"She's hurt. She showed up and I was cleaning the four-wheelers and she took off on one. She went over the edge at the end of the big hairpin. Dad. She's hurt bad. She's bleeding. I'm scared."

"Where's Haley?"

"At the house. Hurry, Dad."

"Don't touch RayAnne. Don't try to get her up. Is she talking to you?"

"She was crying, not making sense."

"Are you with her now?" Mac asked.

"Yes. She doesn't want me to leave."

"Is she still crying?"

Seth's voice choked. "No she's quiet. Just making noises.

"She's probably in shock. Take your coat off and put it over her. Don't let her move. I'm calling an ambulance and I'm on my way. Keep talking to her."

"I don't know if she can hear me."

"Doesn't matter. Keep talking to her. Tell her she's going to be okay, and help is on the way."

Rebecca left.

He could hear Seth talking, but he didn't hear a response.

"Can you reach up and hit the kill switch on the ATV?"

"I think so."

The roaring engine went quiet. "Good. Stay on the phone with me, buddy."

"Okay."

Before Mac got down the steps, Rebecca was back at his side with another phone. "Here's another phone."

He said, "Dial 911 for me. Quick. It's an emergency."

She dialed it and handed him the phone. "Go. We'll handle everything here." She'd already put a BE RIGHT BACK sign in front of his chair.

Mac walked as calmly as he could so as not to frighten the kids and parents still waiting in line, and then sprinted to his dressing room to get his keys. He called for an ambulance as he ran.

"This is Kevin MacAlee." He spit out the address trying to talk slow and clear even though his mind was reeling at full speed.

"What's your emergency, sir?"

"Ten-year-old girl wrecked on an ATV. She's pinned underneath. Bleeding. My son is with her."

"Is there access from the street?"

"Take the dirt road to the right of the house all the way to the back. Go through the gate. Follow the path to a fork. Take a right at the fork. There's a hairpin turn. That's where they are. I'm on my way." He grabbed his keys and turned to leave, realizing he was still in full gear. No time to remedy that now.

"Is the road passable in a vehicle?"

"Yes. I've driven it in my truck." Mac ran through the alley behind the buildings toward his truck.

"Are both of them your children, sir?"

"No. My son is with her. His name is Seth."

"Do you know the victim's name?"

The twenty questions were pissing him off. "Yes. It's RayAnne Ragsdale. Have you dispatched someone yet?"

"Yes, sir. They're on the way. If you can stay on the line with me, I just need as much information as you can give me."

"Fine."

"Your son is still with her?"

"Yes, I have him on the other line." He fumbled with the two phones as he climbed into his truck.

"Keep him on the line. Tell him we're on the way. And tell him to let you know when he hears the sirens."

He bobbled the phone and lifted the other. "Seth. You there?"

"Dad. I'm scared."

"Help is on the way. Let me know when you hear the sirens, okay?"

"Okay, Dad. She's not talking to me. I can feel her heartbeat, but I'm scared. There's a lot of blood on her head."

He needed to contact Sydney, but between a phone in his lap, one against his shoulder, and trying to drive, he was out of options. And just how the heck did RayAnne get to his house without Sydney?

If RayAnne was seriously hurt, Sydney would never forgive him. Head wounds always made for a lot of blood and a scary sight. He prayed it wasn't as bad as Seth made it sound.

He pressed the speaker button on the phone with dispatch and laid it on the seat, holding the one with Seth on the line.

"I hear the sirens," Seth screamed. "I don't see the lights yet."

It was dark. And cold, too. "Stay right where you are. Do you have the flashlight? There's one in the pack on the four-wheeler, remember? Can you get to it?"

"I don't know. Let me try."

Mac stared into the night. His headlights slashing through the darkness as he sped down the street.

Seth's voice was steadier. "I got it."

"Turn on the flashlight and aim it toward the path."

"Okay." Seth's voice was shaky, but he'd regained composure. At least he was responding to direction.

Mac drove as fast as he could. It wasn't but a few miles and by the time he got to his house the road was lined with emergency vehicles and an array of red, blue, and white flashing lights.

He drove as far as he could then jumped out of his

truck, leaving it running. He'd have to run the rest of the way.

Mac knew most of the guys working fire and rescue. He trusted these men, but right now all he wanted was to be there himself.

"Sir?" someone shouted. "I need you to stop right there."

Mac turned to see his old buddy from high school, Johnny Ray, in his deputy uniform.

"Stop," Johnny Ray said again. "You can't go back there, sir."

Sir? Mac's mind spun. *What the heck? We've been friends for . . .*

Then it dawned on Mac that he was still dressed like Santa. "It's me, man. Mac. Seth's back there with RayAnne."

"Mac? Go, man. Your boy is okay." He waved him on, and Mac dug down into a full-out run. He was still another sixty yards or so from the pole gate when the ambulance came toward him. They'd gotten to RayAnne quickly. Thank goodness. In the wash of light from the ambulance headlights, he saw Haley standing with Seth near the gate.

The ambulance blasted by, lights flashing.

Mac ran over to them. Seth's eyes were swollen red, his hair a sweaty mess even in the cool night. He looked confused, and Haley looked shaken.

She'd probably never have kids after all Seth had put her through this week.

"Seth. Are you okay?" He grabbed both of Seth's arms.

"Santa?" Seth said.

"It's me. Yes. Come here." He pulled him into a hug.

"Dad?" Seth looked to Haley, then stepped back looking a little freaked out.

"Yes. You did good, son. I'm proud of you."

"Why are you dressed like that?"

The jig was up now. No way around that. "I'll explain. But right now, come on, we're going to the hospital."

"I'm so sorry, Mac," Haley said. "I didn't even know she was at the house."

"Doesn't matter. Let's keep our priorities straight. Blame is not one of those."

The hospital was a good forty-five-minute drive.

They jumped into Mac's truck. Once they turned onto the main road, Mac tried to call Sydney, but her phone went straight to voice mail over and over again.

The first twenty minutes of the ride no one said a word.

Mac pressed redial to Sydney, but the call still didn't get through. He dropped his phone into the console.

"Are you okay, Seth?"

Seth nodded.

"What got into you?" Mac asked. He was trying hard to keep his cool, but he'd thought he'd taken every precaution to be sure those four-wheelers wouldn't present a danger. He needed answers. "Why would you ride without me? We had a deal."

"I didn't. Dad, I swear." Seth straightened in his seat and crossed his heart. "I wouldn't break that promise. Ever."

"How is she? Did they say anything when the paramedics got there?" Mac looked to Seth, then caught Haley's reflection in the rearview mirror.

Haley pulled her arms tight around herself. "I'm not

sure, Mac. It didn't look good." Her lips quivered as she spoke. "There was a lot of blood and they carried her out on one of those board things. I hope it was just a precaution, but they were hurrying. No one gave us any information. I'm sorry, Mac. I can't believe this happened."

"This is not your fault, Haley."

He turned to Seth. "Tell me everything. Start at the top."

"It's weird talking to Santa."

"I'm sorry. I have explaining to do too. But that's going to wait." Even if he took the suit off, that beard wasn't going anywhere without a little work.

Seth wiped his hand across his forehead. "She showed up on her bicycle. Her dad isn't coming for Christmas now. He's such a jerk."

Mac would normally call Seth out for saying something like that about an adult, but in this case he couldn't disagree. He wondered how someone like Sydney could have been with someone like that. What was wrong with that guy?

"From the top, Seth," Mac said.

"I was out front wiping down the four-wheelers when RayAnne showed up on her bike."

"Did you know she was there?" he asked Haley.

She shook her head.

"I didn't have a chance to tell her." Seth's shoulders rolled forward. "It kind of happened really fast. RayAnne wasn't crying, but she had been. I could tell. She was really mad at her dad. Then, she dared me to go riding, and I told her we couldn't, because my dad . . . *you* . . . weren't home."

Well, at least Seth knew the rules and was strong enough to stand by them.

"She called me chicken. I didn't care about that, but

then she got on my four-wheeler and started it up. I thought she was just messing around. I told her we couldn't ride until you got home. The next thing I knew she took off."

"Did you take my four-wheeler after her?"

"No. I know the rules. I took her bike and chased after her. I went as fast as I could." Seth's mouth pulled into a tight line. "When I finally caught up to her she was over the side . . . upside down. The engine was screaming, wheels spinning in the air, and there was smoke pouring out of the thing. I couldn't even see her under the four-wheeler at first. It was hard to hear."

Seth fidgeted in his seat. "Then I saw her. I tried to help her out, but she couldn't move and she was crying. I didn't know if it would catch on fire."

Mac placed his hand on his son's shoulder.

"I didn't know what to do. So, I called you." He looked over at Haley. "I'm sorry."

"You should be sorry," Mac said. "Haley's doing us a favor, and this is the second stunt you've pulled on her in a week."

Seth's eyes got big. Mac knew Seth was putting two and two together that not only was his dad wearing a Santa suit, but he was also the Santa he'd spoken to the night he'd snuck out.

"Seth, I know you were worried about RayAnne, but you have to be smart. I pray she's okay."

"Me too, Dad." His hands pulled into tight fists. "I don't even care how much trouble I'm in. She just needs to be okay."

Chapter Twenty

Pounding at the front door woke Sydney. She raced from the couch half-coherent and swung the door open without bothering to look out the window first.

"Diane? Are you okay?"

"Why aren't you answering your phone?" She pushed into the room.

"Oh that. Long story. I'm sorry, did I scare you? Come on in. What time is it?"

"You're coming with me. I needed to get a hold of you. Don't do that again."

"It's been kind of a bad night. I turned off my phone."

"Get your purse."

"Why?"

"Sydney, there's been an accident. Tony was part of the volunteer squad called out."

"Who's hurt?"

"It's RayAnne."

Sydney looked behind her to the stairs. "RayAnne is upstairs asleep."

"I don't think so."

Sydney stood there, confused. *This isn't happening,* she thought desperately.

Diane grabbed Sydney by the hand and ran up the

stairs. Sydney raised her hand to knock, but Diane pushed the door open.

The room was empty. Her bed made up.

"No." Sydney covered her mouth with her hand. How long had RayAnne been gone?

"Come with me." Diane tugged Sydney by the arm and they ran back downstairs. "Purse?"

Sydney pointed to the table by the stairs.

Diane swept the purse into her arms, and then dug in the top and lifted out her phone. "Here. Turn this on." Sydney pressed the button on the phone and let Diane lead her outside.

"What happened?"

"She wrecked on a four-wheeler." Diane revved the engine and headed for the interstate.

"Where is she?"

"The hospital is a hike. It's going to take us at least half an hour to get there no matter how fast I drive. I'll see what Tony can find out for us."

"How did this happen?"

"From what I gather she was with Mac's boy."

"I knew that was a mistake." Sydney's head was reeling. She kept thinking she might open her eyes and realize this was a bad dream, because it had all those mixed-up components and people in the wrong roles and places like dreams often did.

Diane's phone rang and she pressed speaker. "Hey, babe. What do we know? I've got Sydney right here next to me in the car."

"Hey, Sydney. She's in the emergency room. They're still assessing the situation."

"How serious is it? Do I need to call her dad? She's going to be okay. Right?"

"You might want to call him and let him know, but

calm down, her vitals were good. I don't think she's in any imminent danger."

"Thank you, God," Sydney whispered.

"She's got a pretty bad head wound," Tony said. "That'll require some stitches, and she lost a lot of blood. I'm sure she'll be in the hospital overnight no matter what."

"How could this happen? I was right there in the house. I must have been asleep on the couch when she left. Maybe she should be living with Jon."

"Don't be silly," Diane said. "Kids are kids. They do stupid stuff. She's going to be okay. Paramedics got there quick and she's in good hands. Right, babe?"

"Yes. Absolutely." Tony's voice was steady and calm. "We don't know much at this point, but I'm going to stay right here. I'll have as much information as possible by the time you get here."

"Thank you. Tell her I'm on the way. And I love her."

Diane concentrated on the road, taking the curves at high speed. Sydney wished they could drive even faster.

"Jon blew her off for Christmas," Sydney said. "RayAnne was so upset. I thought she was in her room asleep. I had no idea she'd left."

"This isn't your fault, Sydney."

"I'd gone upstairs to check on her. When she didn't answer I just thought she was asleep. I didn't even look in on her. This is my fault. I should've checked."

Sydney dialed Jon's number. When it went straight to voice mail she wasn't surprised. She hadn't wanted to talk to him, either. "What's the hospital name, Diane?"

"West Carolina Regional."

"Jon. It's Sydney. There's been an accident. I'm headed to West Carolina Regional. It's RayAnne. I'll

give you a call back as soon as I have all of the details."
She ended the call and dropped her phone in her lap.
"How much longer?"

"We're almost there."

Sydney leaned her forehead against the cool window.
She felt sick to her stomach, and her body shook.
"RayAnne, please be okay."

They came to an intersection and the bright lights of
the hospital hung above the fog settling over the parking
lot. The eerie shadows looked menacing.

Diane pulled right up to the emergency room door
and let Sydney out. "Go ahead. I'll park and be right
there."

Sydney jumped out of the car before it was all the
way to a stop and ran inside.

She ran up to the woman at the desk. "I'm Sydney
Ragsdale. My daughter, RayAnne, was brought in by
ambulance."

A man took her by the arm in a surprise do-si-do.
"Hey, Sydney. It's me, Tony. Diane's husband."

The woman behind the desk didn't seem to be in a huge
hurry. "We're going to need you to fill out these papers,
please." The woman shoved a clipboard in her direction.

"I'm not filling anything out until you tell me how
my daughter is and let me see her."

"Someone will be out to see you in a moment. Meanwhile, if you can get that filled out for me."

Sydney snatched the clipboard from the woman and
held it to her chest.

Tony guided her to a seat near the ER doors. "They've
taken her to x-ray to check for broken bones. She's pretty
out of it. She wasn't wearing a helmet, and she was
pinned under the four-wheeler when we got there."

The double doors opened and a man in a Santa suit

walked in with a woman and a boy behind him. Seth. That was Seth. And Mac.

Anger rose inside her. "You said it would be fine—it would be safe. This is your fault. I don't even know if my daughter is going to be okay. How could you do this?"

"What do we know?" Mac asked.

Sydney stabbed a finger in the air in Mac's direction. "We know this would've never happened if we hadn't let her ride your four-wheeler in the first place."

Seth stepped behind his dad, and Sydney regretted screaming at him in front of his little boy.

"Oh my gosh. What have I done?" Sydney said, turning in a circle.

"You didn't do anything, Sydney," Mac said.

"My little girl is lying back there. I'm her mother. I'm supposed to keep her safe."

Tony excused himself to go get another update.

"Have you seen her yet?"

"No. I don't know anything except what Tony has told me."

"What can we do?" Mac reached for her arm, but she pulled away.

"You've really done enough, don't you think?"

"Sydney, I—"

"What happened? Tell me what happened. I didn't even know she was gone," Sydney said.

"Seth said she showed up at our house on her bicycle."

"That's a long ride." Sydney leaned forward with her elbows on her knees, covering her face with her hands. "I was right there in the house all night. I thought she was upset with her dad. She didn't respond when I knocked on her door. She was probably already gone."

"This isn't your fault." Mac said quietly.

She stared at the three of them. "I think you should leave."

"We want to be here for you."

"I don't need you. Diane and Tony are here with me."

Mac stepped back. "I really want to be here for you, Sydney."

Her heart was heavy and fear gripped her so tightly that it was hard to breathe. "I don't want you here. If I'd never met you this might never have happened. You knew how worried I was about her riding. How could you?" Sydney couldn't get the rest of the words that were flowing through her mind out in the single breath.

Seth spoke up. "But he didn't—"

Mac cut Seth off. "I understand," Mac said. "Will you make sure someone lets us know how she is?"

"I'm not going to sue you if that's what you're worried about." Sydney's hand shook, anger spiraling inside her like a tornado.

"Sydney, that is the last thing in the world that I'm worried about. I'm concerned about your daughter. About you. If you change your mind, please let me come help you through this."

"Why don't you just take your Santa suit and get out of here. You are not Santa. Not some wish granter. I'm not even sure what this whole Santa obsession is with you, but it's not good. It can't be. Look what you've done."

"I just wanted to help."

"Then go. You can't do anything good for me. Just go away."

Mac, Haley, and Seth walked back to the truck.

"That was a long ride to not even know if she's okay," Seth said.

"We need to let them have their space."

"Why didn't you tell her it wasn't your fault? That RayAnne showed up and rode off on the four-wheeler all on her own?"

"Because it doesn't really matter right now," Mac explained.

"She thinks you let RayAnne get hurt. That's really bad."

"It's okay, Seth. She'll know soon enough. Right now, she's worried, and I understand that. She loves RayAnne more than anything in the world. I'd feel the same way if it was you in there."

They rode back to the sound of Christmas carols playing softly on the radio. Seth was asleep by the time they got back home.

Mac pulled into the driveway and Haley got out of the truck.

Mac nudged Seth then got out, too.

"I'm so sorry about all of this, Mac." Haley looked downcast.

"Don't beat yourself up over it."

"I was being so careful, and something still happened. I'm not cut out to be a mother."

"You'll be a great mother. Things happen. We can't protect them from everything. They make decisions. Please don't beat yourself up. I don't blame you." He leaned inside the truck. "Seth. Wake up and go inside and get in bed."

Seth roused, slid out of the seat, and went inside without saying a word.

"I'm going to get out of this costume and get some sleep, too. I guess there's not much we're going to be able to do to help unless she decides she wants our help."

"I know. It feels awful." Haley started to walk away. "Call me as soon as you hear anything. I don't care what time it is."

"I will." He stood there out in the cold for a long time. He checked his phone a dozen times, but there were no calls. No updates.

No sense calling Diane and Tony's house. They were both still at the hospital. He went inside and looked up the number to Tony's garage. He texted the 24-hour service, knowing that the message would get to them.

> Mac: Mac here. Any updates on RayAnne?
> Tony: Broken ankle. Keeping her overnight.
> Mac: Thanks. Please keep me updated if anything changes.
> Tony: You got it.

Mac went inside and lay on the couch. He wanted to call Sydney. To text. To do something, but he also didn't want to add to the stress she was going through right now. He closed his eyes and fell asleep with his phone in his hand.

"Hey, kiddo." Sydney swept RayAnne's hair back from her bruised face. They'd finally moved RayAnne to a private room. "How do you feel?"

"Awful. I was so scared. I thought I died." A tear slipped down RayAnne's bruised cheek.

The thought made Sydney's throat catch. "You're going to be okay. I was scared, too." It was hard to talk without being choked by tears of relief. It was bad. Stitches, a cast, bruises that would be sore for a long time, a concussion, too. But it could have been so much worse. Diane had wanted to stay, but knowing the prognosis was good Sydney had insisted Diane go home to tend to her own family. Selfishly, she didn't want to share the attention to RayAnne with anyone right now.

"I'm sorry, Mom." RayAnne's words sounded thick coming from her bruised mouth and lips.

"Please don't ever scare me like that again."

"I didn't mean to. I'm sorry, Mom." RayAnne sniffled back tears. "I was so mad at Dad."

"I know, kiddo. I don't know why he keeps breaking his promises to you."

"Because he ... he doesn't love me anymore," RayAnne said between sniffling back tears.

"Of course he does." RayAnne sucked in a breath. Sydney found herself in a familiar spot, pleading his sorry case again. "He loves you with all his heart. He's just mixed up and being selfish."

"Mom, I need to call Seth. Can I use your phone?"

Sydney hesitated. "I don't think that's a good idea."

"Why?"

"Because it's the middle of the night, and look what happened when the two of you got together. He shouldn't have taken you out riding on that four-wheeler." Her words bit, although she was trying hard to not let her anger show. Last night could've ended in a real disaster, and Sydney knew that she would've never recovered from a blow like that. "Besides, you need your rest."

"I've been lying here for hours. I can call while I rest. I wrecked his ATV, Mom. Those things are expensive."

"That is not your problem. He should never have let you ride that thing. Especially without protective gear. What was he thinking?"

"Mom! He didn't—"

"RayAnne, you don't have to defend him. I'm just thankful you're going to be okay. You just relax and let's get you well."

"It's not Seth's fault. Mom, he told me we weren't allowed to ride because his dad wasn't home. I took off on his four-wheeler. Without permission. If he hadn't ridden out after me on my bicycle I'd probably still be out there."

"RayAnne?" Sydney tried to comprehend what that meant. "Why would you do that?"

She shrugged it off like a tough guy, then broke down sobbing. "Daddy's not going to love me anymore."

"That's not true, RayAnne."

"Daddy's having a baby with Ashley. He told me yesterday, and he's not coming to see me. He's going to love the new baby more." RayAnne started crying. "I wanted to run away."

Sydney crawled up in the bed with her. "That's not true. Well, they are going to have a baby, but your father loves you so much. I promise you. I get mad at him, too. Sometimes he acts like a fool, but it's not because he doesn't care. He does. He will love you forever. You will always be his first girl. I promise you that."

"I really messed up. Seth is going to hate me now."

"No he won't. They were really worried about you. They even came to the hospital."

"I'm tired."

"It's late. Close your eyes and sleep. I'll be close by."

"I love you, Mom." RayAnne looked so tiny in the bed with her bandaged head cradled in the stiff pillows and foot elevated. Her face and arms looked as if she'd been rolling in mud where the bruises were starting to turn color.

"I love you." She pressed a kiss into the palm of RayAnne's hand, afraid to touch her swollen face.

RayAnne closed her eyes, and no sooner did she fall asleep than the nurse came in to check on her.

Sydney took the opportunity to step out of the room and try Jon again. He still wasn't taking her calls, so she texted him the details in one big honking text.

His text back was short and sweet.

Jon: On my way. Tell Ray I love her.

Sydney stood near the door out of the way as the nurse checked all of the machines and added another dose of pain medicine to the IV.

"She'll probably sleep for a while. You should get some rest," the nurse said as she walked out. "I'll be checking on her."

"I can't leave her. I don't want her to wake up alone."

"I can bring you a pillow and blanket. That chair reclines like a bed. It's really comfortable."

Sydney appreciated the concern, but she was afraid to even close her eyes. "Thanks. I don't think I can sleep."

"I understand, but I'll bring you the pillow anyway. Tomorrow's going to be another long day. You need your rest so you can be strong for her, too." The nurse left without waiting for a response.

She was too tired to talk to Mac, but she also knew she owed him an apology. He must think she's crazy the way she leapt to conclusions . . . again.

That wasn't like her. Or maybe it was. Her life had been so wrapped up in Jon's world for the last ten years that she wasn't entirely sure who she was anymore.

She picked up her phone and brought up Mac's number. She started to text him, then backspaced and started over twice.

> **Sydney:** Sorry I wrongly accused you. Didn't mean to be unkind. RayAnne is going to be okay. Too tired to talk right now, but we should. Soon. I'm so sorry.
> **Mac:** No apology nec. We're all going to be okay.

She wasn't exactly sure what that meant, but she felt better for having sent the note. The nurse came back in with a pillow and a blanket. "Snuggle up under this warm blanket, and get some rest."

"Thank you." The blanket was thin, but it must have just come out of a warmer because it felt like a hug. She relaxed into its warmth, closing her eyes. Exhaustion took over where the adrenaline and worry had kept her moving the last several hours. "That does feel good." She curled up with her knees to her chest.

"You let me know if you need anything," the nurse said. "I'm here for you, too. The kids bounce back from these things way quicker than the parents."

"I believe that. Thank you." Sydney turned her head and watched RayAnne sleep. She was resting comfortably. What a blessing it hadn't been worse. She recited a silent prayer to God. *Thanks for protecting RayAnne, and for strength and awareness to see the right path for herself.* A wave of safe comfort flooded over her and she tuned herself into the sound of her own breaths. In. Out. Until she was dreaming of warm, sunny days filled with flowers and laughter.

A soothing voice echoed in her dream. Deep but melodic, she heard, "You're going to be okay."

Sydney opened her eyes, realizing the voices were not a dream. It was morning. The doctor had come in and was talking to RayAnne.

Sydney pushed the blanket back and got out of her chair. "I'm sorry. I didn't hear you come in."

"That's fine. I'm sure this has been quite a night for you both. I'm Dr. Kelly." He reached over and shook Sydney's hand.

"Your girl's pretty sore this morning," he said. "The swelling at the head wound seems to be under control, but I really want to watch her one more day."

RayAnne moaned her disapproval.

"That'll give us time to get physical therapy in here to help her learn to use the crutches, too." Dr. Kelly turned to RayAnne. "If all checks out in the morning, we'll get you home for Christmas Eve."

"Crutches will be cool," RayAnne said. "I bet everyone in school is going to want to sign my cast."

Sydney patted the bulky cast on her daughter's leg. "I have no idea what you'll be able to wear with that thing on."

"Oh, yeah. My jeans won't fit over this."

Dr. Kelly laughed. "I'll let you girls figure that out. I'll be back tomorrow morning to check on you."

"Thank you," RayAnne said.

He updated the electronic chart, then said, "No riding without a helmet ever again. Right, RayAnne?"

"Yes, sir," she said with a nod. "We have a promise."

"Good." He turned to Sydney. "She'll need to follow up with the orthopedic surgeon on her leg. He'll have some instructions for you on that. As for her head, the doctors there in Hopewell can take her stitches out. We work with them a lot."

"Okay. Thank you."

"Everything should heal fine. She's lucky it wasn't more serious."

Jon strode into the room with Ashley at his side. "Did I hear you say she'd be fine?"

"Yes." The doctor glanced at Sydney.

"I told you she'd be fine, Jon," Ashley said, pushing her hair back over her shoulder.

Jon put his hand up, as if he'd silenced her with the gesture plenty of times in the past.

"I'm RayAnne's father." Jon shoved his hand in Dr. Kelly's direction. "We were on our way to Paris when we got the call. So she's going to be okay?"

"With time she'll be one hundred percent."

"Thank you." The doctor left, and Jon turned and glared at Sydney. "Where were you when all of this happened?"

Sydney's gut twisted. "Let's concentrate on her getting well, Jon."

"I wouldn't have to concentrate on that if you'd been doing your job, and taking care of her. I'm sure as hell this wouldn't have happened on my watch."

"Dad. It wasn't her fault."

"Jon, don't do this. We don't need to upset her. It's almost Christmas and she's been through enough, don't you think?"

Jon leaned over and gave RayAnne a kiss on the cheek. "You okay?"

She nodded.

"What made you do something like that?"

RayAnne looked at Sydney, her eyes wide. "It wasn't Mom's fault."

"I think we need to talk," Jon said to Sydney.

Sydney was not about to get into it with him now. And she sure wasn't going to do it with his little girlfriend by his side. "I don't have a whole lot to say to you right now."

"Well I do," Jon said. "This is not how you take care of our daughter. Nothing like this ever happened back in Atlanta."

"Y'all don't fight," RayAnne said. "Dad, why are you messing everything up? We had a good life before, and now you don't love us." RayAnne took in a stuttered breath. "You didn't even want to see me."

"That's not how it was, RayAnne. You're blowing this out of proportion."

Sydney's heart was breaking for RayAnne. The last thing she wanted was to upset her further. She motioned to Jon and Ashley to follow her outside. And it was a good thing he fell right into step with her because she was about an eighteenth of an inch from snatching him by the hair and dragging him out. "What is your problem?"

"My problem?" He huffed and shoved his hands deep into his pockets. "Don't even get me started. Why on earth would you let our daughter ride on an ATV unsupervised and without a helmet? Are you completely crazy, or just completely incompetent?"

"Don't you dare go there." Sydney's jaw tightened.

"I'm sorry I signed those papers now. I'm really rethinking custody right now," he said.

"Excuse me?"

Ashley folded her arms across her chest.

Just having to look at her was enough to make Sydney want to smack her. Was all of this her doing? The continued letdowns? The custody? She knew it was up to Jon to make those final decisions. She couldn't blame it all on the other woman . . . even if it would make her feel a little better.

"Maybe RayAnne should come live with us after all," Jon said. "It's what she wanted all along anyway." Ashley nodded in agreement.

"You were dead set against that just a few months ago."

"Things have changed."

"So I've heard. And in case you're too dimwitted to put two and two together: your rain check and the news about your new baby are what sent RayAnne off on that dangerous little excursion. So don't talk to me about knowing how to raise a child. You were unkind and a coward. Get your priorities straight."

"I'm *sure*—" Ashley stepped forward, but Jon blocked her with his arm.

Jon looked visibly shaken. "I'm sorry. I didn't know that."

"Well, that's exactly what happened. After your bombshell that you weren't coming on Christmas, either, she locked herself in her room. She was totally devastated. Then she snuck out and went over to her friend's house. That's when all of this happened. You can't keep jerking RayAnne's emotions around."

"I have broken a lot of promises lately." He glanced over at Ashley. "That won't happen again."

"I really hope not." Sydney leaned back to look in the room. RayAnne was hugging her pillow. "Not only is it too much for her, but I'm really tired of trying to resolve all of these issues you are causing. I promised myself I wouldn't badmouth you, but you are making it very challenging."

"We've got to go," Ashley said, nudging Jon. "We can still make it on time if we leave now."

Jon scrubbed his hand across the scruffy whiskers on his chin. "We're going to miss that flight."

Ashley let out an unhappy huff, then went and sat in a chair across the way and started scrolling through her phone.

Sydney resisted the urge to comment. He'd chosen his path. She wasn't part of it, and she was starting to feel very good about that. She had better things to do.

"We're going to need to replace that four-wheeler," Sydney said. "She took it without permission."

"Why would she do something like that? That's not like her."

"She was upset. She was already sad about you cancelling plans. And then the new baby news made her think you didn't love her anymore. Like she was going to be replaced." Sydney glanced over at Ashley. "Kind of like I was. With no notice. On a holiday."

His jaw pulsed. But he didn't argue.

"Excuse me." She turned to see that Mac had walked up behind her. "Hi, Mac."

"Good morning. I don't want to interrupt. I just had to know how y'all were doing. I hope you don't mind."

"Not at all," Sydney said. "Thanks for coming."

"How is RayAnne this morning?"

"The doctor was just here. Things are going to be okay. They're going to keep her one more night just to be on the safe side." She could feel Jon's piercing eyes. "This is my ex-husband," she said. And boy, did that feel good and final. "Jon, this is Mac."

"Jon Ragsdale."

The surprise in Mac's face was pretty clear.

"Oh, you're RayAnne's father. Sweet little girl. She and my son have become good friends. Nice to meet you."

"Your four-wheeler, I'm guessing?" The words held an accusatory edge.

"My son's."

"I understand she took it without permission. I'll replace it."

Mac just nodded.

Jon looked like he was sizing Mac up, then looked at Sydney and said, "I'm going to go back in." Ashley scurried past them and raced to Jon's side, wrapping her arms around his bicep.

Jon looked annoyed, but he didn't say anything else as he went into RayAnne's room, closing the door behind him.

Sydney smiled at Mac. "I'm so sorry I lashed out at you."

"You okay?" Mac asked.

"Yes. Better than I've been in a long time." She glanced over her shoulder. "That's becoming old news."

He smiled. "I still owe you a picnic under the stars. You think they'll let her come home tomorrow?"

"The doctor said he expected she'd be fine to come home Christmas Eve. He wants to keep her the extra night to watch the head injury and get the physical therapist to help her work with the crutches a little. Probably a good thing. I'm going to have to figure out how to get her in and around the house. Those stairs aren't going to be crutch friendly."

Mac nodded, chewing on his lip. "You two should come and stay with us. You can use the bedrooms downstairs. You'll have plenty of privacy, and she'll be able to get around more easily as she's figuring out the crutches. Although you'll be shocked at how fast she'll get the hang of it."

"We couldn't impose."

"Why not? Please do. She and Seth will have fun."

"That's not necessary. I don't blame you, Mac.

RayAnne's accident was all of her own doing. Well, Jon motivated it, but please don't feel bad. She told me everything."

"I'm not making this offer because of guilt. I want to help. Selfishly, I'd enjoy having you in my home for the holidays, too. Come on. What do you say? It'll be so much easier with our help."

Sydney felt things shifting. It was a little dizzying, but in a good way. Her attitude. The walls she'd been holding up. The fear of being hurt again, all falling away.

It was almost like she'd been parked on a hill and someone just took off the emergency brake. The accident had shaken her in an unexpected way. It was Christmas and she wasn't going to be alone. She had her daughter, and new friends, and new opportunities lining up for her. A new world with bright possibilities.

"Let's just roll with it," he said.

And she wasn't really afraid . . . for once. "I think I can do that."

Ashley walked out of the room and right past them, moving down the hallway.

"That was interesting," Mac said.

"Did she look mad to you?"

"Not happy." He watched as Ashley got on the elevator. "Some people don't know how to be happy. That's not us though."

Jon walked out and stood between them. "RayAnne's pretty banged up. Sydney, I've made some mistakes."

And this day was just piled with surprises. An admission from Jon? She'd have put money on that never happening. "Yeah. Puts things in perspective, doesn't it?"

"It really does. I'm going to make all of this right. I'm really sorry I've been such a jerk."

Jon gave Sydney's shoulder a squeeze and shook Mac's hand. "I'll get a check over to you for the four-wheeler. Just have Sydney get the details over to me."

"Thank you."

"I'll call you later," Jon said. "Ashley was going to make some calls. I guess she went downstairs."

Mac shrugged as Jon walked away. "Y'all don't look like a pair."

"We were. Once upon a time we were a really good pair." For the first time in a while she was able to say that without feeling anger or disappointment.

"Sydney!" Diane called out from the opposite end of the hall. She rushed forward in rather a frantic pace, waving one arm above her head.

"I should have called her. I totally forgot." Sydney left Mac standing there as she hurried to meet Diane halfway down the hall. "I'm so sorry. I should've called to give you an update. She's going to be okay. You didn't have to drive all the way out here."

"Oh, I'm so glad to hear the good news. But that's not why I'm here." Diane looked past Sydney. "Hi, Mac." She lowered her gaze and whispered to Sydney, "Did he stay here all night with you?"

Sydney turned her back on Mac and nudged Diane. "No. He just got here, too. Never mind that." She looked over her shoulder then spoke so he could hear. "Why are you here then?"

"It's Bea. Someone found her collapsed in the book-store. Tony heard it on the scanner and called me. I went right over there. They just brought her in," Diane said.

"No. This can't be happening. Is she going to be okay? What kind of Christmas is this? Everything is going haywire."

"I know," Diane said. "It didn't look good. I thought

you'd want to know. But don't worry. Don't give up hope. If there's any time things can work out, it's Christmas."

"There's always hope at Christmas. I sure have been praying for a lot of it lately."

"I'm going to go back down and stay with Bea. She doesn't have any family, you know. I lied and told them I was her granddaughter. I don't think they really believed me, but they let me in."

"She needs someone with her."

"They were putting her on a ventilator when I left."

Sydney held her hand to her heart. "No. I'm so torn. I want to be with them both. Keep me posted. I have my phone. And tell me when I can come see her."

"I will." Diane turned and headed back to the elevators.

Sydney glanced into RayAnne's room. She looked to be resting comfortably. She stepped right into Mac's arms and let the tears go. "RayAnne. Now Bea is in the ER. What more could go wrong?" She regretted saying it as soon as the words left her mouth.

Mac wrapped his arms around her. "You're going to be okay," he said, resting his chin on the top of her head. "I'm here. We'll get through this."

She placed her hand against his chest. His heartbeat was steady and strong, and she felt safe there.

"I can wait here with RayAnne if you want to go down and check on Bea," Mac said.

"Would you mind?"

"Not at all. Haley is with Seth. I can stay as long as you need me."

"Thank you. Yes. I need to see Bea." Sydney leaned back. "Thank you for being here."

He kissed her on the forehead.

The kiss sent an unfamiliar feeling racing through her. She wasn't sure what to even make of it, but right now she needed to get to Bea. She could analyze her emotions later. She jogged down the hall and pressed the button on the elevator. She followed the signs to the emergency room. Diane wasn't in the waiting room.

Sydney walked over to the desk. "My aunt was brought in just a little bit ago. Bea Marion. Can I see her?"

The woman gave her a double-take, then typed on the computer, and then asked her to take a seat near the door. Sydney sat waiting.

A moment later a nurse came out. "Are you here to see Bea Marion?"

Sydney got up. "Yes. Can I see her?"

The nurse led her inside. Then stopped before going any further. "I'm sorry. She didn't make it. Her grand-daughter is back there with her. Would you like to join them?"

"Diane?"

"Yes," the nurse said.

Sydney blinked back tears.

The nurse pushed two tissues into her hand and guided her to a room at the end of the short hall. As soon as Sydney walked in, she and Diane both cried and clung to Bea's hand.

"This can't be happening," Sydney said. "Bea, you were helping me find my way again. I need you."

"You're going to be fine. I promise," Diane said to Sydney. "Hopewell will always be here for you."

Sydney's body felt too heavy to move. And all of the strength she'd mustered to get through the night with RayAnne just crumbled away. "She was such a big part of everyone's life in this town."

"She'd slowed down, but I don't think anyone expected that she'd . . ."

"I know. Did you get to talk to her?"

Diane shook her head. "No. I mean I told her we loved her and needed her, but she was out of it. And that was before I came up to tell you. She didn't respond. I don't know if she could hear a thing." Diane hugged Sydney, the two of them holding hands. "When I came down, she was gone. She looks very peaceful."

Sydney noticed the slightest grin on Bea's face. "Bea talked about going home to be with Henry again one day. I pray he came and held her hand all the way to those streets of gold."

"We'll have to figure out who might know what her final wishes were."

"She'd gone to see her attorney one morning this week before she came to the bookstore, so he must be here in town."

"That makes it easy. There are only two in Hopewell. One is the mayor."

"They seemed to be very close. I'd start with him," Sydney said. "I have a key to The Book Bea. I can look in the office to see if she had any documents on file there tomorrow when we get back."

Sydney wasn't even sure how much time had gone by when an older woman in a cheerful holiday cardigan walked in carrying a clipboard. "I'm so sorry."

"Thank you," Diane said.

Sydney lifted the wet wad of tissues to her eyes again. Fresh tears streamed down her face.

"Do you know who your family would like to handle the arrangements?"

Diane and Sydney looked at each other, then Diane said, "Cooper Funeral Home in Hopewell."

The woman scribbled it down on her clipboard. "I'll give them a call and get things scheduled for you, dear."

"Thank you," Diane said.

Sydney waited until the woman left. "How did you know that?"

"I didn't," Diane said.

"You can't just make a decision like that."

"It's the only funeral home in Hopewell. We'll figure out the rest later."

"Oh." There were more advantages to living in a small town every day.

Diane placed her hands on Sydney's shoulders. "Look, you have been through so much the last couple of weeks, and the last twenty-four hours has been a real doozy. I'll take care of the stuff down here. Go spend time with RayAnne. Call me if there's anything you need me to do before y'all come home."

"Call me before you leave," Sydney said.

"I will. I'm so glad you came back to Hopewell, Sydney."

"Me too." She walked down the hall and stopped in the chapel. She knelt and bowed her head. "Please let my little girl be okay. I'll do anything. Anything at all. Just let her be healthy and happy again. Please take care of the people I love." She then silently prayed for Bea, for RayAnne's speedy recovery, and for clarity about what path she should be following herself. She stood, then knelt one more time and prayed for Jon.

Feeling more at peace, she stopped in the bathroom and pressed a cold rag to her eyes, then went back to RayAnne's room.

Mac was sitting in the chair in RayAnne's room, watching television.

"Thanks," she said quietly.

He got up and nodded toward the door. As they got to the hall, he said, "She didn't even know you were gone. She slept the whole time. You're upset. Is everything okay?"

She shook her head and buried her face into his chest. His hand pressed the back of her neck, holding her tight. Letting her cry. No words. Just his arms around her.

"It's been a rough few days," he said.

"Bea." She pulled in a breath. "Mac, she didn't make it."

A crease formed between his eyes. "Wow. I didn't expect that."

"She's been so great. Making me feel so welcome in this town. Giving me purpose and building my confidence. I can't believe she's gone."

"She will not be forgotten. I can promise you that."

Sydney shook her hair back behind her shoulders. "I know. I should be so lucky to live to be the kind of person Bea was."

"You already are, Sydney. What can I do for you?"

"Nothing. You've already given me everything I need," Sydney said. "I feel stronger just for you being here, and giving me a safe place to land."

"I'm here for you." He pulled his keys out of his pocket. "I don't want to leave you."

"I'll be okay."

"I'll get my place ready for y'all to come stay. Can I pick up anything for Christmas Day from your house?"

"Oh gosh, I could probably do it when I get home tomorrow."

"Just let me help. There's going to be a lot to do with checking her out of the hospital and making the trip back."

"If you could go by Wheelies and get her bicycle that

would be great. It's the one in the window. He doesn't know I'm picking it up, though."

"I know Wes. We go way back. I can do that."

"And there's a bag of stuff in my front hall closet for the stockings. If you could pick up the stockings and that stuff. That's pretty much all I did."

"Perfect. Christmas isn't about the gifts and toys. It's about the fellowship. It's going to be a wonderful Christmas."

"You're right. I just want my girl home with me."

He leaned forward and kissed her on the mouth. Lips to lips. "This is good."

Chapter Twenty-one

The physical therapist had RayAnne standing and maneuvering with crutches in under fifteen minutes. The woman pushed RayAnne to sit, stand, walk, turn, lie down, and get up. Sydney fought the urge to intervene. Her daughter had just had surgery to pin her ankle back together. Her toes were so purple they were painful to look at, much less walk on. What was this woman thinking? Sydney finally walked out of the room to keep herself from telling the woman to ease up and give RayAnne a break.

After the physical therapist left, RayAnne was back asleep, only waking up when dinner arrived and when the nurses came in to check on her through the night.

In the morning Dr. Kelly showed up before eight o'clock to check on RayAnne and sign her release papers. "I hope you have a merry Christmas," Dr. Kelly said.

"Thanks, Doc," RayAnne said. "I can't wait to get back home."

Mac walked in just as RayAnne was trying to move from the bed to the chair in her crutches the way the physical therapist had shown her. "You're pretty good at that."

"Thanks, Mr. Mac," RayAnne said.

Mac handed a paper bag to Sydney. "I thought

RayAnne might need some clothes to change into so I brought her some sweats of Seth's. Figured you could slit the leg if you needed to for the cast. He's outgrown them anyway."

"Thank you. That was really thoughtful."

"RayAnne, do you want to change into these?"

"Yeah. Anything is better than this hospital gown. My clothes were ruined," she said.

"Hope you got some good rest last night, RayAnne. We're going to have a nice Christmas Eve celebration at the house tonight."

"Can we go, Mom?"

Sydney glanced over at Mac.

He cocked his head. "You didn't tell her?"

"I never said for sure yes."

"What?" RayAnne said.

"Mac invited us to stay at their place for a few days. We can use his downstairs bedrooms. That would give us a few days to get you used to the crutches and getting around before having to navigate the stairs at the farmhouse. I wasn't sure how you'd feel about that."

"Cool." She raised her hand in a Girl Scout salute. "And I promise not to do anything stupid. Thanks for forgiving me. You sure Seth isn't mad?"

"Positive. We talked about it again this morning. He thought it was a good idea, too."

"Awesome," RayAnne said.

Sydney laughed. "I guess I was worried for nothing."

"Apparently so." He turned his back to RayAnne. "You're not having second thoughts about me, are you?"

"No. I'm definitely not."

The nurse came in with the wheelchair and went through the final notes on at-home care with Sydney. Then Mac went to get the car, while RayAnne was taken downstairs. Sydney walked out of the hospital alongside her daughter under strength that she didn't even know she possessed. With a sense of purpose driving her, she stood to the side while Mac helped get RayAnne in his truck. Sydney slid into the passenger seat and buckled her seatbelt.

They took RayAnne home and got her settled in Mac's living room for the day. Haley and Seth were working on making food for their gathering later.

"You going to be okay here?" Sydney felt awkward leaving RayAnne behind. "I need to go to The Book Bea to check on a few things." She hadn't yet told RayAnne that Bea had passed away. It just didn't seem the kind of news to share with a little girl who'd gone through something so traumatic.

"I'm good."

"We won't be long, and Haley will hang out with y'all."

"Love you, Mom."

"Love you too, kiddo."

Mac drove her to The Book Bea. The door was locked, but all the lights were on.

She unlocked the door and they went inside. Books were scattered across the floor by the display table near the register.

Mac bent down and picked up the books, setting the stack on the table. "She must have collapsed here and tried to catch herself."

"We were just standing here together talking about this display the other day." Sydney mindlessly arranged the books on the table. "I don't know why I just did that. Oh, Bea. This town will not be the same without you, and this place." She checked the register and pulled the receipts for the day from the register. "I don't even know what to do with this money. I guess her lawyer will know."

"Just put it in the money bag. We can take it to the lawyer after Christmas. I'm sure they'll push the service out until after the holiday just so everyone can come. No one will want to miss the chance to pay their respects."

"Bea said this whole town was her family." Sydney wondered why everyone felt so much a part of Bea's life, when really no one was completely part of her life. "I can't wrap my head around her being gone."

Mac unplugged the Christmas lights. "I'll go ahead and unplug things since no one will be here. We wouldn't want anything to catch fire."

"Good idea. I'm going to go check the office for insurance papers, attorney names, or possibly a copy of her will. If Diane had already sorted that out she would have called, and she hasn't."

"Okay." He unplugged the coffee pot and worked his way around the room as Sydney walked to the back. The office was tiny, but well organized. She sat down in the upholstered wing back chair. The arms were worn thin from years of use. She pulled out the file drawer on the desk and flipped through the manila folders. She pulled three folders. One labeled INSURANCE. Another labeled CONFIDENTIAL, and the third labeled PERSONAL.

"Any luck?" Mac asked.

"Maybe. I'm going through some folders now."

Mac stood leaning in the doorway. He was so handsome. "I found this when I was unplugging the Christmas tree. It has your name on it."

"What is it?" Sydney took the envelope with gentle fingers. "I wonder who put it there?"

"Open it and see."

The envelope was taped across the back. She ran her

finger under the tape and pulled out a card. She immediately recognized it as one of the cards Bea sold on the spinning rack over by the coffee nook. On the front a woman read to a group of children. Inside was written in a shaky cursive:

> Sydney~
> Thank you for carrying on my legacy.
> You were the angel I've been waiting for.
>
> Bea

"That was sweet." Sydney held the card close. "I'm going to miss her so much. She's been a friend and a mentor. I really needed that right now."

Mac flipped through papers in the folder. "She's good people." He lifted a stack of papers from the file. "It looks like the mayor was her attorney. His name is on several of these documents. I don't see a copy of a will in the personal documents, but maybe he knows what Bea's final wishes were."

"We should stop over and talk with him." Weary and fragile, she wished she could turn back the clock and have more time. She and RayAnne had just begun to find peace and happiness here in Hopewell. Bea was a big part of that. Another month with Bea and who knows how life would feel here.

"I doubt he'll be in the office on Christmas Eve. Anything else you need to do here?"

"I feel like I want to straighten up and keep this place going. But I know it's not my place to do that. Without her here I feel a little like I'm trespassing. Even though I have a key. Does that make sense?"

"I get it." He wrapped his arms around her. "I think you're right where you're supposed to be," he said softly.

"You two had a very special connection. I saw it the first day I met you here."

"Yeah. It was like we'd known each other forever. She was such a big part of me falling in love with books when I was a kid. That impacted my whole life. I have a feeling she touched a lot of lives over the years."

"I wonder what will happen to this place?"

"I don't know." She leaned against his arm, hugging his bicep. "I hate to even think about it."

"Maybe there's something we can do."

"Like what?"

He took in a deep breath, then picked her up and spun her around. She let out a shriek and then started laughing. "What are you doing? Put me down."

He spun her around one more time and then set her down, but his hands traced the outside of her arms, leaving a trail of tingles. Then his hands rested on her face, his thumbs at her mouth, and slowly pushing her hair back, he lowered his mouth to hers.

The kiss was tender, but with purpose. His heart raced against her own. With each breath he took, he drew her deeper into his hold, his heart. She'd never felt a kiss with such intimate power.

"Sydney, I want you to know that after Genna I thought there was no way I'd care about anyone again, and it's been a long time. Years. I haven't looked. I haven't yearned for it, but that day I saw you here, behind that counter, you did something to me. You touched something deep inside of me that I don't think anyone ever could."

"Mac?"

"Don't. Please. Let me finish."

She looked into his eyes. Wanting to tell him she felt something too, but patiently she listened.

"I know you're just getting through your divorce. I can't begin to imagine how hard what you're going through has been. I don't want you to think I'm taking it lightly, but I want you to give me a chance. Us a chance. Me and Seth. We're a package deal."

"Like me. And RayAnne. But Mac, I can't make any promises."

"I know. I'll respect your space while you're staying with me. I promise. I'll be a perfect gentleman, but do you feel it? A little?"

She did. But was it just her being hurt and wanting to be loved? Was it real? She couldn't make a mistake. "I'd be lying if I said I don't feel anything. But Mac, I'm not sure what it is."

"Me neither. I just know I want to explore it, and I didn't want to risk not telling you how I felt." He took her hand in his. "Let's take it a day at a time. I have a feeling we will have spent months and years before we take the time to stop and count them."

Her heart felt light, joyous. Was it Christmas hope making her feel this way? She rubbed her thumb on the outside of his hand. "A day at a time."

"Come on. Let's get home and celebrate our first Christmas together."

"I'm not sure this qualifies as our first Christmas."

"Why not? It's Christmas. And we're together."

"Usually that means you've spent a year together."

"Says who?"

She really couldn't answer that. "Fine. Our first Christmas."

She locked up The Book Bea with tears in her eyes. Her phone rang, and she dropped the keys trying to dig for her phone in her purse.

Mac picked them up.

"Hello? Everything okay?"

"Sydney, it's Diane."

"Sorry. Hi, I thought it might by RayAnne. I left her at Mac's."

"At Mac's, huh?" Diane's voice had that little singy-song rise and fall to it that reminded Sydney that there wasn't much in a small town that didn't get around.

"We're just staying there through the holidays until RayAnne gets the crutches down. We thought the stairs might be a bit much on day one."

"For sure."

"It was really nice of him to offer."

"I didn't say it wasn't."

Sydney looked up at Mac, who was smiling down at her. He seemed to be enjoying her discomfort, and he dropped a kiss on the back of her neck as she talked to Diane. She squirmed away from him and went down the steps.

He was beside her before she got to the bottom.

"I wanted to drop over a little something for y'all to-night. Can I stop by Mac's?"

Sydney put her hand over her phone. "Diane wants to stop by. Do you mind if she comes by your house?"

"Mi casa es su casa." Mac took the phone. "Hey, Diane. Come over whenever you like. We've got all kinds of food and goodies. My neighbors and a few friends are coming over, too. Bring the kids and Tony if you like." He handed her the phone.

"Isn't that just adorable," Diane said.

"Stop it," Sydney whispered.

"Oh, quit your worrying. Coach Mac is one of the nic-est men in town."

And Bea's description had been darn near the same. She'd been nudging them together.

"Anyway," Diane said. "I spoke with the mayor. He's at his son's house in Virginia, but he'll be back tomorrow night. He said he has Bea's latest will. She just made some updates this past week. I gave him your number. He said he'd contact you to discuss the details. Probably has something to do with shutting down the store and all since you were her only employee."

"Right. Yeah. Thank you."

"He's going to contact the funeral home too with the details they need," Diane said.

"So everything is being taken care of. That's good." Sydney followed Mac and let him open the door for her. He gave her a hand into his truck, then walked around and got in. "I wish there was something I could do."

"I'm sure there'll be something for all of us to do," Diane said. "The mayor said it could all wait until after Christmas. They'll be making an announcement in the paper and everything."

"That's good."

"I'll see y'all in a little while," Diane said. "I'll bring Jenny. She's been driving me crazy to see RayAnne. We'll keep the visit short."

"That's fine. Thanks for everything, Diane." She laid the phone in her lap. "I think I've made better friendships in this town in just a few weeks than I did my whole marriage in Atlanta."

"Hopewell has a certain kind of magic, doesn't it?"

It certainly had something, and whatever it was, she couldn't imagine ever leaving it behind.

When Mac pulled into the driveway at his house, the lights on the tree were already shining through the window, and Sydney could hear Christmas music all the way out to the driveway. "Is that singing?"

"Sounds like it to me."

He opened the door and let her walk in first. RayAnne was in the easy chair with her leg propped up on pillows on an ottoman. She was stringing popcorn, and Seth was draping lengths of the strands onto the tree. Haley walked into the room with another bowl of popcorn. "Hey, y'all weren't gone long. We thought we'd have this done by the time you got back."

Seth draped the five-foot-long strand of popcorn on the tree, then walked over and high-fived RayAnne. "We might've been done if we didn't eat more popcorn than we strung."

"You're the one eating it all." RayAnne tossed a piece of popcorn in the air and Seth ducked and moved under it, catching it in his mouth. "He's pretty good at that."

Seth pointed to about twenty pieces behind RayAnne's chair. "She's not so good at it."

"No fair. I can't move. I'd totally kick your butt if I was mobile."

"Says who?"

"Says me," she said. "Rematch as soon as I'm back on my feet."

"You're on."

"Smells good in here," Sydney said.

"That's my chili. It gets better the longer it cooks," Mac said. "And I cook one mean cornbread to go with it, too."

"And here I thought ham and turkey were Christmas foods," Sydney teased.

"We'll have ham tomorrow. But Christmas Eve is all about keeping things simple around here," Mac said.

Sydney put her purse on the table and sat on the couch. "That sounds perfect to me."

Diane showed up with Jenny at a little after seven.

Hayley's parents had come over, and all of them shared stories in the kitchen while the kids played a game in the living room.

The playful banter was soothing to hear, and Sydney felt blessed to be there, even if the circumstances that brought them to Mac's had been less than positive.

By nine o'clock, everyone had had their fill of chili and an assortment of cookies and treats Haley's mom had made for the annual tradition.

Diane and Jenny left, and Mac walked his neighbors back over to their house.

Sydney cleaned up the dishes while he was gone, then came back into the living room with a bright red kitchen towel with the word JOY appliqued on it draped over her shoulder. "RayAnne, I think it's time we tried to get you situated in bed for the night."

Mac walked into the room. "Oh, not yet. We have one more thing to do tonight."

"That's right," Seth echoed.

"What's that?" Sydney and RayAnne asked.

It had already been a pretty long day, and Sydney knew if she was tired, RayAnne had to be exhausted, even if it was Christmas Eve.

Mac had hung their stockings on the mantle alongside his and Seth's, and the tree was the biggest one she'd ever seen inside a house, although there were no gifts under it. A big change from Christmases back in Atlanta, where their tree would have so many gifts stacked under it that the bottom branches would be lifted by the height of the boxes.

"You stay right there." Mac dodged around the corner and up the stairs. A moment later he came downstairs with four boxes wrapped in different holiday-patterned paper.

"What's all this?" Sydney had a sinking feeling. She hadn't bought him anything.

"Tradition," he said.

Seth said, "My grandparents used to do this with us every year. Dad is carrying on the tradition. I already know what it is."

Mac gave him the evil eye. "Don't spoil the surprise."

Seth zipped his lip, and then accepted a big box wrapped in shiny red foil with reindeer on it. Mac handed RayAnne a purple glossy package with lime-green, hot pink, and turquoise bells on the paper, and a huge silver bow on top. Mac set a solid red package down in his recliner and then handed Sydney a sapphire-blue box with a shiny gold ribbon. "I thought the paper matched your eyes, and the ribbon matches the little gold flecks in them."

Had Jon ever, in all their years of marriage, mentioned the color of her eyes? "Thank you."

He sat down and they all began to unwrap their gifts. RayAnne was the first to get to the contents. "Pajamas. Mom, look. The coolest camo pajamas ever. And it's shorts so I can get it over my cast."

"That was really thoughtful, Mac. Thank you," Sydney said.

Mac nodded toward her box. "Open yours."

She pulled out a pair of cotton pajamas, so soft they slipped through her fingers. The pajama set was feminine but totally acceptable for wearing in mixed company. Nothing embarrassing or flimsy.

Seth opened a pair of camo pajamas, and Mac opened his box. A pair of pajamas that looked more like sweat pants and a T-shirt, but the good news was they'd all be comfortable in their new pajamas to celebrate Christmas in the morning.

"Thank you, Mr. Mac," RayAnne said. "I love them."

"You're welcome."

Seth got up and crossed the room and gave his dad a hug. "Love you, Dad. I'm going to bed."

"Good night, son."

Seth gave RayAnne a high-five as he walked past. "Night, Mrs. Ragsdale."

"Good night, Seth." She got up and put her hands on her hips. "Okay, shall we get you into bed, RayAnne?"

"Yes, ma'am. I think I can do it myself."

Sydney handed RayAnne her crutches.

RayAnne shifted to the edge of the seat. After a couple of attempts to rock herself up, Mac reached down and lifted her from under the arms. "There you go. If you take too long, Santa might see you awake and skip our house completely."

RayAnne was able to get her crutches under her arms and get back to her room with little problem. "Getting up is kind of hard. But I'll get better at it."

"You'll have to," Sydney said. "Because I don't think Mac and I can follow you around school every day."

Sydney helped RayAnne change into her new pajamas and then tucked her in bed. "I love you."

"I love you, too, Mom. Thanks for not being mad at me. I'm so sorry I messed things up."

"We're going to get through this just fine."

"It feels more like Christmas with a bunch of people around. This is a happy place."

Sydney crawled into bed next to RayAnne. "It is a happy place. This house. This town. The people. I think I could make a life here."

"Me too. I like it here. It's different than back home."

"Do you think it's just Christmas making it seem good?"

"No." RayAnne tapped her fingers against her cast in a little jingle bells rhythm. "I think it's just like everybody is family. I liked the Santa here, too. I think he's delivering what I asked for."

Sydney felt her heart drop.

"Well, not the four-wheeler. I think I'm kind of okay without one of those for now. Maybe forever. Besides I'm pretty sure I'm on the naughty list for this year."

"I couldn't take another accident like that. I was so afraid."

"Mom?"

"Yes, RayAnne."

"Daddy asked me if I want to come live with him."

Sydney's whole body tensed. She braced herself, pasting a smile on her face to hide the devastation rising from her gut. She took RayAnne's hand, and reminded herself of the promise she'd made in the chapel.

"That's what you had wanted," Sydney could barely get the words out.

"He looked really sad when I told him that I didn't want to live with him and Ashley."

"You?" She'd said no. "You told him that?"

"I wanted to live with him, because then I thought you would come too. Dad would have to see that he wanted us to all be together again. But he didn't, and I don't want to be a family without you, Mom."

"Me neither."

"And I like being here. We're a good team. I'm sorry I almost messed up our Christmas."

Sydney needed to tell RayAnne about Bea, but Christmas Eve was just not the time. "You are the best thing about this family, RayAnne. I love you so much. You being okay is the best Christmas gift you could ever give me."

"I know there's another guest room here for you," RayAnne said. "But do you think you could sleep in here tonight?"

"I'd love nothing more than having a slumber party with you tonight, kiddo."

Chapter Twenty-two

The next morning Sydney woke to nonstop chatter in the living room. She rolled over and looked at the clock. She hadn't slept this well since they'd moved to Hopewell. A big part of that was probably the temperature. There wasn't a single draft or chill in this big log home. And there wasn't one space heater situated anywhere in the whole house that she'd seen.

It was just after six in the morning. What was it about Christmas that catapulted even the biggest sleepyheads out of bed before sunrise?

She hadn't even heard RayAnne get up.

She caught a whiff of coffee. That was enough to get her out of bed. She padded out to the living room. RayAnne was in the chair propped with pillows. Her crutches leaned against the side of it where she could reach them. She and Seth were both going through their stockings and comparing the trinkets and candies they'd received.

"I love my bike! Did you see it? I can't believe Santa thought of something so super cool. It's the prettiest bike ever. And when my leg is better Seth is going to teach me to do a wheelie on it."

The last thing she wanted was for RayAnne to be

doing wheelies or jumping over stuff, but that was her kid. A daredevil from day one. She'd love to be able to blame Jon for her little tomboy, but the truth was RayAnne really did love that stuff. RayAnne was a thrill seeker, and Sydney was just going to have to deal with that.

"And Seth got an electric skateboard thing." RayAnne stuck her tongue out at him. "It stinks you're going to be able to practice so long without me. You're going to be amazing at it before I even get to try it out."

"Thought I heard a new voice in here." Mac carried two mugs of coffee in with him. "One for you."

"Merry Christmas, and thank you." She took the mug from him. "Careful, I could get used to this special treatment."

He chuckled then walked over to the hearth and picked up her stocking and tossed it to her.

"What have you done now?"

Mac raised his hands in an exaggerated shrug. "Don't look at me. Santa filled these."

He and Seth exchanged a knowing glance.

Sydney dug into the stocking, and Mac sat down in front of the Christmas tree and dumped his out on the floor.

Seth dove to the floor next to him. "Awesome. We got planes too! We totally need to race them!"

"I already put mine together," RayAnne said.

"I think she's trying to challenge us, son." Mac glared toward Sydney. "I think this is totally boys against the girls."

"Oh you are so on," Sydney said as she started ripping the wrapper from the balsa wood glider that was in her stocking.

"We'll take this championship out to the driveway,"

he said. "Right after breakfast. Which is ready. Let's eat first."

"You made breakfast too?"

Seth jumped up. "Dad makes the best breakfast casserole. It's tradition. He makes it every year."

"You're just full of surprises. And traditions," Sydney whispered as she got up to help RayAnne.

"Stay tuned." And when he placed his hand on the small of her back, Sydney felt as if she'd somehow stepped through a magic portal that had landed her in the middle of a Christmas scene in a snow globe.

I think I will, she silently replied.

She reached over and grabbed RayAnne's crutches, then extended a hand to help her daughter to her feet. RayAnne hopped and bobbled then tucked the crutches under her arms.

"You got it?"

RayAnne bobbed her head. "I'm good."

Sydney watched as her daughter moved through the living room with a click-step-click-step. When she got to the table she set the crutches against the wall and then slumped. "The worst part is the sitting and the standing."

"You'll get better at it," Seth said.

They ate breakfast from paper plates decorated with Santa faces on them.

"That was really tasty," Sydney said. "You're going to have to share the recipe."

"Why do you keep acting surprised when I do things?" Mac asked. "You're starting to give me a complex."

She laughed easily. "Somehow I doubt that."

Seth got up and gathered the plates. "I'll clean up."

"Thanks, Seth," Mac said.

He dropped the plates into the trashcan, then handed

RayAnne her crutches. "We'll meet y'all on the driveway."

"It's freezing outside," Sydney said.

"We have coats, Mom."

"Yeah, Mom. Don't be such a girl," Mac teased.

Seth gave RayAnne a hand up and they raced, as much as RayAnne could, to the door.

"No fair practicing," Mac called out.

"Competitive much?" Sydney teased.

"Oh, you just wait and see."

"It ain't over yet, mister. You might want to be careful just how many words you might have to eat."

"A challenge. I like that." He grabbed her hand and squeezed it. "I'm really glad you're here."

"Me too." Her phone rang from the other room. She raced over to get it, glancing at the number before she answered. "It's Jon," she said to Mac. "He must want to wish RayAnne Merry Christmas." She pressed the button and answered with a hearty "Merry Christmas."

"You're in a good mood this morning." He sounded less than enthusiastic.

"It is Christmas morning, Jon. Don't be a scrooge."

"Where are you?" His words were short and snippy, like she'd become accustomed to over the past year. For someone getting his way he did always seem to be in a mood about things.

"What do you mean where am I?"

"It's a pretty straightforward question. I mean I'm here at the house and you and RayAnne are not. It's Christmas morning. Where the hell are you?"

"I thought you weren't coming to see RayAnne. Don't you have a date in Paris or something?"

"Change of plans. I wanted to surprise her."

"You will. She sure didn't expect to see you. You should have let me know."

"Maybe I wanted to surprise you, too."

His attitude aggravated her, but she knew RayAnne would want to see him so she tried to swallow her opinion and be polite. It was Christmas after all. "The stairs at the farmhouse were going to present a challenge until RayAnne gets some practice on her crutches. We're staying with friends."

"What's the address?"

Panic rushed through her. Her divorce was final, so why did she feel so guilty? "Sure. You can come by."

She shrugged and gave Mac an I'm-sorry look.

He smiled and shook his head.

He didn't mind. That made her feel a little better. She gave him Mac's address.

"How far away is it?" he asked.

"About a mile as the crow flies," Sydney said with a smile.

"Whatever that means. I'll put it in my GPS." Jon ended the call without a goodbye. That was one of those little things that had started irritating her like crazy once they'd split up. Funny how things that didn't bother you at all while things were good could turn into high-blood-pressure moments once things went south.

She put her phone back into her purse. "Jon decided to surprise RayAnne."

"That's a good step."

It was, and she should be thankful that he'd come through. But then why did she feel so bothered by his call today?

Mac went to the hall closet and got out two heavy coats. "Here, you can wear this one." He held it up and she slipped into it.

She stood there, swallowed up by the coat. "If I didn't know better I might think you're just trying to handicap me to be sure you have an edge to win." She raised her arms, but her hands didn't even peek to the end of the sleeve.

"Oh, you think you even have a chance?"

"For sure!"

He put on his coat. "Well, then I guess RayAnne must be really good."

"Are you insinuating I can't hold up my end of the team?"

"Well, you know."

"I'll have you know that I'm quite talented at a lot of things. And competitive. You better brace yourself."

Instead he braced his hand against the wall, blocking her from the door, then scooped her close with the other arm. "I know a few things you're good at."

He kissed her slowly and thoughtfully. "You look good in this place. This is a really good Christmas."

She kissed him, then playfully nipped his lip. "Don't distract me."

She pushed past him and stepped outside. The cold air immediately stung her eyes. "Y'all are crazy to want to be out here."

Before she got down the sidewalk, a black sedan pulled into the driveway. Jon must have flown up from Atlanta and rented a car, because there was no way he'd be seen driving a car like that any other time.

RayAnne seemed unaware until Jon stepped out of the car. "Daddy!" She hopped and bobbled then crutched toward him.

"Hey, baby girl!" He stopped and opened the back door and took a large box out of the back. "Brought you a present."

At least it wasn't a four-wheeler.

"Thank you, Daddy!"

Sydney stayed put. No need to walk over and chat with Jon. He was here for RayAnne, and somehow she felt like, for once, she didn't need to make an effort. She stood there, an observer, watching as Jon and RayAnne talked and RayAnne proudly introduced Seth as her new best friend.

Jon carried the box up the driveway with a forced smile—that fake toothy one he used when he was at business social events. She'd know that look anywhere.

"Hi, Mac," Jon said. "Didn't expect to see you again so soon. Mind if RayAnne and I go inside?"

"Not at all."

"Thank you." He settled his gaze on Sydney. "Join us."

She glanced up at Mac.

"Go on in," Mac said. "Seth and I will set up the measuring lines for the big airplane race."

"You sure?"

"Positive." He and Seth headed to the driveway, and she walked inside behind Jon. She shed her coat near the front door, and they settled into the living room.

RayAnne handed Sydney her crutches and sat down. She ripped into the paper of the big box. "No way! This is the newest gaming system out there! Hardly anyone can even get these yet."

"I have connections."

Of course he did. He always was quick to name drop. A peacock always strutting his stuff. There was a time when she'd practically swoon with pride over him. Now it just made her tired.

"You're the best. Seth and I are going to have so much fun with this. And I can do this with a broken leg."

Sydney shrank. The bike was almost a cruel joke, but it had been purchased long before the accident. *It's not a competition,* she reminded herself.

"That was a really thoughtful gift, Jon."

He looked around the room. "So you two are staying here?"

"Just until RayAnne gets on her feet. It was really nice of them to offer."

"Plus I won't be as bored here with Seth," RayAnne said.

"You could always come back to the house if you need to." Jon's eyes clung to hers. Her heart hitched. What was he saying?

Her mouth hung open slightly, then went dry. For months she'd hoped for this. Wanted, prayed, even wished for it.

RayAnne looked at her, then back at her dad.

Sydney would give a million dollars to know what was going through RayAnne's head right then. But maybe not knowing was better.

Sydney stood. "Why don't I go get Seth so he can see your new gaming system?"

"Thanks, Mom. I bet he knows how to hook it up. It's going to be a blast."

Jon reached into his pocket. "I almost forgot. Here's a gift card to order games online. I wasn't sure which ones you'd like to play."

"Thanks!"

"And Sydney," Jon said, "I'm serious. We can go home now. Find out what I owe Mac. I'll pay him while we're here."

Sydney had already turned to go to the door. The last words, "while we're here," hung in the air like a bad smell. Did he really think he could just waltz in and suggest they come home and they would run adoringly to his side?

No. Things had changed.

She had changed.

There was no going back to Jon.

She hoped RayAnne wouldn't be distraught, but she had to do what she knew was right for her. For once. And maybe the bookstore wasn't going to be a part of it, but Bea's strength and independence were qualities she planned to embrace in Bea's honor in everything she did going forward. And being happy was going to be at the top of her list.

Bea's advice echoed in her mind. *The happier you are with yourself, the happier your daughter will be. Be the example of a strong, independent woman without ever saying a word.*

Sydney stepped outside feeling strong and oddly in control. She cupped her hands to her mouth and yelled, "Hey, Seth. RayAnne wants to show you her present. Can you come inside?"

Seth handed Mac his airplane and ran past her. "What'd she get?"

"You'll have to see for yourself."

He flung through the door. Sydney could hear his reaction all the way outside.

"From the sounds of Seth's *yeeha*, I'd say it was a good gift." Mac walked over to her. "Aren't you freezing?"

"A little. Come in with me. This is your house."

"I wanted to give you some time as a family."

"Don't be silly." She tugged on his hand. "Come on. He's not my family anymore."

They walked inside and went to the kitchen. "Coffee?" she asked.

"Yeah, that would be good."

RayAnne and Seth were already taking components out of the box and comparing details about the new system that they'd seen online or heard about at school. "This is the coolest game ever."

When Mac and Sydney walked back into the room, Seth held one of the controllers, making exploding ammo sounds as he pretended to blow up stuff.

"Want to hook it up?" Seth asked.

"Totally," RayAnne said.

Jon straightened. "Or you could just wait and hook it up when we get back to Atlanta."

RayAnne looked confused.

Seth said, "You're leaving?"

Mac's eyebrow shot up, but he didn't look her way. Sydney cleared her voice. "No. Seth. We're not leaving."

"Well, you don't have to come today," Jon said.

"RayAnne can certainly visit, but I don't think it's a particularly good idea for her to do that until we get past the next few doctor's visits."

"We have the best doctors in the country in Atlanta, Syd. You know that. And Ray, you know we'll find something to do back home. Your old room is ready and waiting for you."

"Jon, can I speak with you?" Sydney wasn't even exactly sure what she was going to say, but whatever the conversation, it did not need to take place in front of their daughter. "Outside?"

Mac crossed his arms, and then backed into the kitchen.

"Sure."

There was that toothy grin again. Sydney marched outside, grabbing Mac's coat on the way.

"I'm sorry, babe," Jon said. "I'm sure this caught you

off guard. Merry Christmas." He dug into his coat pocket and took out a small box. "Here. I made some mistakes."

She didn't take the box. Jon had always thought he could gift away problems. "Some mistakes?"

"RayAnne made me realize that. When I was talking to her in the hospital, it just became really clear."

"Clear that you couldn't have your cake and eat it too? Or that I wouldn't know you were eating cake elsewhere if I came back to you?"

"Sydney. I wouldn't do that. Come on. We can be a family again. I'm sorry."

"Really? Seems you're getting to be a pro at abandoning families." She cocked her head, but what she'd like to have done was cold-cock him right on the jaw. "Don't do this. I'm not interested. The divorce is final. And finally, I'm actually over you. Go back to Ashley and don't make the same mistakes with your new child."

"Don't throw that in my face." Jon's mouth twisted. "Wait. What? Are you sleeping with the tall, sporty guy?"

"As if it was any of your business, but no. We are not sleeping together."

"He's probably just being nice to you to keep us from suing him over the four-wheeler incident," Jon said.

"I can't believe you just said that. Belittling me is not a way to get points. Do you think so little of me that no one could possibly be interested in me?"

"I didn't say that. Don't twist my words. We were good once."

"You're right. We were. You broke that trust. It can't be fixed. No matter how much you spend or how much jewelry you throw at me."

"Open it," he said. "You'll like it."

She raised her hand. "Stop. We were great once, and

you broke that. There's no going back. I'm staying here in Hopewell. Forever. If you'd like to have RayAnne spend time with you once we get over these hurdles, fine. But I won't take her out of school to do it. We have a custody agreement, and we are divorced."

"That is just paper. You know you still love me."

"No. What I know is that I am completely capable of taking care of myself. And I plan to. I am not in love with you. You made this situation. Deal with it. And do not make me part of your future plans. Because that will never happen."

He looked at his shoes. Then back at her. No toothy grin this time. "You're just going to live in that old farm house? You could come back to what we had."

"I'm fine in that old farmhouse."

"Or live here like some Davey Crockett wife?"

"That is none of your concern."

"It's my concern if my daughter is living here."

"Well, we'll just cross that bridge if we ever come to it. As of now, Mac is my friend, and he's been here when I needed him. Do you want to say goodbye to RayAnne before you leave?"

He paused. Then turned and walked to the car.

She should've known he'd take the easy way. And yes, again, she'd be explaining his bad behavior to their daughter.

Sydney stood there in the cold. Puffs of vapor rising in front of her as the cold stung her cheeks. She watched Jon drive away. Mac opened the door.

"What just happened?"

She walked up to him. "He's predictable. He doesn't get his way and he runs. I know RayAnne is going to be upset. I can't believe he said all of that in front of her."

"He was trying to push your hand."

"His style."

"RayAnne is okay," Mac said. "She said as much to Seth when y'all walked out."

"She did?"

"Yes, she did." He nodded. "So you really don't have feelings for him anymore?"

"No. I definitely do not. She slipped her hands underneath his coat. His warmth comforted her. "I think I'm falling in love with a competitive sporty guy with a flair for surprises."

"Moi?"

"Definitely you."

"Does this mean the airplane race is back on?"

"You better believe it."

Chapter Twenty-three

Despite the freezing temperatures, Sydney and RayAnne were determined to outlast Mac and Seth in the Christmas morning balsawood airplane fly-off. During the first two flights, the four of them laughed so hard that they had as good a workout as if RayAnne had been in bicycle shape.

The four of them stood side by side at the line Mac had scraped across the driveway with a tree limb.

"One. Two. Three," RayAnne counted off, and all four of them let their planes sail.

Seth's plane was a clear winner, landing almost in the street.

Three more times ended with the same results.

"The Christmas Day champion!" Seth ran to retrieve his plane, then ran in a circle with his airplane held over his head. "I can't be beat."

"And just as humble as his dad, I see," Sydney teased. "Come on, RayAnne. We're the losers. It's our duty to make the hot chocolate."

"With marshmallows," Mac reminded her.

"We've got this. No gloating necessary." She and RayAnne went inside. Sydney's cheeks stung when they walked inside the warm house. She found a box of instant hot chocolate, but just behind it was a can of cocoa powder. She pulled it out of the cabinet. "Look what I found!"

RayAnne's face lit up. "Oh goody! I bet they've never had really good hot cocoa. They're going to die when they taste yours."

"Let's keep them alive. They are kind of fun to hang around with."

"They are." RayAnne crutched over to the refrigerator and got out the milk.

Sydney grabbed the canister of sugar and vanilla, then put a pan on the stove and started mixing ingredients. "RayAnne, do you want to talk about what your dad had to say earlier?"

"No. Not really."

"You know I would never stand in the way of you spending time with him."

"I know, Mom."

Her heart tightened at just the thought of it. "If you wanted to live with him in Atlanta, I'd leave that decision up to you."

"I want to be here with you. I think he was just saying that because I told him he messed everything up when I was in the hospital. He looked really sad when I said that."

"I'm sure he was sad. He loves you."

"I like our life here. It's different. And cool. We're happy here, right?"

"We are. Except for the part where you crashed and ended up in the hospital." Sydney gave RayAnne a squeeze and stirred the cocoa. "I love you."

"Hey, Mom," RayAnne said, her voice softer. "Seth told me Miss Bea died."

Sydney stopped stirring. "I'm sorry. I was trying to

find the right time to tell you. It happened while you were in the hospital."

"That's really sad. She was nice. I'm going to really miss her."

"I know. Kind of breaks my heart." Sydney swept a hand under her nose to stop that tickle that meant she was getting ready to cry.

"Are you going to run The Book Bea for her?"

"Oh, RayAnne, it doesn't work like that. I'm sure she's made arrangements for her estate. She'd been talking about selling."

"We should've bought The Book Bea. Then when I grew up I could work there."

Sydney had been wishing for that herself. "That would have been my dream job when I was your age, too. But for now it's Christmas, and we're here. And this is pretty good. Let's focus on today."

RayAnne nodded. "I'm glad we're spending Christmas here."

"Me too." Sydney hadn't had this much fun in a long time. They were all so relaxed around each other, like they'd been lifelong friends.

The doorbell rang.

"I think we might have to make a double batch of cocoa, Mom."

"You might be right. Go see who it is."

RayAnne clomped off on her crutches to the front door.

Sydney finished up the first batch and began pouring it into the mugs, floating six small marshmallows on the top of each one.

"Hi, Sydney," the mayor said from the kitchen door.

"Hi there. Would you like some hot cocoa?"

"Don't mind if I do. It's a bitter cold day out there."

"Sure is." She handed him one of the mugs, then poured another mug for herself with what was left in the pan. Just enough to go around.

"This is without a doubt the best hot chocolate I've ever had," Mac said.

"That's because it's not hot chocolate. It's homemade hot cocoa," RayAnne said. "My mom makes the best.

Sydney was pleased with the resounding approval.

"I had all the stuff in my kitchen to make this?" Mac took another sip.

"Sure did."

"Dang, Dad. We've been missing out on this stuff for no reason?"

"There is a reason. I don't know how to make it."

"I'm not giving up my recipe," Sydney teased.

"No problem. We'll just beat them at every game we know," Mac said with an exaggerated wink to Seth.

"Easy as pie." Seth slurped the marshmallows from the top of his mug.

"You wait until I'm out of this cast," RayAnne said. "It's game on, then."

The mayor seemed to be enjoying the banter from the depth of his laugh.

"So what brings you by on Christmas Day, Mayor?" Sydney hadn't thought the mayor and Mac were all that close, but it was certainly possible.

"I wanted to talk to you about Bea."

"To me?" Sydney set her cocoa down. She hoped he wasn't going to ask her to say a few words at her funeral. She'd never get through it without turning into a blubbering mess. She felt as close to Bea as she had to her own grandmother. Maybe some of that was due to the things that she'd been dealing with when she hit town. Bea had given her comfort and advice, and a part-time job to keep her busy while RayAnne was supposed to be gone for the holidays. It had given her purpose and helped her find her way.

She braced herself for the inevitable.

The mayor pulled an envelope from his coat pocket. "First things first. I've spoken to Cooper over at the funeral home. He'll be handling the cremation and all of the specifics that Bea had requested. That will all happen on Sunday afternoon. At noon."

Sydney nodded, and put an arm around RayAnne.

RayAnne snuggled closer. "You okay, Mom?"

"I'm okay," she said just above a whisper.

"I have a couple of questions for you, Sydney," the mayor said.

"Okay."

"Are you planning to stay in Hopewell?"

She felt a smile tug at the corner of her mouth. She looked at Mac first. He simply nodded. She wasn't even sure if it was intentional or not, but she took that as a sign. Then she looked at RayAnne, who piped in, "Yes. We're staying in Hopewell. Right, Mom?"

Sydney nodded with a smile, and Mac broke out into a wide grin.

"Excellent. That makes all of this so much easier."

"All of what?"

"Bea's estate."

"What's that got to do with me?"

The mayor handed the envelope over to Sydney. "I'll go through all of this in detail when you're ready, but here's the short version. Bea had no family. She firmly believed that someone would be sent to her who would love The Book Bea as much as she did, and who would carry on her works. Sydney, she thinks . . . thought . . . that person was you."

"Me?"

"Yes. I think she made a wise decision," he said.

"Mom?" RayAnne nudged her. "Does this mean . . . ?"

"Bea's entire estate has been left to you. With the exception of her house, which will be turned into temporary housing for families in need and run by the town."

Mac stepped forward. "The Book Bea is Sydney's now?"

"Yes," the mayor said. "That's exactly what I'm saying."

"What will it cost me?" Sydney asked.

"Nothing. You'll take it over as is. The building is paid for. The taxes are up to date. It's even insured through December next year. You'll simply step in and take it over."

Sydney felt as if she were in a dream. "This can't be happening."

"She'd like you to reopen within ten days of her funeral. That was the only stipulation."

"I was supposed to start a job after the first of the year at Peabody's," Sydney said. "We'd talked about me buying the bookshop, but I was going to ease into it, working both for a while to get my money right."

Mac said, "Peabody's will have a couple weeks to figure out what they're going to do about the position you won't be filling, then."

Sydney walked over and sat at the table. It was a lot to absorb. "This is really happening? Mayor, I will make her proud. This town proud. I promise."

"Mom, it's like a dream come true. I can take it over when you're old like Bea."

The mayor shook her hand. "We hope you'll also step into her position in the city business sessions. Bea always brought a cool head and innovative ideas to the table."

"Yes, sir." A swell of pride filled her. To think Bea trusted her to carry on her legacy was overwhelming. "This is the best Christmas ever. The only thing we're missing today is snow."

"That's always a possibility in Hopewell," the mayor said as he stood. "If you could come by and see me tomorrow around eleven I can walk through all of the details of the funeral and of your inheritance."

"I'll be there."

Sydney shook the mayor's hand, and then Mac took her hand and they walked the mayor to the door.

They stood on the porch arm in arm, and just as Sydney raised her hand to wave, the first snowflakes fell over Hopewell.

Chapter Twenty-four

At noon on the Sunday after Christmas nearly everyone in the whole town of Hopewell gathered to pay their respects to Bea Marion, long-time owner of The Book Bea. There wasn't anyone in the town of Hopewell who hadn't been touched by her kindness in some way.

The gardens in front of the bookstore were filled with people. And neighbors and friends lined the walkway and sidewalks for as far as Sydney could see.

Two days ago there'd been snow. She and RayAnne spent their first white Christmas together with Mac and Seth, but today the sky was bright, the air fresh, and the temperatures unseasonably warm.

The church organist had set up his organ on the front porch of The Book Bea and played a continual cascade of hymns.

The preacher stood next to the mayor in front of The Book Bea sign. It was there that Bea's ashes would be forever entombed. And Bea had even made provisions for the landscaper who took care of the grounds in front of the store to continue to maintain the area surrounding the sign, her final resting place, for the next five years.

PARTINGS COME AND HEARTS ARE BROKEN,
LOVED ONES GO WITH WORDS UNSPOKEN.

NEVER SELFISH, ALWAYS LOVING AND KIND,
THESE ARE MEMORIES YOU LEAVE BEHIND.

OURS IS JUST A SIMPLE PRAYER,
GOD BLESS AND KEEP YOU IN HIS CARE.

"Amen," said the preacher. The word seemed to wrap around the block as others chimed in.

The organist played and the mayor did the honor of setting the urn in place beneath the sign, just as Bea had requested. Nothing fancy.

The mayor placed a kiss on his fingertips, and then to the urn.

The preacher's voice rose, reaching the deep crowd of friends and neighbors. "Our love for Bea Marion should flow from friend to neighbor today and forever. You are invited to partake in the refreshments and at Bea's request you are invited to share your stories and fond memories with one another."

The crowd peeled back.

Sydney walked up the steps to her store. The Book Bea. Diane, RayAnne, and Mac all followed her inside.

Many of the townsfolk wanted to remember Bea with a purchase from the store, even though the news had spread quickly that Sydney was the new owner and the store would remain open.

Sydney helped customers while Diane rang up the steady line of friends and neighbors.

Mac and Seth came up to her as she helped someone choose a book on photography.

She lifted a finger, hoping they'd give her just a minute and not leave.

"I think your niece will really enjoy this book. It's got lots of practical advice, but look, it's filled with photographs, too. Kind of a picture book and text book all in one."

The woman beamed. "It's perfect. You know, Bea was right. You have her same spirit."

Sydney's breath caught. "That might be the nicest compliment someone could ever give me. Thank you."

"I'm Helen. I run the annual Christmas in July parade. Maybe you can help out."

"Happy to." Sydney was eager to be a part of as much as she could work in.

"Great. I work for the dentist here in town. Let's chat when you come in for your checkup."

Which reminded her that she and RayAnne both needed to get into the dentist. Especially after all the sweet treats this holiday. "We'll see you after the first of the year, then," Sydney said.

She spun around toward Mac and Seth. "Sorry."

"Don't be sorry. This place is buzzing," Mac said.

Seth nudged Mac. "Buzz. Like bees. Good one, Dad."

"We've been working on something out front with the mayor. Can you come with us?"

What was he up to now? "Am I going to like this?"

Seth grinned. "You're going to love it."

"I'll hold down the fort," Diane said.

"Then what are we waiting for?"

Seth and Mac each took one of her hands and led her outside to the lawn. As they walked up to the sign in front of The Book Bea, RayAnne stood there waving and holding a camera.